# Behold the Mighty Dinosaur

# Behold the
# MIGHTY
# DINOSAUR

*Edited by*
David Jablonski

ELSEVIER/NELSON BOOKS
New York

Copyright © 1981 by David Jablonski

*Library of Congress Cataloging in Publication Data*

Main entry under title:
Behold the mighty dinosaur.
Bibliography: p.
CONTENTS: Taylor, B. L. The dinosaur.—Taine, J. Before the dawn.—Miller, P. S. The sands of time.—[etc.]
1. Science fiction, American. 2. Science fiction, English. 3. Dinosauria—Fiction.
I. Jablonski, David
PS648.S3B4   1981   813'.0876'08   80–25831
ISBN 0–525–66704–0

Published in the United States by Elsevier-Dutton Publishing Co., Inc., 2 Park Avenue, New York, N.Y. 10016. Published simultaneously in Don Mills, Ontario, by Nelson/Canada.

Printed in the U.S.A.     First Edition
10  9  8  7  6  5  4  3  2  1

# ACKNOWLEDGMENTS

"The Dinosaur" copyright 1912 by The Chicago Tribune.

"Before the Dawn" copyright 1934 by The Willams and Wilkins Company; reprinted in *Famous Fantastic Mysteries* for February, 1946.

"The Sands of Time" copyright 1937 by Stret & Smith Publications Inc.; copyright © 1965 (renewed) by The Condé Nast Publications, Inc. First published in *Astounding* for April, 1937. Reprinted by permission of Mary E. Drake.

"A Sound of Thunder" copyright 1952 by Ray Bradbury. First published in *Collier's* for June 28, 1952. Reprinted by permission of the author and his agent, Harold Matson Company, Inc.

"Poor Little Warrior!" copyright © 1958 by Mercury Press, Inc. First published in *Fantasy and Science Fiction* for April, 1958. Reprinted by permission of the author and his agent, Scott Meredith Literary Agency, Inc.

"The Wings of a Bat," copyright © 1966 by The Condé Nast Publications, Inc. First published in *Analog* for May, 1966. Reprinted by permission of Pauline Whitby.

"The Runners" copyright © 1978 by The Condé Nast Publications, Inc. First published in *Analog* for April, 1978. Revised version published here by permission of the author.

"During the Jurassic" copyright © 1966 by Joseph McCrindle. First published in *Transatlantic Review*, reprinted in *Museums and Women and Other Stories*, by John Updike. Reprinted here by permission of the author and Alfred Knopf, Inc.

# Contents

# Introduction

Dinosaurs have a great fascination for many of us. They are strongly entrenched in our minds as symbols of ferocity and strength, and of lumbering hugeness and mindless obsolescence. The most familiar dinosaurs were gigantic and often bizarre animals, and they vanished with an abruptness and finality that is still puzzling paleontologists, the scientists who study dinosaurs and other ancient forms of life. Thus it is not surprising that science-fiction writers have found a rich source of inspiration in these long-extinct but always engrossing creatures, sometimes expressed by evoking an ancient, lost world (as in "The Sands of Time") or playing with dinosaurian symbolism (as in "During the Jurassic").

In recent years, the scientific study of dinosaurs has undergone an exciting renaissance, and the ideas published in technical journals sometimes surpass even the most imaginative fantasies envisioned in science-fiction magazines. James O. Farlow's prefatory chapter is a state-of-the-art report on dinosaur studies by an important researcher who has a number of fine technical papers to his credit.

Bert Leston Taylor's "The Dinosaur," whose evocative first line provides the title for this collection, is a *Chicago Tribune* columnist's playful response to the misguided notion that *Stegosaurus* had two brains: one "brain" was actually an enlargement of the spinal cord in the hip, and it presumably played a part in coordinating the powerful hind limbs and massive spiked tail. "Before the Dawn" by John Taine (Eric Temple Bell) is a classic example of 1930's pulp science fiction, a wonderfully vivid and action-packed rendition of the long, painful final disappearance of the dinosaurs and their kin. The dim-witted massiveness of his water-dwelling herbivores may be a bit overdone, but the author's admiration for the magnificent tyrannosaur Belshazzar shines through, in a slightly abridged version.

On somewhat less flamboyant scientific (and stylistic) ground is P. Schuyler Miller's story from 1937-vintage *Astounding,* "The Sands of Time." Dinosaurs have lured many science-fictional big-game hunters into the Mesozoic, as we see in two of the stories included here, "A Sound of Thunder" by Ray Bradbury, and "Poor Little Warrior!" by Brian W. Aldiss. Who can soon forget Bradbury's riveting depiction of the hunters' first sighting of their quarry, or Aldiss' exodus of dinosaur parasites?

"The Wings of a Bat," by Paul Ash, is a fine, rarely seen story of a mining operation in the Cretaceous, in which we learn why pteranodons make good friends. Bob Buckley's "The Runners," especially revised for this book, incorporates many of the most recent paleontological ideas into a tale of the dinosaurs near the end of their reign and at the pinnacle of their evolution. And John

Updike's "During the Jurassic" is a delightful story in a class all by itself.

Since space limitations permit me to include merely a fraction of the provocative, exciting stories that dinosaurs have inspired, I have included an appendix listing some additional dinosaurian science fiction for those whose appetites may have been whetted for more. Like the stories collected here, they will transport you into the long-vanished world of the Terrible Lizards.

*David Jablonski*

*Preface*

# Behold the
# Mighty Dinosaur

by James O. Farlow

I suppose most youngsters go through a phase when they think dinosaurs are the most wonderful things that ever existed; that's exactly how I felt upon seeing the dinosaur sequence from *Fantasia* on the Mickey Mouse Club as a five-year-old. No doubt the reason for a child's fascination with dinosaurs is the great size and strength of so many dinosaurs. (If I were a *Tyrannosaurus rex,* then Mommy and Daddy and Big Brother and Teacher and that Bully on the Next Block couldn't push *me* around!) Whatever the reasons may be, this enthusiasm is eventually displaced by more adult concerns such as fast cars, flashy clothes, money, and sex—except in certain individuals who are developmentally stunted like me and grow up to be paleontologists. Even so, most adults remain interested enough in dinosaurs to keep museums more or less financially solvent and motion-picture stars like Godzilla, Rodan, Gorgo, Gwangi, the Giant Behemoth, and the Beast from 20,000 Fathoms off the unemployment lines.

Until recently, however, the general public's enthusiasm for dinosaurs was not shared by paleontologists. By and large, dinosaurs were considered to be scientifically uninteresting; their long reign, it was felt, signified nothing more than that for over 100 million years there was nothing better in the way of animals to supplant them. As a teenager, I once heard a paleontologist remark that the extinction of the dinosaurs was no mystery; what *was* puzzling was that they managed to survive as long as they did.

During the 1970's, however, the scientific image of dinosaurs changed to the point where many paleontologists now hold an almost diagonally opposite view. Dinosaurs are now regarded as anatomically advanced, active, alert, and, to some extent, even intelligent animals, which, until their mysterious extinction, prevented the animals that ultimately replaced them, the mammals, from breaking out of their ecological role as small, secretive creatures. Not all paleontologists agree with every aspect of the dinosaurs' new image, but most of them feel that the big lizards' traditional image as dull-witted, ponderous behemoths was wrong to some extent.

Some of the new interpretations relate to the habitats and modes of life of certain kinds of dinosaurs. For example, sauropods (or brontosaurs, if you prefer) traditionally have been seen as aquatic animals. The standard scenario had them bolting for the drink the moment a big carnivorous dinosaur showed up, leaving the water-hating meat-eater haplessly hungry on shore. Reexamination of the fossil evidence has resulted in drastic modifications of these ideas.

The ultimate source of the aquatic theory of sauropod

habits was Sir Richard Owen, the British anatomist and paleontologist who proposed recognizing the dinosaurs as a distinct taxonomic group of reptiles and who was a bitter foe of Darwin's theory of evolution. On the basis of relatively poor fossil material, Owen described the sauropods as a group of crocodilians and went on to speculate that they were aquatic or even marine animals. Even when new evidence was found that revealed the noncrocodilian nature of these dinosaurs, most paleontologists, perhaps unconsciously biased by Owen's earlier interpretation, continued to view brontosaurs as largely aquatic animals.

At any rate, both Robert T. Bakker and Walter P. Coombs have recently presented cogent arguments in favor of a more terrestrial mode of life. For one thing, the reason for the dorsal position of the nasal opening on the skull of sauropods, which was often cited as an adaptation to permit underwater snorkeling, has been questioned. Some aquatic vertebrates do indeed have their nasal openings in such a position, but then so do other, more terrestrial animals. Furthermore, it is doubtful that a fully submerged sauropod could expand its lungs against the weight of the surrounding water. It has even been thought that the size, shape, and position of the nasal opening suggest the presence of some kind of proboscis in the living dinosaur. Other skeletal structures are less ambiguous. The overall shape of the body, the structure of the vertebrae, and the shape and positioning of the limbs and feet are more consistent with a terrestrial interpretation of brontosaur habits. In addition, the remains of these dinosaurs are usually found in sedimentary rocks that formed in moist lowland, floodplain, and river deposits, the type of environment in which fossils of typically dry-land animals are found—seldom in rocks formed in large lakes and swamps, where the remains of aquatic animals like fishes, turtles, and crocodilians are common.

Bakker visualizes the various kinds of sauropods as having fed on the foliage of trees and shrubs growing at different heights above the ground. Some were quadrupedal, but others, like the well-known *Diplodocus,* may have been able to rear up on their hind legs, and, bracing themselves with their tails, browse on vegetation thirty meters or more above the ground. Some sauropods had large, spoon-shaped teeth, whereas others had slender, rodlike teeth; these dental differences presumably reflect dietary differences.

Although the sauropods were probably primarily land animals, it would be a mistake to suppose that they never entered the water. Modern terrestrial animals, such as elephants and moose, frequently enter the water to feed and soak, just as hippopotami, generally thought of as aquatic animals, wander long distances from water on nocturnal feeding excursions. There is a famous trackway in Texas which records the passage of a floating sauropod dragging itself along by its forefeet alone. I imagine that brontosaurs frequently splashed into rivers or lakes to feed on choice aquatic delicacies or merely to cool off on a hot day.

Another idea that has been revised relates to the posture and gait of the bipedal dinosaurs, in particular the theropods (meat-eating dinosaurs: small theropods are called coelurosaurs, large ones, carnosaurs) and the ornithopods (duck-billed dinosaurs and their relatives). Most older skeletal mounts or flesh restorations show these creatures stalking about with a rather dignified, erect bearing, in which the backbone is held at a 45-degree angle to the ground, and the tail itself is dragged on the ground. However, work by John H. Ostrom, Peter M. Galton, B. H. Newman, and others indicates that these dinosaurs walked and ran with the backbone held in a horizontal posture and the tail well off the ground. Some of these reptiles were rather fleet (some ornithomimids, or "ostrich dinosaurs," were probably faster runners than ostriches, although not as agile), but my favorite dinosaur, *Tyrannosaurus,* was described by Newman as a pigeon-toed behemoth whose "gait was an ungainly waddling rather than the formerly postulated majestic striding." You can't win them all.

One of the most interesting sets of new ideas about dinosaur biology relates to their intelligence and behavior. The alleged stupidity of dinosaurs has become a hoary cliché, but, like many clichés, it is only a partial approximation to reality. Casts of the cranial cavity of the skull (of the brain area) and endocranial casts (of the inner surface of the cranium), can be used to estimate the size of the brain in fossil vertebrates. Several years ago, Harry J. Jerison showed that, contrary to popular belief, the brains of dinosaurs were not exceptionally small for reptiles of their body size. This is because, as vertebrates get larger, brain size does not increase as rapidly as overall body size. More recently, James A. Hopson has expanded on this study by comparing estimated brain sizes in various dinosaurs with those of hypothetical crocodilians of dinosaur size. (Crocodilians are the closest living reptilian relatives of dinosaurs.) For each dinosaur studied, Hopson computed an encephalization quotient

(EQ), which was the ratio of the estimated size of the brain of that dinosaur to the predicted size of the brain of a comparably sized "megacrocodile." An EQ greater than one (1) indicated that the dinosaur in question had a larger brain than you'd expect in a crocodile of that size: an EQ less than one indicated a smaller brain.

Sauropods had the smallest EQs, about 0.2–0.3. Ankylosaurs and stegosaurs had slightly larger EQs, 0.5–0.6. The horned dinosaurs, or ceratopsians, had EQs of about 0.7–0.9; ornithopods had EQs of 0.9–1.5. Large meat-eating dinosaurs, or carnosaurs, had EQs of around 1.0–1.9. The small meat-eater, *Stenonychosaurus,* had a very high EQ, about 5.8; relative to its body size, its brain size was as large as that of some living birds, and this appears to have been true for many other small carnivorous dinosaurs (or coelurosaurs) as well.

Hopson noted a striking correspondence between EQ and the inferred speed and agility during locomotion of the various dinosaurs. Sauropods had the lowest EQs, and studies of brontosaur trackways by R. M. Alexander indicate that the beasts were ambling along at only about one meter per second. Neither ankylosaurs nor stegosaurs were built for running; ankylosaurs were heavily armored dinosaurs whose antipredator tactics consisted of crouching low and/or waving a bony tail club around, and the stegosaurs had dorsal bony plates that may have made their appearance threatening to carnivores, as well as a spiked tail that may have been used as a more concrete defense. Ceratopsians probably used their horns both in fighting with members of their own kind (e.g., males squabbling over access to a female) and in actively resisting the attacks of meat-eaters; both kinds of behavior would involve more speed and maneuvering than anything inferred for sauropods, ankylosaurs, and stego-saurs. Ornithopods were at least partial bipeds and, lacking any real offensive weapons of a type suitable for deterring predators, probably relied on keen senses and fast running to avoid becoming carnosaur dinners. As we shall see later, the social behavior of at least some ornithopods was probably fairly elaborate. Of course, one might expect the meat-eaters to have had relatively large brains; among living fishes, lizards, and mammals, active carnivores tend to have fairly large brains.

If brain size says anything about intelligence—and one intuitively would think that it does, at least to some extent—then it is a fallacy to think that all dinosaurs were equally intelligent. Coelurosaurs, carnosaurs, and orni-thopods were probably smarter than the other dinosaurs; furthermore, many of the coelurosaurs were probably as smart as some living birds. Even the smaller-brained dinosaurs were probably nearly as smart as the average living reptile.

This means that the behavior pattern of dinosaurs might have been as complex as that of living reptiles and, in some cases, considerably more complex. Even the behavior pattern of some living lizards and crocodilians appears to be more sophisticated than was previously recognized. Lizards have been observed to move about and forage in small social groups. Crocodilians sometimes engage in what seems to be cooperative food-gathering or food-carrying activities, as well as in elaborate courtship, and they display distinctive territorial behavior. The degree of parental care seen in some crocodilian species is also striking. Nests are guarded by a parent and opened when the young hatch. The parent may even crack the eggs open in its jaws and carry the young to the water in its mouth. After hatching, the young remain near one and sometimes both parents and receive protection from them for up to several weeks. The evidence of brain size suggests that dinosaur behavior could have been equally as or even more elaborate.

And, indeed, the fossil evidence seems to support such a belief. John H. Ostrom recently noted that fossil trackways of certain sauropods, ornithopods, and theropods strongly suggest gregarious habits. This is because many trackway localities have multiple parallel trackways of the same kind of animal, all going in the same direction. It is unlikely that these animals were all forced to head in the same direction because of some physical barriers on either side, because other trails, frequently made by a different kind of dinosaur, cross the main set of tracks at a high angle to the main group's bearing. Furthermore, in a sauropod trackway site in Texas, the footprints of young brontosaurs are surrounded by those of much larger individuals; R. M. Alexander's study showed that all the sauropods, young and old, were moving at the same speed, supporting the idea that this site does record the passage of a herd, and suggesting that older animals were surrounding the juveniles to provide protection during the march. Finally, both Ostrom and I have argued that some flesh-eating dinosaurs may have hunted in packs of some kind, basing our argument on the evidence of trackways, on fossil assemblages where several individuals of meat-eaters are found associated with smaller numbers of large herbivores, on the relative brain size in theropods, and on the occurrence of group-foraging in living reptiles.

Certain behavior traits can be deduced by studying the

bones of dinosaurs. Many kinds of duck-billed dinosaurs (hadrosaurs) had cranial crests of startling size and shape. Different species had different crest shapes, and Peter Dodson and J. A. Hopson have shown that within any particular species, presumed males had larger and showier crests than presumed females. Hopson has argued that individual hadrosaurs could recognize other hadrosaurs of the same species, and could distinguish between males and females (a useful distinction during the mating season) on the basis of their crest shapes. The crests were hollow and housed part of the nasal tubes; in addition, there were depressions around the exterior nasal openings on either side of the animal's face. Hopson believes that the hollow crest served as a vocal resonator, and that the depressions on either side of the nose housed inflatable sacs of skin. Thus we have the delightful image of immense reptiles with heads of outlandish shape blowing balloons out of their noses as they honked their ardor to the world. And there are those benighted fools who consider paleontology a dry science.

Sexual dimorphism has also been recognized by Dodson in the bony neck frill of the primitive horned dinosaur, *Protoceratops*. Like hadrosaurs, the various kinds of ceratopsians are distinguished by differences in head shape, in particular in the size and shape of the neck frill and cranial horns. Dodson and I have suggested that these differences in head shape were related to differences among the various species in courtship and aggressive behavior, just as Hopson has argued for hadrosaurs.

Pachycephalosaurs were a group of ornithopods characterized by a thick, bony dome on the top of their heads. Here, too, sexual dimorphism has been recognized. P. M.

Galton proposed that males butted their heads together, like living mountain sheep, in order to win the right to mate with female pachycephalosaurs. The shape of the skull and the nature of its articulation with the vertebral column support such an interpretation.

You have probably noticed that much of the speculation about dinosaur behavior stems from functional interpretation of various structures of the skeleton. Other aspects of dinosaur biology can be deduced from studies of the functional morphology of the skeleton. For example, the dinosaur *Stegosaurus* is characterized by upstanding bony plates that ran in an alternating double row down its back. The function of these plates has long been debated. For one thing, their alternating arrangement, contrary to a paired-plate arrangement that would be in keeping with the bilateral symmetry more characteristic of external structures in vertebrates, has been hard to explain. As noted earlier, some scientists have suggested that these plates may have made the animal look bigger and tougher to predators and other stegosaurs. Although this interpretation seems reasonable, I believe that the plates had another function as well.

A few years ago I was struck by the highly vascular appearance of stegosaur plates. The external plate surface is deeply grooved by the traces of blood vessels, and the interior of the plate is very spongy and probably had a rich blood supply. X rays of intact plates revealed traces of a well-developed, branching venous system inside the plate. This made me wonder if the plates could have been used as sites of heat exchange between the animal and its environment, much as the dorsal sail of the earlier-living fossil reptile *Dimetrodon* had been theorized to operate as a device for collecting heat from the sun when the animal was cool and for radiating heat to the environment when the beast was too warm.

I discussed my ideas with an expert on heat exchange, Daniel E. Rosner of the Yale School of Engineering and Applied Sciences, and we designed some simple model stegosaurs for testing the heat-exchange properties of artificial stegosaur plates in wind-tunnel experiments. These studies strongly supported a temperature-regulating function for stegosaur plates. The plates seemed to be designed for dissipating excess body heat by forced convection—that is, when the wind was blowing over them. The alternating arrangement of the plates was particularly suitable in that it allowed the animal to take advantage of breezes blowing from any direction without changing the orientation of its body with respect to wind direction.

This conclusion leads to an obvious question: Why didn't other dinosaurs need such a system? I would guess that other dinosaurs, because of differences from stegosaurs in body size and shape, habits, and habitat, relied on other kinds of temperature-control mechanism.

This in turn brings us to a matter that has received a good deal of attention in the popular press: the whole question of "hot-blooded" dinosaurs. The possibility that dinosaurs, like living birds and mammals and unlike living reptiles, may have had high rates of heat production and been capable of vigorous, sustained activity is not really new. G. R. Wieland made such a suggestion during the 1940's and in 1965 Loris S. Russell argued that, since in many ways dinosaurs are more like birds than like crocodilians in their skeletal anatomy (birds and crocodilians being the closest living relatives of dinosaurs), they may have been correspondingly more birdlike than crocodilelike in their soft anatomy and physiology. Since the late 1960's, the idea has been championed with varying degrees of enthusiasm by such workers as Armand de Ricqlés, John H. Ostrom, and especially Robert T. Bakker.

The arguments, pro and con, on this question are too complex to be satisfactorily discussed here, but I think it is fair to say that there is no consensus among paleontologists at the present time. Some believe that dinosaurs were warm-blooded; others are convinced that they weren't, and the majority, with me included, are probably not convinced either way. Some scientists believe that many dinosaurs could have had a fairly high, constant body temperature simply by virtue of their large size and consequent great thermal inertia. It is possible that the various groups were not at the same level of suggested physiological advancement. J. A. Hopson has suggested that the amount of brain tissue in a vertebrate may be related to the total amount of activity sustained by members of that species, and that this in turn may reflect the energy expenditure of that species. If this chain of causality is correct, then dinosaurs with low EQs, like stegosaurs, ankylosaurs, and sauropods, were probably more like living reptiles than like birds or mammals in their physiology. (To head off the obvious question, I think that even a cold-blooded *Stegosaurus,* because of its size, might frequently have become warm enough to need the cooling system described earlier.) This makes some sense; it is hard to picture monsters like *Brachiosaurus* and even larger sauropods being able to pass enough food through their relatively tiny mouths to fuel warm-blooded bodies of that size. Dinosaurs with higher EQs, like ornithopods, carnosaurs, and especially coelurosaurs, may have been closer to having birdlike or mammallike metabolic rates, and coelurosaurs may even have been fully "hot-blooded."

A final thought on this matter: Has anyone ever considered how much more sense the fiery-breathed Godzilla makes on the assumption that dinosaurs were indeed hot-blooded?

No less puzzling and controversial than any other aspect of dinosaur biology is the question of why that biology ceased to be. The extinction of the dinosaurs was part of a wave of mass extinctions that hit the organisms of our planet about 65 million years ago. Dale A. Russell has estimated that perhaps 75 percent of the species of plants and animals living at that time became extinct. Hardest hit were large terrestrial vertebrates and large marine animals (both vertebrates and invertebrates); freshwater organisms, on the other hand, were nearly unaffected by whatever it was that killed their contemporaries.

Some of the traditional explanations for dinosaur extinction can be quickly discounted. For openers, the great reptiles didn't die off because of a taste for dinosaur eggs on the part of contemporary small mammals. Mammals and dinosaurs originated at the same time, so it seems unlikely that after all that time together the mammals should suddenly go on an egg-eating binge. Neither can the replacement of conifers and their relatives by flowering plants as the dominant terrestrial plants account for the extinction. Although it has been proposed that dinosaurs couldn't adjust to the new fodder, the main floral replacement occurred well before the great extinction, and R. T. Bakker has argued that changes in the fauna of herbivorous dinosaurs were at least partly responsible for the floral change. Not only that, it is probable that the evolution of some groups of herbivorous dinosaurs happened in response to the floral change. In other words, there was a mutually beneficial "coevolution" taking place between dinosaurs and flowering plants. Finally, neither the mammal nor the flowering-plant theory accounts for the contemporaneous marine extinctions.

Leigh Van Valen and Robert E. Sloan recently presented a theory of dinosaur extinction that drew upon their extensive studies of the rocks containing the last of the dinosaurs in Montana. According to them, there was a gradual replacement (over a period of about 100,000 years) of a subtropical plant and vertebrate (dinosaurs and certain primitive mammals) community by a temperate plant and advanced-mammal community that invaded Montana from the north. This ecological change was in response to a gradual decline in winter temperatures. Van Valen feels that the advanced mammals were better able to live in the temperate forest than dinosaurs (but he does not know why), and consequently were able to prevent the dinosaurs from adapting to this floral change in the way they had adjusted to the even greater floral change (replacement of conifers and their kin by flowering plants) earlier in their history. As a result, the dinosaurs had to retreat to the tropics; eventually, the mammals became better able than dinosaurs to exploit food resources in the tropics as well, and the terrible lizards vanished for good. An interesting corollary of this theory is that dinosaurs may have survived well into the Age of Mammals in some tropical areas. Sloan, on the other hand, has difficulty visualizing any Mesozoic mammals outcompeting dinosaurs (even baby dinosaurs); he thinks that, in Montana at least, the cooling climate decreased the amount of plant food available to herbivorous dinosaurs, resulting in their demise and in the consequent extinction of the carnivorous dinosaurs.

Unfortunately, the situation may be more complicated than admitted by the scenarios of Van Valen and Sloan. First of all, R. T. Bakker notes that crocodilians continued to live as far north as Saskatchewan after the dinosaur extinction; if crocs could survive the climate change, why couldn't dinosaurs, he asks, particularly when they'd weathered climate changes of equal or greater severity in the past? Surely some of the herbivores could have adjusted to the diminished food supply postulated by Sloan. Second, Dale A. Russell argues that we know of no temperate forest communities (of the type Van Valen and Sloan say replaced the subtropical communities dominated by dinosaurs) that are *both* of late Mesozoic age *and* lacking in dinosaurs. Finally, although the gradual replacement of dinosaurs and primitive mammals by more advanced mammals can be seen in the rocks at some localities in Montana, at other nearby localities the dinosaurs and primitive mammals remain abundant nearly to the very top of sedimentary rock units deposited during the Age of Reptiles. Work by J. David Archibald and others suggests that in some local environments, dinosaurs and primitive mammals were replaced, but in others they survived and even thrived until the end of the era.

Robert T. Bakker has noted that the extinction of the

dinosaurs was only one of several mass extinctions that have occurred during the history of the earth, and has put forward a theory that attempts to explain these recurrent mass extinctions. Bakker observes that vertebrate fossils are found in rocks which formed from sediments that accumulated in lowland areas on the margins of continents or in continental interiors. Thus, upland environments are only indirectly sampled in the fossil record. Furthermore, Bakker contends that species diversity is richer in topographically high (and diverse) regions than in the lowlands, and that the evolution of most new species occurs in the uplands. Some new species that evolve in the highlands eventually disperse into the lowlands, where they may leave their bones as fossils.

Species are always going extinct for a variety of reasons, such as abrupt, but minor, climatic changes, changes in their food supply, the appearance of new predators or parasites, or some combination of these. However, there are usually new species evolving to replace them. Thus, during most of the Age of Reptiles, as one dinosaur species became extinct, it was replaced by a newly evolved species that was either its descendant or the descendant of some other dinosaur species. This led to an orderly change in dinosaur faunas through time. At the end of the Mesozoic Era, however, something happened that prevented the evolution of new dinosaur species, and when existing species died off for the usual reasons, there were no new species to replace them. What was it that prevented the evolution of new species?

Bakker contends that it was what geologists call the Haug effect. It is now well established that the continents are carried along on crustal plates by sea-floor spreading;

new crust rises from the earth's interior to push the continents across the surface of the planet. However, the rate of sea-floor spreading is variable through time. At times when the rate of spreading is rapid, the areas from which new crust spreads are elevated with respect to the rest of the sea floor. This displaces water from the ocean basins onto the continents, producing large inland seas on the continents. At the same time, however, the increased crustal activity increases the rate of mountain building on the continents. Thus, the Haug effect results both in an increased amount of continental flooding and, paradoxically, in greater elevation and topographic diversity in those parts of the continents that aren't flooded. When the rate of sea-floor spreading slows, on the other hand, the shallow inland seas retreat and the mountains erode away. The result is more land surface, but land surface that is monotonously low in topographic relief.

Bakker argues that periods of mass extinction, such as the one at the end of the dinosaur age, occur when the rate of sea-floor spreading slows. The uplands of the continents become drastically reduced in area, resulting in a drop in the rate of origination of new species (at the end of the Mesozoic era, Bakker argues, the rate of origination of dinosaur species dropped all the way to zero). When the existing species are gone and they have few or no replacements, a mass extinction ensues. When sea-floor spreading picks up again, species diversity begins to climb and keeps increasing until sea-floor spreading slows down again, at which time there is another mass extinction.

I like Bakker's theory. First of all, it provides a common explanation for vertebrate mass extinctions in the fossil record, and I agree with Bakker that this may be preferable to looking for ad-hoc explanations for each mass extinction. I also like his emphasis on changing rates of species origination, as opposed to the emphasis on extinction per se.

However, I have some reservations about his theory. Geologists are not unanimous in their belief in the Haug effect (even though nearly all geologists now accept sea-floor spreading and continental drift): that is, not all agree that periods of mountain-building coincide with periods of continental flooding.

In 1971 Dale A. Russell and Wallace H. Tucker suggested that a supernova in our stellar neighborhood might have caused the mass extinctions at the end of the Age of Reptiles. It is estimated that supernovas occur in a galaxy like ours about once every fifty years, and it is likely that there was a supernova within 15 parsecs (one parsec equals 3.26 light-years) of our sun in the last 70 million years; within a few hundred parsecs, the number of likely supernovas within that time period becomes much greater.

If there were a supernova within about 15 parsecs of our planet, Tucker suggests that within three to thirty years after the supernova became visible from earth, we might be hit by a cosmic ray pulse from a relativistic shock wave generated by the explosion. The cosmic-ray background might increase by a factor of about 5000, resulting in a heavy or, for many organisms, even lethal annual dose of radiation that would last about ten years. Such a bombardment would also greatly disrupt the ozone layer, increasing the ultraviolet flux reaching the earth's surface and greatly altering the climate. Within three thousand to thirty thousand years after the explosion, the expanding shell of the supernova remnant itself would reach the earth. This time the cosmic-ray flux would increase by a factor of about 300 over normal background levels, and there would be sublethal, but perhaps cumulative, annual doses of radiation that would last for thousands of years. Again the ozone layer and climate would be affected; there would be violent storms and perhaps a lowering of temperature.

All this sounds pretty scary, and if such a series of events did cause the terminal Mesozoic extinctions, then it's a wonder that any organisms survived. But is there any hard evidence that a nearby supernova was responsible? Not really. For one thing, normal supernova remnants only last up to a few hundred thousand years; thus any traces of such a supernova at the end of the age of reptiles are long since gone. However, there seems to be an expanding elliptical ring of interstellar hydrogen in the neighborhood of the solar system. This structure, called Lindblad's ring, may be the remnant of an exceptionally powerful supernova that occurred about the time the dinosaurs became extinct. Still, as Paul A. Feldman notes, it has not been proved that (1) Lindblad's ring really does exist; (2) that, if it does, it is a supernova remnant; and (3), if it is, that the supernova did actually coincide with the time of mass extinction. Thus astronomical evidence may not support a supernova theory, but it does not really disprove it either.

Russell argues that although we know that the upper limit for the amount of time during which the extinctions occurred is about two million years, we cannot at present really establish a lower limit. In the most complete sedimentary rock successions where the interval has been identified, it is present as a single bedding plane (or brief cessation of sediment deposition), which may represent as short a time span as from one to a hundred years. Russell contends that the sediments immediately above the extinction plane were deposited under conditions of more energetic water flow than those below the plane. Could this be evidence of increased storminess due to the effects of a supernova? I don't know; to me, it seems pretty flimsy evidence on which to build a theory. Still, I agree with Russell that the supernova is a possibility that cannot be completely excluded at the present time.

So there you have it; the extinction of the dinosaurs remains nearly as mysterious as ever. Perhaps continued research and new research methods will eventually yield an answer to the puzzle.

But that needn't concern us right now. Let's get on with the stories. Dinosaurs *are* great fun, whether your interest in them is professional or, for the science-fiction fan, recreational. So, the final thing I want to say to you is: Enjoy!

# The Dinosaur

## by Bert Leston Taylor

Behold the mighty dinosaur,
   Famous in prehistoric lore,
Not only for his power and strength
   But for his intellectual length.
You will observe by these remains
   The creature had two sets of brains—
One in his head (the usual place),
   The other at his spinal base.
Thus he could reason "A priori"
   As well as "A posteriori."
No problem bothered him a bit,
   He made both head and tail of it.

So wise was he, so wise and solemn,
   Each thought filled just a spinal column.
If one brain found the pressure strong
   It passed a few ideas along.
If something slipped his forward mind
   'Twas rescued by the one behind.

And if in error he was caught
    He had a saving afterthought
As he thought twice before he spoke
    He had no judgment to revoke.
Thus he could think without congestion
    Upon both sides of every question
Oh, gaze upon this model beast,
    Defunct ten million years at least.

# Before the Dawn

## by John Taine

## Chapter 1

THE LITTLE FOLK

An invisible needle of light pried its way into the minute cavities of an uncut diamond.

Of the three watching that epochal experiment with the electronic analyser, Langtry alone was at ease. He had invented the "clock," as he called his ingenious decipherer of the secrets of light, and he felt confident of success. Bronson, the stocky, practical president of the American Television Corporation, breathed heavily and kept his eyes on the diamond. Old Professor Sellar, the archaeologist, erect and tense, tried not to seem too expectant, although it was his own restless curiosity that had started the whole series of experiments of which this was the climax.

"Watch for the violet—it is coming," Langtry warned.

As the invisible needle-point of light found its mark in the heart of the diamond, a soft violet radiance shimmered on the air, bathing the crystal.

"We've got it," Bronson exclaimed, starting forward.

"Yes; but what?" Sellar muttered. "How far back, Langtry?"

"I can't tell. Wait and see if anything condenses."

The violet light palpitated and gradually expanded. From a globule the size of a cherry it swelled to a huge ball, five yards or more in diameter, and seemed to live. Through the clear violet atmosphere of the pulsating sphere swift flashes of crimson and yellow, of blue and green, like the changing colors of a fire opal, flashed and instantly disappeared.

"Do either of you see anything?" Bronson demanded. "The focus is all wrong. I get nothing but a blur of color."

"Wait," Langtry counselled confidently. He stepped back a few feet. "We are not looking at it in scale," he said. "Ah, I see the trouble. The image is upside down." He made a delicate readjustment of the "clock." "How's that?"

"I still see nothing—" Sellar began. Before he could finish they all saw it—the first record of television *in time* ever to be seen by human eyes.

The record was stimulating but disappointingly brief. The swirling crimson and yellow wisps of light suddenly rushed together near the center of the violet globe, shimmered indecisively for a second, and congealed. A monstrous curved talon like a vulture's, but as long as a man's arm and twice as thick at the base, hovered for an instant in the violet haze. Then, still crimson and smoking with the blood of its prey, the murderous claw flashed down and out of the solid picture.

For some moments there was silence. Then Langtry spoke.

"Well?" he queried.

"We've done it," Bronson agreed to the inventor's unexpressed question. "That was no figment of our disordered imaginations!"

Langtry made the basic discovery while engaged on a purely practical and humdrum detail of ordinary television engineering. He modestly insists that it was all a lucky accident and perhaps he is right. If so, it was that fortunate kind of mischance that happens only to the right man looking for the wrong thing—like Röntgen, when he surprised himself by discovering X-rays.

Langtry's "clock," or "televisor," or electronic analyser, to give the devise its scientific name, does for light what a phonograph does for sound. The records which the televisor "plays" are nature's, and the older they are the clearer.

But one serious defect remains to be overcome before the televisor can be marketed profitably, that of "unscrambling" a particular record and reassembling it in the natural time sequence. At present this has been done only at enormous expense in the laboratories. The difficulty is similar to that of getting a perfect symphony out of bucketfuls of badly smashed phonograph records. Before the symphony can be played, the puzzle of fitting the shattered fragments into smooth, whole records must be solved.

To return to Langtry's "accident," for which Professor Sellar was directly responsible. For over thirty years Sellar had devoted all his working hours to the apparently hopeless puzzle of reading the grotesque stone records left by the Mayan priests and astronomers.

All his mature life he had been tormented by a vague feeling that there must be some exact *physical* means for dating historical monuments. Must not something happen to a slab of polished limestone or granite in the course of centuries, to store up forever the record of the days and nights, and dawns and the sunsets, the frosts and the scorching summers it has taken, year after year and century after century? That every dead or living thing must carry with it the whole of its history, in some readable shape or another, seems obvious to anyone who believes, as Sellar did, that nature is something more than a welter of utterly lawless accidents.

Granted that Sellar's belief was not baseless, his problem came down to finding what language is nature's own, and in what script she conceals her secrets from too curious eyes. The script is light itself, and the language is the simplest and most direct of all, the moving record of events as they happen. Only when the very atoms of the rocks are dissipated into their primal electricities and smoothed out in eternal nothing, will nature be inscrutable and the past forgotten beyond recall.

Unable to believe wholeheartedly in his various rivals' theory of dating the eclipses, and not being a physicist, Sellar consulted his old friend Bronson.

"I'll ask young Langtry to think about it," he promised. "If he gets an idea, I'll let you know."

The result was that Langtry resolved to devote all his spare minutes to the "clock."

At the time, he was perfecting an intricate amplifying device for measuring the exact degree of worn-outness of the large and expensive grids used in the television tubes of his company. The theory behind these practical measurements was simple in the extreme. When light impinges on a smooth metal surface, some of the outer electrons in the atoms are knocked off—to speak the older language of a much modified theory. By measuring the amount of electric current thus liberated by the light, it was possible to calculate for how long the surface of the metal had been bombarded and pitted by earlier impacts of light or other intense radiation. The earlier light left its own record in the metal.

From that hint to the end was a long way, but one marked at every step by legible signposts. Langtry read the easier of these; it required the combined efforts of the world's greatest engineers and experts on theories of quanta and radiation to decipher the rest. But the signs were finally read, and by properly amplifying the variable photoelectric current emitted by a lump of dead matter, men at last deciphered the unaging records of all the light that ever shone on the lump.

Just as the phonograph restores the music recorded in the serrated grooves of a disc, which apparently are as unlike sound as the roughened surface of a crystal is unlike a living picture of events long past forgotten, so the televisor unweaves from the slightly modified atoms all the history of the light which, ages ago, robbed them of a few electrons.

Sellar offered his most treasured possession for the ultimate test of the "clock." This was a beautiful Mayan calendar stone, as smooth in its polished perfection as it was the day it left its maker's hands.

"See in what year this was finished," he directed Langtry. "If your tubes date it within a century of the lunar eclipse recorded upon it, I'll begin to believe you may have something. I'll not tell you my date till you give me yours. Bronson can be our witness."

Langtry adjusted the calendar stone on the revolving steel platform and prepared to focus the exploring needle of monochromatic light. The inventor turned a screw switch, and announced that he was ready.

A switch was closed, and the invisible needle began feeling its way into every microscopic cavity of the polished stone and finally stopped.

"I date your calendar stone with a probable error of less than a year as 704 A.D.," Langtry said.

For a moment Sellar's face was blank with astonishment.

"A wild coincidence, eh?" Langtry smiled. "Let's see if I can hit another. Anything else you want me to try?"

Flushing slightly, Sellar fished about in the roomy pocket of his work jacket, and somewhat shamefacedly produced a greenish lump of translucent crystal. He held it up for their inspection.

"This was found in the gravel near Xlitctl. The gravel bed had been buried under a lava outflow eight feet thick." He paused for a moment with a wry smile. "No geologist will risk his reputation guessing when that outflow occurred. They admit that it must have been before the Christian era, because the lava itself is buried under three distinct strata of rubbish from prehistoric ruins, and the strata are separated by layers of silt washed down from the mountains. So," he concluded confidently, "whatever this is, it is at least as old as anything human in America." He passed it to Bronson. "See what you think it represents." Bronson turned the greenish lump over and over till he accidentally found which position was intended to be right side up. "Why," he exclaimed, "it's a crude statuette of a woman in a sitting posture."

"Precisely," Sellar agreed. "And there's not a legible scratch anywhere on her to give a clue to her age. The crystal is calcite—fairly soft and quite easily worked. Well, Langtry, see what you make of this. I'll accept anything up to two thousand B.C."

What followed will doubtless be remembered long after our time as one of the great moments in the history of the world. Langtry adjusted the calcite statuette in the apparatus, and Bronson stood ready to take down the readings. Slowly, at first, then jerkily in great staggering jumps, the pointer swept over a full two-thirds of the scale. Gradually the pointer came to rest, trembled as if struggling to exceed the limit of its feeble strength, and then, so gently that it seemed to die, slid back over the scale. The life-giving impulse of the light was spent, the story told.

Langtry hesitated long before venturing to announce the result of his carefully checked calculations.

"The date is preposterous," he began diffidently. "But I can't help how absurd it may seem. I've run that clock backwards and forwards, and I know it can't lie. Your calcite woman dates 35,937 B.C."

"That woman may be ancient," Sellar remarked dryly; "but she is not that old. Try it again."

"Another test," Bronson suggested, "and we'll call it a day. If this agrees, we can't beat your clock. Whatever Sellar says, that woman was chipped out of the crystal over thirty-six thousand years ago."

Why this run should have proved the turning point,

neither Langtry nor any of the radiation experts of the world understands to this day. Did Langtry accidentally expose some deep, invisible fissure of the calcite image to the penetrating needle of light, letting light meet light in a clash of transcendent remembrance? Or had the prolonged exposures at last broken down the resistance —"darkness"—of the hardened shell of the image, thus permitting the prisoned history of a thousand million years to escape in one blinding revelation of age that the very minerals of the earth have forgotten?

There was a faint, sharp hiss; the greenish lump of crystal melted and became a shapeless, soapy mass of yellow glass; a blinding violet light filled the room, and for one brief moment the three amazed spectators caught fleeting glimpses of a cosmic tragedy which flashed up and out with the speed of light.

No two of the three agreed on what they had seen. Each remembered but a fragment of the whole that slowly developed, like the image on a photographic film, on their over-stimulated retinas. Sellar still insists that he saw teeming cities and vast battles flash by; Bronson recalls only the upheaval of a colossal mountain range as it seemed to shoulder its bulk up through the crust of the earth—a vision of millions of years compressed to a fraction of a second; while Langtry saw nothing but a whirling fire compact of the tragedies of worlds, stars and galaxies.

Their first thought when their eyes again became normal was the same. They had blundered onto a greater thing than they had sought. Bronson broke the silence.

"We must learn how to slow it down. Then we shall really see."

"Perhaps," Sellar agreed. "But what?"

"Everything that lump of calcite has seen," Langtry spoke up with quiet confidence. "It may take a thousand years, but it will be done. And it will be worth doing."

Success was delayed, but not for so long as Langtry had anticipated. It was early discovered that crystals had preserved the best light records of the past. From there it was but a short step to use the diamonds almost exclusively in the earlier experiments.

The first actual image, that of the gigantic talon, was obtained by the use of a diamond, as has been described.

Of all the prehistoric objects analyzed by the televisor, fossil plants consistently gave the best results.

The dramas which we witnessed were soundless. Their last echoes passed into the eternal silence hundreds of millions of years before the human race emerged from the compelling shadows of the past.

So real were those intangible shapes of solid, moving color evoked by modern science, that we frequently found ourselves fleeing in instinctive terror, although we realized that the gigantic actors had vanished from the face of the earth ages ago—ages before the Andes slowly heaved up their massive bulk above the desolation. In the perfected records the actors were life size and the stage acres in extent. We too walked upon the stage, but as spectators, not actors.

Often we were surprised into striking out blindly to protect ourselves from the hurtling onslaught of a hundred tons of snarling, reptilian fury, only to realize that the attack was aimed, not at us, but at another actor in the drama. Both had passed from the scene of life millions of years before the first cave dwellers crouched shivering over their smoky hearths. We passed through the bodies of the combatants as if they were air. They were not air, but insubstantial, living light.

If at times we felt dwarfed and puny in the presence of nature's giants—her masterpieces so far as almost brainless feeding, fighting, and breeding machines are in any sense masterpieces—we usually recovered when we remembered that we, after all, survived, while they perished. And if nature had tried to erase forever the record of a futility which took all of nine million years to work out to its predestined failure, we flattered ourselves that men had succeeded in exposing the records of her blunder for all to see.

The technicians like to think that their first real success with the televisor recorded the birth of that superb brute of the later records whom they have affectionately named Belshazzar.

Encouraged by Langtry's success with the uncut diamond, the engineers at once repeated his experiment, using the same diamond. They first worked to get a more extensive globe of violet light. Having accomplished that, they labored for three months to slow down the speed of the color condensation.

It was difficult to realize, when a perfect image was at last achieved, that we were looking at a mere image, painted in light, and not at the tawny sands of a real desert sweltering under a tropical sun. The transparent air quivered above the yellow sands in the heat haze, and we all but felt the vast silence crushing us down into the burning desolation.

The scale of the image at first puzzled us. Was this a mere patch of the desert, or were we seeing thousands of square miles focused into the blinding intensity of a fifty-foot image? At the first glance there was nothing to give us the scale. No unmistakable horizon was visible, and no distant peak loomed up to set a relative standard.

An exclamation from Sellar directed our eyes to a spot on the sand about five feet from the centre of the image.

"Eggs!"

We followed his finger, and instantly adjusted our eyes to the true scale. It was a patch of sand we were viewing, and not the whole desert. What some of us had mistaken for a curious, haphazard three dozen or so of brownish stones the size of large potatoes, was revealed as a badly scattered bushel of smooth, long eggs. The depression in the sand which had formed the nest was still plainly visible. It was obvious that the eggs had only recently been scattered. By whom? We soon discovered. Langtry saw her first.

"There!" he exclaimed. "In the nest."

She was a beautiful little creature with her tawny, hairless skin mimicking the desert sands, and her quick enquiring brown eyes. Although it was only a guess in the absence of any absolute scale, we judged her to be about the size of a large house cat. Somehow she reminded us of a greatly overgrown but very young mouse.

When we first spied her she was busy with both forepaws readjusting her troublesome young. These she carried conveniently in a capacious pouch on her stomach. She might have been a small kangaroo, except for her sharp-pointed ears and the long whiplash tail which rested on the sands behind her in a graceful sinusoid. Art could not have devised a curve more pleasing to the eye than the careless grace of that resting tail.

Having seen that her young were getting their proper food, the mother concentrated her mind on her own wants. The tail flickered, and she hopped forward. One of the long potatolike eggs was her objective. Settling down luxuriously in the warm sand, she reached quickly forward and picked up the egg in her paws. Then for the first time we saw her dainty teeth, sharper than needles. They were ideal for piercing the tough skin of that snaky egg. With one expert nibble she punctured the leathery hide. In two minutes she had the egg dry, and hopped to the next.

This time her lunch was not so good. Possibly the egg she coveted had been the first laid, or had rested in the hottest spot of the nest. Anyway it was ripe to the hatching point. Unable to obtain any liquid nourishment, the hungry mother ripped open the sac with her incisors, and thrust her nose into the vent.

Something in that evil purse disgusted her, for she quickly flung it wide. As the egg struck the sand a feeble, squirming reptile like a salamander fell out and sprawled on its back, pawing at the sky. Its ridiculously short forelegs were mere vestiges of hands, but its hind legs already gave promise of tremendous muscular development and invincible brutality. If that puny wriggler was indeed Belshazzar, his entrance was extremely undignified and no prophecy of his heroic exit.

The voracious little robber of reptile nests was about to attack her third egg when she stiffened, as if suddenly frozen. Her intelligent brown eyes widened and she clutched frantically at the pouch containing her young. In her alert wary tenseness she made a perfect picture of listening.

We of course heard nothing. But the nervous rigidity of

that small creature's body conveyed more to us than a cannonade. Before the battle began we felt the barrage and sensed the enemy's charge. Her anxious, intelligent awareness made us her allies—across the abyss of millions of years. She was of our own kind, her enemy was not.

In viewing the charge we were in the position of a cavalryman who has been thrown from his mount and who sees nothing but the flash of galloping hoofs. Our diminutive ally saw the charge coming, and through her wary movements we also followed every maneuver of the advancing enemy. She waited till the charge was about to overwhelm her. Our instinctive but futile shout of warning coincided with her own sideward leap as she deftly evaded the plunging foot. One talon of it would have obliterated her family. The huge birdlike foot with its four vicious talons, each the length of a man's arm, buried itself in the sands, flashed up, and again plunged down with the impact of a triphammer, only again to miss its mark.

Blundering brute force proved itself a poor second against the spark of intelligence behind that insignificant mammal's eyes. Wherever the huge birdlike foot blundered and smashed its futile fury into the sands, she was simply absent, often by a margin of an inch, but still absent.

We began to wonder what our ally's strategy was. One rigid forepaw was clutched tightly over the pouch on her stomach. If she was solicitous for her young, why did she not flee? Instead of seeking absolute safety, she skirted its margin with a reckless deviltry that brought our hearts into our mouths. Two plunging feet, eight terrible talons in all, now menaced her. One of the talons, we noted, was crimson with smoking blood. The gigantic brute whose feet alone were visible in that first partial image had blundered from one battle, in which he—or possibly she—had triumphed over an enemy his own size into another, only to be baffled and defeated by an opponent who might have perched like an inconspicuous mouse on the tip of the least claw of the attacker.

Our ally received not so much as a scratch. We surmised that she was waiting for the fury of her brainless enemy to fritter itself out in futile stamping. Then she would calmly resume her feast on the enemy's eggs. Few were now left; the outraged parent had smashed most of them in a stupid, instinctive attack to safeguard an unborn generation. Against a single spark of intelligence the gigantic brute had less chance than an animated tractor.

All but three of the eggs had now been pulped in the sand. Belshazzar—if indeed it was he—had also escaped. During the battle he had somehow managed to flop over on his belly. When we next noticed him, he was wriggling pathetically toward our ally, feebly propelling himself in spasmodic jerks by his hind legs. He was favored with one quick, bright glance from our ally just as she gracefully sidestepped a flashing talon. There was something not altogether kind in that swift, direct glance.

"What a murderous look," Sellar muttered. "That little devil means business."

Indeed she did. Before the wriggler came within a yard of her safety zone, she changed her tactics. The long whiplike tail stiffened, and she was off. In three hops she was out of the picture.

For some minutes the brainless attacker continued to dent the sand, unaware that his foe had withdrawn. Worn out at last—we simply could not credit the owner of those blundering feet with sufficient intellect to organize a pursuit—the enemy staggered off and vanished from the narrow compass of the image. The huge birdlike feet were all we saw, but their shuffling exhaustion was as complete a picture of hopeless frustration as any masterpiece of Napoleon's flight from Moscow. He was beaten, and he did not know it.

Our bright-eyed friend did not delay her return long. As cooly as if there had been no recent unpleasantness, she hopped back into the arena. The three eggs were still intact, as was also the wriggler. First she disposed of the eggs. All were evidently fresh and palatable. Then she turned her attention to the child of her enemy and the enemy of her children. With bared teeth she hopped toward it. As clearly as if she had spoken across the abyss of ages she told us by her every movement what her purpose was. She had no intention of devouring the helpless wriggler. She merely wished to kill it by nipping it in the neck.

A fair, brainy fight is not unpleasant to witness. Cold-blooded murder revolts normal intelligence. We wished she would not do it. But she had no conscience, only a fierce and natural loathing for the hereditary enemies of her parvenu race. Fortunately for our squeamishness she was balked.

Not till many months later did we fully understand what urged the rout which we now witnessed. The tantalizing meagreness of the image exasperated us, but the engineers could do nothing at the time to widen the narrow horizon. What we saw was a mere patch, about fifty feet in diameter, of a teeming panorama which must have occupied hundreds of square miles.

Just as she was about to nip the helpless reptile, our friend stiffened and jerked erect. For two seconds she was a rigid statue of fear. Then she wheeled on her haunches, pressed both forepaws over her pouch, and leapt from our view.

The manner of her disappearance was so incongruous that we shouted with laughter. She vanished as if she had plunged through an invisible wall. It all happened in less than two seconds. First her head vanished, then her body, and finally the stiffened tail was rammed into the void after her. She had merely leapt through and clear out of the spherical image projected by the televisor. Millions of years now separated us from her.

The wriggler also seemed to be anxious to get away. Crude, automatic reflexes urged it into desperate, floundering efforts to move faster. We ourselves almost sensed the sudden drop in temperature as the air above the scorching sand ceased to quiver and the sand dimmed from blinding yellow to dusky gold.

Although we saw no vegetation in the patch of desert visible to us, we could only hope that some dry twig lay not far beyond the range of the televisor. Even a newly hatched reptile is entitled to a sporting chance for his life, and we trusted that the young son of our late enemy would manage to crawl aboard some seaworthy ark. For we could almost feel the approaching deluge.

Long before it came—we did not see it—the rout of the valiant mammals was in full tide. What must have been their multitude could be guessed from the fleeing horde which streamed across the narrow circle of our vision. For the most part they were smaller than our vanished friend, although now and then a larger hopper of a different species bounded over the rabble.

The spark of intelligence which we had admired in our friend's eyes was absent from those of this precipitate mob. Fear, and fear alone, animated them. Whatever it might be that had routed their host, it was no ordinary enemy that courage might face and intelligence overcome. They were vanquished by one whom it would be folly to resist.

A swift change came over the image. The gold of the sands deepened to brown; the routed mammals became blurs of fleeting purple, and the whole image quivered uncertainly as in the throes of death. The light which millions of years ago had left its record in the atoms of the diamond was dying.

The engineers' efforts to amplify the expiring light failed. But their ineffectual effort gave us one last fleeting vision, as the crystal canted—a black sky ablaze with stars. In that glimpse we recognized an old landmark of our race. Sirius glittered in all his flaming brilliance, and almost at the zenith a cluster of stars like a bunch of grapes glistened icily. We recognized the Pleiades. But their aspect was unfamiliar, as if the cluster were richer in stars than our race has known it. Orion too was strange, but recognizable. We were gazing out on a younger heaven.

One of the most obstinate difficulties with the early televisors was that of superposed images. The same specimen—crystal or fossil—frequently threw into the projector a wild confusion of several conflicting scenes, so that it was all but impossible to follow a particular action clearly from setting to climax. The trouble was similar to that which a careless amateur encounters when he takes a dozen photographs on the same film.

To overcome this difficulty it was necessary, in the experimental stage, to study large-scale images intensively. For this purpose Bronson ordered the construction of a twenty-acre arena, where events of considerable magnitude might be reproduced precisely as they had happened without distortion in any detail.

The project was less formidable than it sounds. All that was necessary was twenty acres of level, hard ground suitably screened from premature publicity and idle interference. A circular fence forty feet high, enclosing twenty acres of level, packed dirt covered by an inch of concrete, was finally constructed as an ideal outdoor laboratory.

For technical reasons the projecting lenses, condensers, analyzers, amplifiers and the rest of the scientific necessities were assembled in the centre of the arena. Under the steel roof of the open rotunda sheltering the scientific apparatus, the engineers toiled day and night, in all weathers, to perfect the images and bring ordered sequences of events out of a whirling chaos of conflicting dramas.

Another strange effect of these vast outdoor pictures may be mentioned, as we never got used to its dreamlike quality. In midwinter, when the thin concrete of the stage was cracking and snapping under the intense cold, the blinding heat of sun-smitten deserts, or the sticky humidity of tropical jungles, sweltered on the biting air. It was perhaps even more strange to witness the frozen glare of a dying continent on an August afternoon when the thermometer registered 90 and the humidity stood at 80.

A raw February day gave the engineers their first satisfactory full image.

Promptly at eight the morning of the test, Bronson met

Langtry outside the arena, and they proceeded at once to the engineers' rotunda.

"Infernally cold, isn't it?" Bronson remarked to Sellar, who had arrived half an hour earlier.

"Ugh," Sellar grunted. "Hullo! What the dickens is that? I could swear I saw those mountains in Guatemala thirty years ago. Am I . . . ?"

"Not in the least," Langtry reassured him. "The technicians are just feeling out the true focus of the projectors."

"But those mountains—"

"I know. If they're anywhere near Guatemala, they're probably buried under thirty thousand feet of slime, mud, sand and rock at the bottom of the Caribbean Sea. They were wiped off the map before Guatemala lifted itself out of the ocean."

"But I saw them—"

"Take another look." Langtry shouted an instruction to the three men struggling with the projectors. "Distort it eight to one for a second or two. Professor Sellar wants to see the vegetation on the foothills."

The purple and azure mass of the distant range quivered, vanished like a mirage, and instantly in the air, forty feet from the rotunda, a streaming jungle of stunted conifers, tall ferns and clublike palms shimmered in sultry silence.

"Ever see trees like those in Guatemala?"

"No, or anywhere else," Sellar admitted testily. "Phew, how hot it is." He stripped off his heavy topcoat, only to put it on again in a hurry as the image blurred and the precipitous range once more sprang into purple and azure shadow in the distance.

"It's coming up clear now," one of the engineers

shouted. "Better get out near the wall if you want to be in the best of it. Over there—due north."

As they hastened toward the indicated location, the color condensations on the concrete floor of the arena began to swarm into definite images. Again the scene was desert sands. But this time they saw the horizon, a dark blue band of dense vegetation, deepening mile after mile to the base of the shadowy mountains.

The image condensed with startling rapidity. If the reader has ever enjoyed one of those old-fashioned indoor panoramas of vast scenes which were popular a generation ago—there was a very fine one of the siege of Paris at the old Crystal Palace in London—he will appreciate the dwarfed feeling experienced by the three men as they penetrated this incomparably vaster panorama taking solid shape all around them. These images were not mere paint on plaster or canvas. They were solid light, and it required a conscious exertion of the will to walk resolutely forward instead of weaving one's way around jagged outcrops of glistening black rock.

Bronson was the first to betray himself. Directly in his path an enormous gray boulder blocked further progress. Changing his course he skirted its edge, and looked back to see whether the others were following. Langtry was doubled up with laughter; Sellar stood stock still, waiting to see what Langtry would do before committing himself. Langtry straightened up, walked into the boulder, emerged on the farther side, and rejoined Bronson.

"That is the most extraordinary thing I have seen yet in all of this," Bronson remarked when he could speak.

"There's nothing to it," Langtry remarked. "You just

walk through. It's nothing but light. Try it yourself."

"I wasn't referring to the apparent solidity of the image. There's nothing new in that. But do you know what you did just then?"

"No," Langtry admitted, somewhat crestfallen. "Except that I walked through the image. There was nothing to stop me."

"Why, man, you disappeared. When you walked into that boulder you vanished as if you had been annihilated. Then you suddenly materialized on the other side."

We had been so intent upon this conversation that we did not see the condensation of the panorama about us until it had risen to its full solidity of intense color. We found ourselves standing in a dry river bed of majestic distances. Our eyes quickly adjusted themselves to the natural scale of the vast panorama. A reasonable estimate of the breadth of the stony bed put it at twenty miles. We were almost exactly midway between the precipitous walls which seemed to cut the blue-black sky miles over our heads.

The river bed was drenched in sunlight—no milder word can describe the stunning, all-pervading intensity of that withering light which beat down upon the tumbled boulders as if to stamp them flat in the gravel. Every particle of dust had been scoured from the dry bed by the rushing of innumerable torrents dumped into the gorges of the mountains for century after century of violent cloudbursts and unrestrained tempests from torrid seas.

Only the most brainless of reptiles would ever blunder into this blazing death trap. No mammal with the least glimmer of a dawning intelligence would ever gamble its life away against such odds smiting it in the eyes.

By an effort of the will we remembered where and what we were. But we could not restrain the instinctive habits of countless generations of intelligence and foresight bred into the very marrows of our bones. We stared apprehensively at the distant banks of the trap. Ten miles, or possibly nine by the shortest route, separated us from our one chance of escape. Could we make it if suddenly we should see the torrent wheel round the slow curve of the river bed, a scant twenty-five miles away? Obviously not. We were as helpless as rats in a sewer.

"Let's get out of here," Bronson suggested, fingering at the muffler about his neck. "It's stuffy."

"We can't," Langtry reminded him, "unless one of us can find his way out of this maze and tell the engineers to alter the scale. I wouldn't undertake to get out inside of twelve hours on a bet. I know, because I tried last night."

"What's the difference?" Sellar spoke up. "Nothing material can happen. Keep your head and let whatever comes pass over you."

"I'll keep my head all right," Bronson retorted. He rewrapped the muffler tighter around his neck. "But what about my mind? Why didn't we choose a warmer day for this? Come on, I'm freezing. Anyone coming?" He glanced back. "I'm going to warm up at the rotunda."

"You think you are," Langtry chuckled, "Try it. Which way is south? We came north, you know."

Bronson did not deign to reply. We followed at a safe distance. When put out, Bronson could be quite explosive. Presently he stopped short. "What the devil's the matter with me? I must have walked five hundred yards, and I'm no nearer that bank than when I started. On the scale of this image we should be halfway out of it by now."

"Perhaps the image condenses 'round as you walk," Sellar suggested maliciously. "What you think is ten miles off is only a few hundred yards at most. The perspective does the trick. I shouldn't be surprised if all this moves more or less with us. That bank is just as far off in time as it would be if it were real. Langtry, suppose you lead us back?"

"I can't," Langtry confessed. "Once into an image of these dimensions you're lost. It is precisely as real, optically, as the original."

"Then how are we going to get back to the rotunda?" Bronson demanded. "Hang it! I wish we had chosen a cooler day. That infernal sun is baking me like a potato."

"Merely your eyes," Sellar reminded him. "I'm shivering. But at that I'm the one practical mind on the lot." He began shouting to the engineers to cut off the projection. Nothing happened. Langtry looked on with an amused smile.

"The boys won't hear you," he remarked. "They follow the racket of the electrons by means of head phones specially constructed to keep out all external noises. I told them to give us exactly sixty minutes of this. We've had about thirty."

The remaining thirty minutes passed swiftly enough, for they were crowded with action. The excitement began when Bronson blundered into a sizeable, lizardlike reptile taking a siesta in the shade of a large blue boulder. The brute was a mere pigmy compared to some that we might equally well have met. From the tip of its tail to its snout it measured probably nine feet and in bulk it did not exceed a large calf.

With one yell Bronson vanished into the image of a blue

boulder. Instinct kicked us in after him. We had merely sprung high and wide, not knowing where we should land. Our previous experience with solid images should have prepared us for the total darkness in which we found ourselves. For the moment we thought we had gone blind. We had merely leapt into a spot totally devoid of light.

"Let's be quiet," Langtry cautioned. "We don't want to waken the brute."

We walked round the boulder to the image of the sleeping reptile. It was sleeping the sleep of starved exhaustion. The stark ribs all but burst the drum-tight, leathery hide of its thorax, and the dished-in pelvis was like that of a mummy. Yet the devil was not dead. The chest rose and fell like that of a man fighting off death.

The whole appearance of the sleeper was that of an incredibly old devil. Something about the glistening white teeth, sharper than a shark's, which the starved lips had bared, made us wish to kill the sleeping fiend. The utter irrationality of our murderous impulse could not check it; we were answering an instinct. Although none of us knew enough about the anatomy of such a reptile to have a competent opinion, we felt that at least two of those teeth were needles for the injection of venom. And we wondered what hapless creature this sleeping devil dreamed of in its starved exhaustion. Its dirty yellowish-green hide reeked of evil. We turned from it in disgust.

An ominous blue shadow was sliding over the distant north wall of the water course. Quickly it slipped down to the gravel bed and raced toward us. Glancing up we saw massive clouds, black as pitch, gathering above the chasm. The deluge was about to burst upon us. Instinct prevailed, and we started running toward the north wall, only to come to an embarrassed halt after a few yards. No one made any remark; we had all been tricked by our senses. We wished the engineers would have a breakdown with their infernal projectors.

"Let's sit down," Bronson suggested. "There can't be over fifteen minutes more of this torture." He carefully lowered himself to sit on a smooth boulder, when he remembered that it wasn't there in the material sense. Straightening up, he stared anxiously toward the distant bend in the river bed. "I feel something coming," he muttered. "Whatever comes, I'll not turn my back. I imagine there's a very considerable cloudburst coming down right now a few miles beyond that bend."

But the particular climax that we dreaded did not happen—at least it did not sweep on to its overwhelming finality while we retained our faculties. What if it had? Should we now be living?

Sellar saw it first. "The bend," he shouted. "Run!"

Twenty-five miles away a tumbling flashing wall of water a quarter of a mile high wheeled round the bend and swept toward us. Bronson stood like a rock staring at the rushing wall. True to his determination, he never flinched. Sellar stumbled off toward a high outcrop of black shale, and stopped, his back to the plunging flood. Langtry stood by Bronson, white-faced and alert. What transpired next ran its course in less than a minute.

Between us and the rushing wall, two gigantic runners pelted down toward us over the gravel. Both were in the last stages of exhaustion. The roar of the pursuing flood, which of course we could not hear, urged them on to the last spark of their vitality. They reeled toward us, blind with brute fear. Of course they did not see us, although we stood directly in their path. As they lurched, panting, toward us, we photographed every detail of their monstrous bodies on our eyes.

First the lumbering, three-toed splay feet, like those of a gigantic and awkward bird, fascinated our attention. The shuffling rise and fall of those blundering feet spelled out the utter exhaustion of the runners in showers of scattered gravel. But the reeling brutes continued to cover the ground, twelve feet or more at a stride. The massive muscles of the legs contracted and expanded with the regularity of a well-balanced machine.

Behind each runner the short, massive tail arched well over the gravel, maintaining the precarious balance of the lurching body as it strained forward to attain the limit of speed. The huge, baglike bellies sagged till they all but interfered with the piston motion of the legs, and each reptile, whether by purely mechanical reflexes or instinct, clutched frantically at the swaying obstruction in an effort to hold it up and free the legs. The hand clutching the belly was more plainly seen than the other, which sawed the air in clumsy arcs to aid the tail in balancing. That hand was grotesquely human. The sloping shoulders joined directly into the massive, columnar neck. All the hopeless struggle was pictured in the tense neck as thick as the body of an ox and rigid with great cables of muscle strained to the limit of endurance.

One of the runners began to outdistance the other. It foraged swiftly ahead, urged by its keener senses as its body all but felt the ram of waters upon it. As it reeled by, the knee joint of one colossal leg passed well above the level of our heads, and we caught a vivid image of a blunt, flattened reptilian head thirty feet above us. That inadequate head, with its compressed mouth snapped close shut like a turtle's beak, was a living portrait of a brainless stupidity animated by brute fear. A mere crested ridge of horny hide surmounted the staring reptilian eyes to contain whatever brain the lumbering creature possessed. Such a machine of ponderous bone and muscle could respond but slowly to external stimuli, and the momentum of any response would carry it far beyond the reasonable limit.

The laggard stumbled toward us, on the point of collapse, its strangely human arms whirling desperately and unavailingly to maintain a balance. The massive stubby tail sank; the runner had lost his race. Death was upon him. Less than five miles behind the merciless deluge came trampling after him with the speed of a nightmare. But he was not to drown.

A shout from Sellar wheeled us sharply about. We thought at first that he was calling our attention to the faster runner, still pounding its ponderous way down the river bed. Then we saw the object of his consternation. The sleeping yellow devil beyond the boulder had roused itself, and was gathering all its dying strength for the supreme crime of its life. The clamor that we could not hear had broken the reptile's poisoned stupor. Crouching low like a cat about to spring on a bird, it glided toward the exhausted runner.

The doomed brute saw its enemy. All the life it was about to lose surged to its great heart. The massive muscles stiffened, the tail sprang up, and the sinews of the neck stood out like cables. Its two horribly human hands shot up to guard the softer flesh of the chin. The attacker was a lizard to a crocodile beside the defender.

For the first time we apprehended the curious aspect of the defender's hands. Each had four stunted fingers and a thumb. But the thumb did not oppose the fingers as in a human hand; the brute could not have picked up so much as a club or a stone with its futile hand. Of what conceivable use could it be? Was it just another of nature's cruel jests?

We never learned the purpose of the stubby fingers. All that the ungainly hand was intended to be was concentrated in the thumb. This was the creature's weapon of defense, a murderous, overgrown, horn-like excrescence nearly two feet long and sharper than a stiletto.

The starving yellow devil crouched and leapt for the other's throat. It was a good leap, for one in the last stages of starvation, and the evil fangs found their mark. A shudder of intolerable pain convulsed the massive neck. Evidently the yellow devil was indeed venomous; even the brainless mass of bone and muscle felt the penetrating fire and sting of that venom. But it was a quick and merciful execution.

The great legs collapsed, and the creature tottered to its death. But in dying it shot one convulsed arm up to its head and spitted its slayer on the dagger-like thumb. A second more and the trampling water overwhelmed the dead and the dying.

All but Bronson turned instinctively to flee. Less than a second . . .

"How's that?" It was one of the technicians shouting from the rotund. The sixty minutes were up. We tried to shout back and choked.

"Oh, this blessed, solid concrete," Sellar sighed, as he

sat down on the floor of the arena and pressed it hard with both hands.

## Chapter II
### THE LOTUS EATERS

Even the earliest successes with the televisor were not hit-or-miss shots in the dark of a forgotten past. As the engineers became more proficient in the technique of analysing, they saw clearly that every apparently trivial incident fitted into one superb picture of a vanished epoch. And as they progressed they perceived that all the histories they deciphered were records of a conflict between two great races. One of these early split into two hostile factions and warred upon its own kind. Finally, both factions were exterminated by a fourth combatant, whom they had overlooked, and before whose irresistible strength they perished, while the nimbler third party fled to safety.

We who followed the unrolling of the histories conceived a new respect for an old doctrine—that of the four "elements," earth, air, fire and water. Our modern, sophisticated knowledge recognizes none of these as an "element," except as a metaphor. Our more imaginative ancestors went to the root of the matter and put their finger on the eternal tetrad of destruction.

If our parvenu race vanquishes the "invincible four," as we came to call the major protagonists of the conflict, it will be the first in the history of the world to do so. But, as has been pointed out by Sellar, who is something of an historian, nature seldom repeats herself. The particular weapon she has reserved for us is probably of a totally different calibre than that which sufficed for the vast, brainless and near-brainless hordes whose decline we witnessed.

Measured against the ages of that forgotten struggle, the whole slow rise of our race from brutehood to manhood is as a second to a day. So perhaps it is premature to make predictions from the records we saw. We, after all, may have it in us to win.

Bronson, who is a practical man with a tinge of pessimism, thinks we shall lose. Intelligence, he believes, is the subtle weapon which nature has reserved for our undoing. However, as he says this only after he has had a bad night, the rest of those who saw the records discount it to zero and predict the exact opposite—as does Bronson himself when he is feeling fit. Anyhow, as Sellar remarks, it was a good show, and we shall have done our part if we can put on one half as entertaining.

As there was little in all the records that could justly be called a picture of lazy peace and contentment, I shall give the one that qualifies in this respect more than its due share of space. The finishing touch to the picture may be disregarded if desired; in face the assemblers have suggested that it be cut from the completed record. But as Sellar insists that the cut be not made in the interests of historical accuracy and fidelity to nature, I shall leave the record intact.

This particular episode was followed from the roof of the rotunda. We thus obtained an unobstructed view of the whole panorama. Behind us stretched the milky-blue placidity of a vast lake or fresh-water inland sea. Vision set no limit to the expanse. We might have been gazing out over one of our own Great Lakes, except for the peculiar chalky appearance of the water. Directly opposite us in the other direction, and about a hundred yards distant at the nearest point, the almost level shoreline ran for league after league to the limit of seeing.

The shallow water between us and the shore was the scene of the lotus eater, as we named the happy harmless creature enjoying himself beneath the sunny ripples. The afternoon was one of those flawless fragments of eternity which we remember for a lifetime. Time seemed to stand still against the motionless masses of white cumulus clouds piled mountain high around the horizon, and the lush reeds in the boundless marshes shone with an unforgettable, quiet green, unstirred by the passing of any breeze. Even the ordinarily drab mud of the shoreline dividing the marshlands from the water was a band of delicate violet, like another, softer sky, in which the stately masses of the clouds shone as in a mirror of infinite depth.

We waited.

When the image first condensed we saw no living creatures. Their presence however was recorded in the spoors criss-crossing the mud of the shoreline in all directions. Having adjusted the perspective, we got the true scale and made a rough estimate of the size of some of those fresh footprints. The deepest of them could easily have accommodated a large wash tub. From that they ranged down to mere pockets the size of a teacup.

Following out one of the larger spoors, we easily deduced the kind of monster which had made the tracks. Whatever its usual habit, it had lumbered along on all four feet over the mud, letting its enormous tail drag. Once in its slow journey it had rested on its belly. The outline of the roughly oval depression could have embraced the bulk of four cows without undue crowding.

Where were the inhabitants of this lush paradise? We guessed them to be off in the tall reeds gorging themselves into insensibility. Our guess was only partly right. The first inhabitant appeared from a totally unexpected quarter. The surface of the water all round our rotunda was completely covered by dense masses of some aquatic plant with fleshy green leaves and large, lily-like scarlet blossoms. If we had stopped to think we would have realized that this flaming cress would make an ideal salad for frequenters of mud flats.

Langtry was admiring the gently rising and falling mantel of scarlet when suddenly he gave a violent start.

"Am I seeing things? There it is again—quick!"

The scarlet water weeds were thrust aside, and a bland, expressionless face the size of a bathtub beamed up at us with a welcoming smile of complete and amiable imbecility. To say that the face smiled is an exaggeration. A smile presupposes at least the rudiments of a central nervous system. There was none behind that vast, vacuous face. The huge slit of the tight-lipped mouth, slightly tilted at the corners, did however give the empty face a semblance of intelligence to which it was not entitled. Even the surly countenance of the dullest hippopotamus would have sparkled with vivacity beside that vacant dishpan of a face.

The lidless pig eyes opened to their fullest extent, the slit of a mouth became less compressed, and the stupid face opened to the sky in an abysmal yawn. It was the most perfect expression of indolence imaginable, and we furtively covered our own sympathetic imitations.

The red chasm into which we peered was as innocent of teeth as the mouth of a mud sucker. A bony ridge along the gums might conceal degenerated teeth for all we could see. But if so, the teeth were tired to cut through. We marvelled that such a mass of laziness could command energy enough to breathe and keep alive. Probably its too bulky ancestors had taken to the shallow waters in order to float and save their legs the fatigue of supporting inert tons of superfluous flesh.

The gaping mouth closed, apparently of its own weight, for the sluggish creature seemed to lack the energy for even so simple an act. For some moments the huge flat head floated lazily among the scarlet blossoms, rising and falling listlessly on the gentle swell.

We thought the beast had gone to sleep. But it had not. It was merely trying to make up what passed for its mind whether or not it was hungry. At last it decided. Feeding time had come again. The flat head seemed to open six or eight inches like a split pie, and very slowly it began to glide over the water, skimming off the cress. As that efficient natural skimmer slid over the surface of the water, a perfectly straight path four feet wide and twenty feet long was swept clean of the floating plants. Not so much as a single fleshy leaf or one scarlet petal eluded the scoop. That mouthful alone, sucked down into the creature's invisible interior as fast as it was skimmed, must have weighed at least a ton. We thought it enough, but we underestimated the beast's capacity for food.

For perhaps two minutes the head rested on the water at the end of the lane it had swept. Then, with exasperating deliberation, it was withdrawn to the starting point. If enjoying a meal was no more exciting than those loutish movements seemed to indicate, we wondered why the sluggish beast bothered to feed itself at all. It would have required less effort to drown in peace.

Again the head rested, this time for over five minutes. Once more the flat face split open just wide enough to take in the plants, and again a twenty-foot lane was skimmed clean. Another ton of unnourishing vegetation disappeared into the invisible interior. Surely it should now be satisfied. But the meal had barely started. Fifteen tons or more of the flimsy stuff vanished before the feeder desisted. It stopped, apparently, merely because it had skimmed the water almost clean in the semicircle it could reach without budging on the muddy bottom. What it could reach by merely extending its neck was the natural limit of its ambition.

"That thing hasn't the brains of a worm," Sellar remarked disgustedly. "By the way, where's the rest of it? We've only seen the head, and by interference the neck. There must be a body floating somewhere nearby to absorb all that fodder."

"Not necessarily," Langtry objected. "I shouldn't be surprised to find the bulk of this beast in the next county. They seem to have gone in for size in the good old days."

"Bigger and stupider lummoxes." Bronson added. He seemed to dislike the harmless creature whose face alone we had seen so far. "Living on salad like that it must be as flabby as a dead cod. I wish there were some way of making it move."

As if in response to his wish, a huge ripple moved out from the base of the rotunda and sped out to the floating plants. The main bulk of the monster was hidden by the rotunda. There being no way of shifting the centre of the image, we had to wait patiently till the beast floated into view.

It did not hurry; it merely drifted. A slate-colored island bobbed up slowly and moved toward the muddy beach. This was the creature's rump. The smooth hide looked like rubber. There was not a protective wart or scale anywhere on that vulnerable, open expanse. Small wonder the beast was in no hurry to wade ashore. The devil only knew what might be lurking in the towering reeds. Certainly that defenseless mass of flesh did not. Otherwise it would have taken to the water for good and have abandoned the atavistic attempt to be half a land animal. Possibly the rubbery hide was tougher than it looked, but we had our doubts. We had seen some pretty sharp teeth in contemporary records.

The sluggish wader slowly approached the shore, and its body emerged from the water. The twenty-foot neck now rose stiffly from the water, elevating the head like a periscope. To our intense surprise the massive flat head now turned twice slowly through an arc of nearly 180 degrees. The great beast had sharper instincts than we had given it credit for. It was spying out off the coast before going ashore. Apparently satisfied with its observations, the wader proceeded.

From our vantage point on the roof of the rotunda we had a somewhat better view of the marshes than was possible to the wary reptile. Had we been consulted we should have counselled watchful waiting. Yet we had observed a suspicious tremor pass over the top of one lush thicket of reeds.

To give any adequate idea of the enormous bulk of that

vegetarian reptile as it appeared when it finally floundered onto the beach is difficult. We judged that its total length exceeded that of two freight cars. The awkward rump, the highest part of the beast, would easily have overtopped the largest locomotive.

What use the clumsy tail might be we could not fathom. It began nowhere in particular as a meaningless prolongation of the creature's vast hinder parts, and tapered out to a blunt nub sixty feet behind. We could not believe that the listless encumbrance of flabby flesh dragging in the mud had ever been used as a weapon of defense. There was not a ripple of hard, healthy muscle anywhere down its whole, futile length; it was nothing but an unnecessary parody of a vigorous tail. Nature had endowed her offspring with the hugest tail in history. The recipient might do with it what he pleased. It was no longer any concern of hers.

As a final crowning piece of irony, the useless tail was nearly three times as long as the inadequate neck. To have made a reasonable job of her idiotic masterpiece, nature should have stuck the head on the end of the tail, as indeed one famous paleontologist did when he articulated the skeleton of a similar monster. Then the sluggish brute would have had a not utterly inadequate periscope.

Viewing that imbecilic jest, Bronson suddenly lost what remained of his respect for natural law as manifested in living matter. If, he declared, nature has a purpose in evolution, that purpose is wholly sinister. A half-witted child of sadistic tendencies could not be so stupidly cruel as to devise a meaningless, helpless monstrosity like that poor brute shuffling along the beach. Sellar calmed him by pointing out that the creature probably enjoyed life in its own simple way, and got more happiness out of it than the most complex human being ever has imagined. After all, it had evidently relished its late dinner.

Feeding did indeed seem to be the monster's only function. Dragging the useless tail laboriously after it, the sluggish reptile squashed its way over the mud flats to the reeds. Reaching a lush clump, it extended its neck, tilted the flat head sideways, and began to feed gluttonously on the tender tops. Such watery stuff would have to be sucked down by the ton lot to furnish sufficient heat to keep the mountain of flesh alive. A vegetarian the size of this beast must spend all of its waking hours in feeding. Here again nature had gone the limit. There was no denying that the feeding machine was efficient. The vast creature epitomized the final and complete confusion between eating to live and living to eat.

Feeling the need of roughage to digest the bale of fodder it gulped down unchewed, the beast began ripping at the thicker stalks of the reeds. We looked on in silent apprehension. The utter defenselessness of the feeder had won us over to its side, and we did wish it would show a flicker of common sense. The inviting slimness of the unprotected neck filled us with dread for an accident that might easily happen down there near the roots.

The insatiable feeder moved forward a few feet over the space it had cleared into the thicket. At this spot the reeds were less dense, and it was possible to catch glimpses of an enchanting bayou just beyond the shelter-ing screen. Enormous orange lilies floated on the brown water. Evidently these were a special delicacy, for our friend greedily thrust his head through the sparse reeds and began skimming off the largest. He advanced a yard of two and stopped—quite suddenly.

The huge body bounded twenty feet into the air as if electrified and smacked down on the mud with an impact that shook the beach and sent long ripples scudding over the lake. The writhing neck flashed up and out of the reeds, spraying them with torrents of blood like water from a fire hose.

The hapless creature had lost its head. Some efficient devil lurking beneath the water lilies had severed the neck about two feet below the head at one snap.

The creature did not immediately expire. Its last moments recapitulated the whole tragedy of its inhibited instincts and its inherited futilities. The loss of its head did not incapacitate the blundering machine of bone and flabby flesh. So far as intelligence was concerned the dying reptile was almost precisely as it had been before the accident. As most of us were aware, the monster's main nervous system was concentrated in the rump, above the haunches, and conveniently near the tail. Whatever coordinated the slow movements of the legs was probably distributed all along the spinal column. All of this now came into violent action. The severance of the head had jarred the whole body into one supreme effort to live.

Showing a speed it never could have been capable of while uninjured, the dying monster bounded over the beach in terrific leaps that shook the lake, drenching the mud with the last of its life. Instinct, resident in its ganglia, urged it to the water. Twice it smashed belly down on the scarlet cress thirty feet from the shore, only to rebound as if made of rubber, and plunge its writhing withers deep into the mud. The crimsoned wash of its desperate plunges surged over the dying creature, bathing it in its own blood. It lay where it had fallen, twitching convulsively.

"Pretty fierce," Bronson muttered. "Damn nature."

"It's not over yet," Sellar remarked. "Here comes the murderer, or the appointed instrument of fate, or evolution or whatever you want to call him. Engaging devil, isn't he?"

To have wrought the irreparable havoc which he had done, the executioner was strangely undersized and insignificant. What he lacked in size he made up in grotesque repulsiveness. He emerged from the reed screen walking erect.

There was not much to him but jaws, sagging belly and hind legs. The forelegs were mere vestiges of what might once have been powerful arms weaponed with ruthless talons. They flipped against the palpitating wrinkles of his throat in a disgusting parody of lighthearted, jaunty dandyism. He was tripping out to dinner and he was in a merry, mischievous mood.

His total height, had he held his broad snout vertical instead of horizontal, might have reached that of a very tall man; certainly it was not over seven feet. Fully three feet of him was absorbed in the powerful jaws, still red with the insignia of their victory. Head joined belly without the intermediary of a neck. From his horny armor we judged that he too spent most of his days and nights in blind terror of his life. Probably he quarrelled with his friends when easier food was scarce.

For the moment however he was in good humor. He minced daintily toward his prospective meal. Others no doubt would soon join him, but for the moment, he, the victor, would enjoy the choicest spoils of his valor.

What followed caused Bronson to modify slightly his somewhat harsh verdict on natural mercy and justice. The balance was partially restored—when he could do the injured party neither harm nor good. Still, it was restored.

The executioner, being a reptile himself, should have remembered that it takes many, many hours for his kind to die completely, especially when the victim is of vast proportions. But, being a reptile half of whose body was belly, and half jaws to rend flesh in sufficient quantities to appease the constant voracity of his hunger, the executioner was incapable of remembering anything. The inherited experience of his forefathers had not yet registered on his rudimentary instincts.

The luscious softness of the quivering tail attracted the feaster first. For a second or two he stood erect, contemplating the prospective banquet. Then, opening his huge jaws to their fullest extent, he plunged in, about six feet from the tapered tip. The cruel, incurved teeth ripped at the flesh like sabres. Although the dying tail quivered excessively, the feaster managed to tear out a huge gobble of smoking meat. He stepped back and raised his enormous jaws skyward, like a bird drinking, the better to swallow the morsel.

All the vestigial instincts of the dying monster awoke once more before they died forever, and the posterior brain remembered its functions. A last reflex contraction of the flabby tail muscles sufficed. Just as the executioner swallowed, his belly was driven clear through his backbone by the terrific impact of twenty tons of outraged, dying flesh.

As the technicians have been largely responsible for the selection of records in this series, I shall follow their preference and describe only those which have an unmistakable reference to their special hero Belshazzar. To understand his history it is necessary to consider several broader records in which he played no part. These have been carefully chosen by the technicians from the complete series, of which they form only a very small sample.

For many weeks we had been puzzled by the frequent recurrence of one type of record which seemed to have no particular bearing on the history we were striving to unravel. We first observed it incidentally in the episode of the decapitated vegetarian. This was the peculiar milkiness of the lake water. Thereafter in scores of records we encountered the same inexplicable feature—boundless inland seas whose placid waters invariably were as turbid as dirty milk.

A radical improvement in the technique of projecting the televisor records was necessary before the riddle of the lakes was solved. The scale of what we were trying to decipher was evidently vast, both in space and time. The mere extent of the lakes offered no difficulty; the time factor seemed to present an insuperable obstacle. This was finally overcome in a ridiculously simple manner, suggested by the similar problem in motion pictures.

The history of years, of centuries, and perhaps even of thousands of centuries had to be condensed and reproduced in a sequence which the human eye could follow clearly in a total exposure of only a few seconds or minutes, or at the most two hours. The record of a long-time event was simply speeded up, like the moving pictures of, say, an opening rosebud.

Such was the simple solution suggested by experience and common sense. Unfortunately it did not work. The speeded records turned out confused gray blurs of swirling fog, in which no detail was visible. These disappointing records were obtained by letting the exploring needle of monochromatic light play continuously for several days on a specimen—crystal or fossil—instead of for a matter of minutes or hours.

The cause of the trouble was so simple that the rankest amateur should have foreseen the difficulty before the experiment of long exposures was ever attempted. The exploring needle was not at fault. It understood the commonest fact of everyday life better than did the engineers—the fact that a night is always interposed between two consecutive days. The needle analysed the hours of daylight and then superposed a blank corresponding to the unstimulated motion of the electrons during the night-long absence of light.

Once that elementary fact was grasped, it was a straightforward problem in laboratory mechanics to devise the proper automatic shutter or interrupter to filter out the nights and leave the recorder open to the days. This of course was no crude mechanical contrivance of diaphragms like a camera shutter. The fastest camera shutter ever made would have been quite useless. The actual device finally used with complete success was a battery of delicately balanced selenium cells—a hint the engineers got from the astronomers.

The first test of the interrupter was made on the lake of the lotus eater. By speeding up the recording, the technicians restored the history of approximately ten thousand years in a total exposure of two hours. At such a speed no details of life were visible; we saw only the milky expanse of the lake and its muddy shoreline.

Again the image was unsatisfactory. This time the difficulty was spotted at once. A slower shutter was devised to filter out the sunless days, whether the absence of full sunlight was due to a mere cloudy day or two or a whole winter season. This improvement produced entirely satisfactory records, until a third, vaster-scale obstacle of perfection, which will be described later, gradually blurred the records in a most puzzling way.

The history of that first ten-thousand-year stretch when accelerated to a one-hour record for exhibition presented a singularly restful picture after some of the ruthless violence we had witnessed. The cloudiness of the water dissolved, and the lake changed from a milky-blue opal to a transparent aquamarine. So clear was the water that we saw the chalky floor of the lake at a depth of hundreds of feet as clearly as if we were looking through a lens.

The speed of the recording was so great that of course we could make out no minor details. But we saw much, some of which puzzled us. Whatever action might be taking place, we observed only as the gradual shading of some vast patch of red into a softer expanse of russet, or as the mazy interplay of irregular patterns of color that seemed to meet, interpenetrate, and separate, both transformed into more intricate mosaics of color. The slow changes which we witnessed actually were flashing by at the rate of about a hundred and seventy years of real, historical time for each second of the projected image.

The technicians continued to run the analyser at the

same prodigious speed for eighteen hours longer, thus restoring the history of about ninety thousand years after the water of the lake first became transparent, giving a total run of one hundred thousand years.

Through all that ninety thousand years we detected no variation in the quality of the water. It remained as clear and as transparent as a flawless crystal. Nor could we observe any significant change in the sweep of the shoreline beyond a slight rhythmic advance and recession, as the image recorded the periodic recurrence of long stretches of exceptional drought followed by more abundant rain-falls for perhaps a millennium or two. Beyond that slow, regular breathing of the sleeping waters we observed nothing worth recording.

Continuing the exposure slightly beyond the hundred-year mark on the scale, we noticed that the water of the lake was growing turbid. The milkiness reappeared first on the colorful floor of the lake. Before following this history further, we reset the analyser and sampled the hundred thousand years at every thousandth-year mark all down the long record. These samples were slowed down to the speed where visibility of details fell just within the powers of the human eye.

The living panoramas were of course still greatly accelerated at this threshold of speed, but they sufficed for our purpose. We wished merely to see what happened to the tribe of lotus eaters in a stretch of one hundred thousand years. As there were ninety-nine such sample records, it is out of the question to report on the whole series. One or two specimens must suffice.

The first significant change appeared when the waters of the lake finally cleared—about the ten-thousand-year mark. In the slower record we noticed that the huge wading reptiles were now venturing out into the water much farther than they had previously dared.

Bronson suggested a plausible explanation for this apparent increase in boldness: all of those reptiles which were incapable of long absences from the land had fallen prey to the rapacious flesh eaters lurking in the marshes. Only those with the capacities for keeping themselves floating and comfortable for considerable periods without having to return to the beach eluded their enemies long enough to have a reasonable chance of reaching maturity. The offspring of this better-adapted breed inherited their parents' superiorities of lung and muscle, and made it increasingly difficult for the flesh eater to earn a substantial living.

Sellar pointed out that the flesh eaters had probably not been idle in the meantime. Only the offspring of the wariest, most voracious, strongest and quickest devils of the tribe would be able to come through the lean centuries unscathed. Their race was now probably a marvel of Spartan endurance and modern efficiency. The balance had not been destroyed; the conflict had merely grown fiercer and the competition keener.

Wishing to see something of the facts and check up on facile theorizing, we stepped down the projections to a more easily followed speed. The effect was at first ludicrous in the extreme, as the action was still transpiring at about twenty times the natural rate at which it had actually happened. The transparent waters of the lake for five or six miles from the shoreline teemed with enormous monsters skimming the scarlet weeds with frantic industry, or darting like electrified swans, their periscopes elevated in tense alertness, from one field to another of the watery pasture.

A stiff breeze freshened far out on the lake, rippled the surface of the water, and blew in vast beds of cress from the inexhaustible supply blanketing the deeper waters. Sensing the breeze, the paddlers faced it, impatiently waiting the arrival of fresh fodder.

The epoch was evidently one of unprecedented abundance. To keep abreast of the unlimited food supply, the huge feeding machines had increased their bulk to the very limit fixed by the laws of mechanics. Ten centuries more of such inexhaustible low-grade nourishment and the huge consumers would be unable to support their own weight on dry land. They must inevitably take to the water permanently to keep from collapsing of their own massiveness. But nature, as we were to see presently, had not yet decided to evolve the whales—or their equivalent, for the whales took to the water down another channel. For the time being, wind and weather conspired to glut the champion vegetable feeders of all time with an excess of food which they had not the wit to refuse.

Along the muddy shore the greatly accelerated action also presented a ludicrous parody of animated vivacity. The ungainly monsters shuffled busily hither and thither like gigantic rats, thrusting their snaky necks into the reed thickets from time to time, or browsing with feverish haste on the succulent tops. Now and then a glutted feeder would lurch back to the water like a runaway locomotive and plunge in. The absence of the prodigious splash which we anticipated only made the scene more ridiculous. Even the greatly accelerated projection could not create a splash where the deliberate beast itself was too indolent to lift its lumbering feet more than six inches out of the mud. But the ripple which the monster set up would have done credit to a freighter.

We were beginning to think the lotus eaters utterly incapable of anything but feeding when a lucky chance, just below the three-thousand-year mark of the record, shot up a comedy which revised our estimate. Probably the episode was a mere accident, the sort of happy chance that occurs only once or twice in a hundred thousand years—like tossing heads twenty times consecutively with an honest coin. Given time enough, any event not sheerly impossible is as likely as not to happen. But we had no wish to disparage the lotus eaters. We agreed to give at least one of them full credit for his apparent exhibition of intelligence, although not one of those who observed the great beasts really believes that a single giant of the lot had the wits of a worm.

The scene was that of early morning. For fully three miles from the shore the water was bare of cress. Either the gluttonous reptiles had pumped the entire week's supply into their vast bags, or an unfavorable wind had blown it all far out beyond the reach of even the most daring waders. The whole population resident in that section was ashore, greedily browsing on the reeds or cavorting—under the greatly accelerated rate of projection—in ungainly evolutions on the mud.

Where was the enemy? Why did he not take advantage of the bountiful windfall right on his own doorstep? Could he possibly be overawed by a mere display of numbers? Not he surely, with his invincible superiority of jaw and sabre teeth, to say nothing of his all but impenetrable armor of horny plates.

The enemy was not bluffed by the impressive concentration of the lotus eaters. But he was a cowardly sort of reptile in spite of his superior armament, and he would take no chances. Not until his victims were delivered practically bound and helpless to his jaws would he venture to attack. Chance—or stupidity—gave the enemy his chance, and he seized it immediately.

One enormous feeder had lurched away from the main herd on its way to the water. It was glutted and moved even more sluggishly than usual. Instantly five of the enemy darted from the reeds and made at top speed for the isolated monster. Like grotesque, squat crocodiles they raced erect over the mud on their stout hind legs, flipping their feeble hands in anticipatory ecstasy, their murderous horny jaws already agape to their widest. This was to be a quick victory and an easy banquet.

Chancing to turn its head sideways, the helpless monstrosity of flabby flesh saw the enemy coming. The five raced over the mud in a compact squad. Their objective, curiously enough, was not the defenseless neck, but awkward, upstanding rump. Not till long afterwards did we comprehend the full significance of that instinctive but nevertheless intelligent strategy. The rump certainly was vulnerable enough, but the neck, we should have guessed, would be an even safer place to attack.

What the intended victim now automatically did avenged the murder of its helpless fellow creature —thousands of years before. Like a mechanical toy operated by surprising springs, the startled monster sprang straight up off the mud, partly by reflex action of its flabby tail, partly by the equally automatic action of the shoulder muscles. The vertical leap shot the huge body up a good fifteen feet. When gravity brought it down again with an impact that jarred every monster on the beach, the five fierce attackers vanished. Their too eager momentum had carried them directly under the ponderous creature's enormous belly, distended and stodged as it was with tons of undigested vegetation.

For some minutes the unconscious victor squatted in the mud incapable of motion. It was paralyzed with fright. Probably it just brooded in the mud in helpless resignation to the momentarily expected slash and rip of the sabre teeth. It might have continued to squat there till the wash of the lake buried its bones in the mud of centuries, had not the precipitate retreat of its own kind roused it to sluggish motion. Terrified by the unprecedented leap of their fellow monster, and urged into motion by the subsequent jarring of the mud flats, all were lumbering toward the water as fast as their stunted legs would take them.

The paralyzed victor instinctively got to its feet and followed the herd. As it rose we saw the five attackers, their vicious jaws still agape, reposing in their last sleep. Squashed flat in the mud they offered a perfect museum exhibit, to be exhumed and chipped out of the rock millions of years later by some ingenious paleontologist. If ever we see that particular group of five in a museum, we shall know where it came from and how five complete warriors all happened to be caught together in the same attitude of arrested flight. The hind legs of all five were extended as if still straining forward to the limit of speed. Even Sellar, usually so sympathetic, could find no softer epitaph than "serve the vicious brutes right."

Having witnessed this unique example of prehistoric justice, we were loath to tempt our luck by searching for another. Accordingly we speeded up the record and passed directly to the hundred-and-ten-thousand-year mark. The water of the lake was again growing turbid, but slowly. Then suddenly, so great was the speed of the record, the whole lake flashed out in a vast sheet of slate gray. The technicians cut off the projection in order to carry the analysis forward half a million years.

\*      \*      \*

## Chapter III
# THE BRIDGE

All the ingenious or terrible variations of the reptilian pattern were worked out at one time or another on that lost continent of the north. As the record swept forward in time, a hundred thousand or half a million years at a stride, we paused now and then for an occasional glimpse at the dying age. What was a vast inland sea teeming with life in an early record became a sand-filled sink in the later histories, too far from greenery to support even the hardiest of the heat-loving reptiles. A still later record showed the same sink again inhabited to saturation with a ravenous population, as torrential rivers from younger mountains again filled the basin and made life possible.

Still later the resurrected sea dried once more as the aged mountains were levelled and the rivers ceased to flow. What had been a lush paradise in the golden age slowly withered as the lake shrank to streaks of alkali marsh. Those whose natural habitat was the water struggled to adapt themselves to the land, while those that had developed beyond all reason on the land made a feeble attempt to lead a half-watery existence as their food supplies diminished and finally disappeared beneath the advancing sands.

In the last slow struggle opposing instincts met and locked in a ruthless conflict which rapidly eliminated all but the fiercest and wariest, until in the end those who would overtake the retreating water were annihilated by those who sought a foothold on the starving land. Migrations in search of fresher seas ended in disaster in the deserts after centuries of futile struggle and ever sharper war of like upon like, and only the birds made the journey.

Everywhere the record was the same. At first the strong, vigorous races responded magnificently to their changing environments, and rapidly reached the peak of their superb efficiency. Then nature forgot them.

The horny armor that had made one giant invincible against the attacks of its most powerful enemy continued to develop like a horrible disease. Utterly useless excrescences of bone or horn impeded every movement in the jungles and forests, and drove the clumsy creatures into the open, to be slaughtered by enemies that loved the sunlight. Overdeveloped claws forced those who had leapt lightly as birds upon their prey to hobble lamely after the punier offspring of degenerating herds, and what had been a joyous battle in a more vigorous age became a disgusting exhibition of starving senility pursuing spiritless cowardice. Often the shambling tracker was sheerly incapable of killing his quarry. In the end the pursuers became scavengers of carrion.

But all these consequences of nature's forgetfulness

were of minor importance. These tragedies of indifference counted as nothing beside those of the major offensives of the revolution.

To render the creeping advance of the ocean over the land visible, it was necessary to compress a million-year analysis into an hour's projection. The engineers hurried the televisor through the next half million years.

At first we failed to appreciate what we saw under the greatly accelerated rate of projection. The scene might have been that of the vast fertile central plains of North America. A stopdown gave us a glimpse of teeming reptilian life at the very peak of its glory. The boundless prairies, paradises of luxuriantly tall grasses, rich shrubs and edible trees, were populated to the limit of their capacity to support life. Speeding the projection again we let the image flash out in smooth green in which no detail of life registered.

For long the green expanse remained precisely as we had first projected it. Then, like ice beginning to split on a frozen river in the spring thaw, a jagged fissure severed the plain in two. In a second the fissure brightened and lived like a streak of fire. Another second and the crimson was blotted out in rapidly spreading black. Other fissures opened from the first, these in turn branched and glowed, until finally the whole plain cracked in a million places and seemed to crawl.

We stopped down and followed the beginning of the record at its natural rate. Red-hot lava was oozing from every crack and creeping over the plain. As it crept it blackened, and dense, dun smoke rolled lazily up, blotting out the last stampedes of the few that had not been suffocated by the first outgush of deadly gases.

The interpretation of the other yellow flash which was analysed in detail was quite similar. It chanced to be near the ocean.

The water heaved convulsively and sent wave after wave toppling over the headlands far back onto the plain. The terrified monsters were swept by swarms into the sea. Those farther back on the plain, beyond the reach of the tidal waves, collapsed where they stood. No living thing could stand on the pitching ground that rolled and tossed like a stormy sea. As the fissures burst open and the lava gushed out, the violence of the earthquakes abated, and the stunned reptiles got to their feet.

Where to flee? Some ventured onto the blackening crust and plunged steaming into solid fire. Others stampeded toward the sea, blind with terror, the pursuing lava rolling after them. At the edge of the cliffs they milled back and forth, seeking a way down to the water. Again the floor of the sea heaved, and a wall of black water hurled the refugees back on the lava. Clouds of steam overwhelmed the day in impenetrable darkness for a moment. Then the marriage of fire and water was consummated in a cataclysm that split the sky.

The last we saw on that record was a rolling mountain of yellowish smoke trampling over the sea, and we imagined that it hid the last flight of the birds, still cleaving the air on steady wings.

To get an intelligible record we went on slowly, at ten-thousand-year steps.

The fate of those who perished in the volcanic outbursts was happier than that of those who survived. As I have tried to indicate, there was never, at any stage of the revolution, any such disaster as universal and continuous volcanic activity. Even at the peak of violence at least one vast plain escaped lava. It was a period of furious earthquakes and devastating invasions of the land by the oceans, but even these appalling violences lost their full terror when eased over the course of a hundred thousand years. The constantly terrified herds gradually adapted themselves to accept violence as the immemorial order of nature, and a more alert race, swifter of foot and keener of muscular sense, survived from the merciless discipline. They grew immune to the terrors which had paralyzed their untried ancestors. But for all their courage they dared not oppose the invincible enemy which nature brought up as her last reserve for their annihilation.

All the spectacular fury of earthquakes and volcanic fires was but the nerve-racking barrage before the charge. It did comparatively little damage—except to the land. Here the time scale played its fatal part. If the pulverized ash of the eruptions had been released a thousand times more slowly into the air, the cold-blooded reptiles might have won. But in what amounted to no more than a few days in the life history of their tribes, their heat supply was cut down a full two thirds. A dense blanket of fine pumice blocked the sun's radiation in the upper lanes of the atmosphere circling the pole. The reptiles had no time to adapt their shivering bodies to the cold, or to evolve a resistant race.

The great migration toward the south began. But retreat had been cut off. Only a long, narrow bridge of barren basalts united the dying continent and the sunny southern land, with its boundless green plains and open inland seas, which was the emigrant's promised paradise. On that bridge only stunted shrubs and wind-blown low grasses grew. The seeds might suffice for ratlike mammals on the trek, but not for the lumbering reptiles. These required bales of fodder at a meal, and their horny mouths were not adapted for cropping.

A thousand years before the hardiest explorers of the kingly reptiles accidentally blundered onto the narrow bridge, the first snow had fallen far behind them, and the thin ice had floated on the surface of the northernmost inland sea. Had more than a thread of barren rock united the continents, whole nations would have escaped. But long before the first reptile dared put out on the long hungry journey across the bridge, millions had perished on the bleak cliffs.

Few ever discovered the bridge. The majority endured centuries of slow starvation as season after season of sleety cold stunted the grass and killed the shrubs. As the winters lengthened and the chilly summers grew steadily colder, the vitality of the struggling survivors ebbed and they became incapable of sustained journeys. Starving and listless they crawled like dying flies over the ravaged plains in search of a tuft of living reeds. The flesh eaters dogged the emaciated browsers, waiting for one to collapse of exhaustion. They had grown incapable of killing all but the youngest, and few young now survived more than a day after emerging from the egg.

If only the listless hosts had discovered the bridge they need not have perished. Heat and food in plenty lay less than a year's journey to the south. Yet almost in sight of the promised land they perished of cold and hunger, dying miserably. But one remnant did escape. These were the geniuses of their tribes.

The continent shivered in one final, feeble outburst of

volcanic activity. It was nature's last gift to those of the reptiles who had not discovered the bridge and her welcoming threat to the newer race which had already passed over. As the slow lava oozed down to the ocean the emaciated reptiles swarmed around it in a last effort to restore their ebbing vitality. For half a generation the dying remnant marooned on a dead continent recovered a tithe of their ancient vigor in the grateful heat. The herb eaters scoured the quaking plain in search of food, and the flesh eaters followed and attacked. Presently the powdered ash sifting down day and night, month after month, and year after year smothered the last of the herbage and the final starvation began. The flesh eaters outlived their cousins by less than a month.

That final gift of heat for a brief season was the marooned reptiles' undoing. Within a half a year's journey of the bridge the last survivor on the continent perished. A sterner climate would have urged them ever southward to warmth and safety.

We reset the analyser and followed the bolder remnant which, half a generation before, had ventured—probably without intention—onto the bridge.

\*       \*       \*

Belshazzar belonged to the same tribe as the great reptiles we had seen in an earlier record of blindness and starvation. But no disease had ever thriven in this superb body, and no enemy had ever so much as scratched a single plate of the protective armor down the back. The muscular tail was long and fully developed. Even the exposed chest was amply protected by short but powerful forelimbs armed with stout claws that could either grapple or rip. And nothing short of plates of bone or horn six inches thick could withstand the slash of the huge talons of the feet or the snap and crunch of the broad jaws.

The whole head was a perfectly balanced engine of aggressive destruction. At least five feet long and three broad where it joined the massive neck, its entire length was jammed full of teeth that could slash or tear as occasion demanded or rage inspired. Not one of those splendid teeth had been broken, although many a horny shield or thighbone far back on the plains bore deep grooves which fitted some of the teeth exactly. Some few of the larger bones that had been cracked for their marrow showed what Belshazzar could do when he was really hungry.

Nature never surpassed this magnificent reptile in any of her creations. If he lacked human intelligence he exhibited a substitute—fierce cunning and a consummate skill in forcing his inhospitable environment to yield him the necessities of life—which was singularly like the power of reason.

Possibly we who now saw him in action judged him too sympathetically. Had we looked at him critically according to our present ethical standards we should have condemned him as a brutal tyrant. But we could not. Belshazzar fought his battles himself. If any life was to be risked, and possibly sacrificed, it was his own which was placed in jeopardy.

Further, he fought the entire world, for the whole age was against him and his kind. That he had the instinctive, brute courage to face insuperable odds, even without knowledge of what was against him, instead of accepting the inevitable defeat before he was forced to, was not evidence of stupidity but of sportsmanship. He would see it through to the end, and be damned to it. No apology from any human being is in order. Having seen Belshazzar we respect him, the more perhaps because he was totally devoid of what we somewhat arrogantly called our higher faculties. He was a brute, some would say, but God had made him and he would walk the earth unashamed before his maker, as he had been made.

Belshazzar's advance must have been almost noiseless. Neither of the duelists was aware of his approach, and the female heard him coming only when it was too late. As her head shot 'round and she jumped erect, Belshazzar leapt thirty feet through the air like an agile bird. All the tremendous muscles of his legs were behind that leap.

Before the terrified female could turn her head again preparatory to flight, Belshazzar had unbuttoned her. One expert slash by the middle talon of his foot down her back, from the nape of the neck to the root of her stubby tail, exposed the backbone, and in another second she was stripped. He killed her on the spot, one fierce eye fixed on her fighting mates. They were next on his program. But they were too quick for him. As he sprang to the slaughter the enraged brute trampling the other leapt into midair, his sharpened dagger aimed for Belshazzar's throat. Belshazzar kicked the maddened reptile squarely in the chest, hurling him forty feet, to land flat on his bleeding back. The other, with the two sound daggers, was now on its feet, running like a bird. We never saw him again. Belshazzar strode toward the prostrate reptile he had kicked.

It heard him coming, but it was still too stunned to rise.

Instinctively it thrust its strong hind legs straight out to meet the expected leap. Its single sound dagger stuck straight up from the stubby hand clutched tightly over the middle of the belly. The stunned brute could not have devised a more effective defense in the full possession of all its senses.

Belshazzar's reptilian eye took in the possibilities. Changing his course, he circled so as to get at his prostrate enemy's head. One snap of his jaws could have crunched it to a pulp. The detour squandered many precious seconds. Before Belshazzar had completely worked out his plan of attack the wounded duelist was on its feet, running as it had never run in all its athletic life. It was not a cowardly retreat; only a fool stands up to the devil of his particular race.

For a moment Belshazzar seemed to hesitate. Prudence urged him to devour the kill he had already made, while sport impelled him to pursue. What followed looked like an act of self-sacrifice, but to interpret it as such is probably a libel. No reptile, so far as we observed, ever gave up anything it wanted for itself. The strange capacity for appreciating the feelings of others to the possible hurt of one's own seems to be peculiar to the birds and the mammals. So what Belshazzar now did need not be ascribed to anything but his preference for a good fight over a mediocre meal. After all, the flesh he had killed was too close to his own to be really tempting.

Two battered reptiles of his own magnificent tribe now emerged somewhat diffidently from the shelter of the watercourse. Although both had evidently been splendid specimens of their race in their prime, neither approached Belshazzar in size. From their gait and the many scars on their sagging hides it was clear that both were much older than Belshazzar. From his tolerance of their rather timid intrusion we judged them to be old acquaintances, perhaps even close friends of his infancy. For even the most ferocious of tyrants must have protectors when he is too feeble to fight for himself.

But again it is dangerous to impute altruism where none exists. As a baby, Belshazzar no doubt had been lively enough to stick pretty close to the strongest of his tribe. Otherwise he would have been eliminated. As he grew up, habit and the lifelong association of seeing the old folks around would accustom him to tolerating their humble presence and letting them share the less lordly of his feasts. In time he might even imitate very closely the behavior which in higher mammals is analysed into filial affection or less pleasing complexes. Indeed, from the manner in which the middle-aged couple clung to one another for better or for worse all through their troubled record, it is not impossible they were lifelong mates. If such was the case, then Belshazzar might well have been their son, which would account for much. On the other hand, we found no evidence that any of the reptiles believed in monogamy, as some of the birds and a few of the mammals seem to, nor that any of them were capable of either constancy or affection.

However, speculation as to the precise degree of kinship—if any—between the members of that strange trio is not without interest, especially to those who have endeavored to analyze Belshazzar's behavior in the light of modern theories. One thing is certain, whatever may have been the relationships of those three: Belshazzar's character cannot be explained in terms of any of the classical complexes which have received Greek names. If he had any sort of complex or fixation, it was of a new kind and it deserves a name of its own. He was a reptile, and he cannot be pigeonholed in any mammalian psychology.

For similar reasons the engineers refused to name Belshazzar's two middle-aged camp-followers after any of the Greek or Roman heroes and heroines. The lady they called Jezebel, simply because she looked like what they thought Jezebel should have looked like. The other looked as if his name were Bartholomew. These labels have the advantage of not suggesting any possibly non-existing kinship among the three.

*       *       *

## Chapter IV
## THE SCIENTIST

Nearly half a century elapsed before our friend with the three-foot dagger and a passion for dueling found his way across the bridge. We recognized him instantly by his one broken dagger and the two scars symmetrically placed below his shoulder blades.

By sampling the record at five-year intervals we had learned that a steady but alarmingly slim stream of refugees trickled over the bridge all through the fifty-year period. Most of these were so exhausted when they finally set foot in paradise that they fell an easy prey to Belshazzar, Jezebel and Bartholomew, who seldom strayed very far from the source of supplies.

Our friend however came over romping in splendid

condition. Although he must have been approaching middle age—for a reptile—he was more active and fuller of the devil than he had ever been in his youth. Possibly the lack of a mate through his lonely years had something to do with his aggressive devilishness. We felt morally certain that he was the last of his kind.

His sound three-foot dagger was still intact. It had earned him a good living. The harassed herd of exhausted herb eaters which preceded him by several hours bore many a mark of his efficiency as a herdsman on ill-protected backs. He seemed to have specialized in rounding up the sturdiest survivors of the fleet-footed chargers with the five horns—or sometimes as many as seven. These fierce creatures he had herded like cows after he succeeded in stampeding them onto the bridge.

Semi-starvation did the rest, till the roughest of them could not have launched a charge more dangerous than a kitten's. His first fights of course had been fair enough. That his stiletto and quick legs were superior to his cattle's numerous horns and nimble feet accounted for his own lusty buoyancy and their emaciated dejection. He had hustled them to the best of his ability, but they could not cover many miles a day on practically nothing to eat.

As this skillful dueler and expert herdsman was probably the last survivor of his tribe, the engineers felt that he deserved a name. Taking everything into account—his striking appearance, his almost human cunning and his bachelorhood, they decided to call him Satan. The rest of us thought this somewhat of a libel on both parties, but let it pass. Indeed Sellar objected quite violently at first, claiming that the dueler had no right to be called after Milton's great hero, as Belshazzar, not he, was the undoubted ruler of the green paradise.

Belshazzar unfortunately was not present to receive Satan as the latter stepped jauntily off the harsh basalt of the bridge onto the first patch of bright green grass. At the moment the tyrant was fifteen miles away, giving all of his ingenuity to the solution of a difficulty which was rapidly becoming desperate.

The food supply was steadily diminishing, and what did find its way over the bridge made pretty lean picking. Bartholomew and Jezebel of late had even been reduced to faring farther and farther afield and smashing what diminutive mammals they could with their poor old awkward feet. Belshazzar left them practically nothing now. What he got was barely sufficient for his own gigantic frame. Soon it would be less than sufficient and then—well, it was better not to look too far into the future.

By his praise-worthy attention to the needs of himself and his camp-followers, Belshazzar missed the liberal supply of fresh meat which Satan imported. In all Satan contributed about twenty souls to the population. Bartholomew's dunderheadedness and Jezebel's greed squandered Satan's considerable gift in utter folly. Had Belshazzar been present, things might have gone otherwise.

The herd preceded Satan by about ten hours. Probably he had stopped for refreshments before undertaking the last lap. The smell of fresh greenery put new life into the starving monsters. Here was peace, here was food beyond their power to consume, here, in short, was heaven at last. They rushed into the thickets and tore at the ferns and shrubs.

For nearly ten hours the refugees stuffed themselves. Incidentally they completely incapacitated themselves for anything even faintly resembling a defense should they be suddenly attacked. So when Jezebel and Bartholomew returned from a three days' shopping expedition on a plain beyond the jungle, the plums almost fell into their jaws. Jezebel was so hungry that she attacked the herd from the rear without a moment's forethought.

It was the stupidest thing she could have done. Even the gorged quadrupeds were still capable of flight. Seeing one of their flock brutally murdered on the very threshold of what they had thought was paradise, they crashed through the shrubs and vanished down a deep ravine, swept along by the old familiar fear. That they would ever return to the vicinity of the bridge was extremely improbable.

Belshazzar would have patrolled the herd and kept it within easy reach. Jezebel had blundered precipitately and fatally, betrayed by her treacherous hunger. She was so hard pressed in fact that she permitted poor old Bartholomew to snuggle down beside her and share the feast.

Their foolish enjoyment did not last long. The racket of the fleeing herd as it crashed down the ravine reached Satan's ears as he stepped onto real grass at last. For a second or two he stood listening. Then he seemed to sniff. He smelt the old folks' dinner. The stubby tail flicked up perkily and he leapt forward in a joyous, skipping gallop. This was almost more than he had expected of heaven —to be met at the gates with a fresh dinner which he had not been forced to prepare himself.

The poor old folks had barely started when Satan burst in on them. Both heard him coming long before he arrived, but Bartholomew saw him first. To the old lizard's credit he instantly forgot his interrupted dinner.

Here was a dangerous rival entering the field to compete for what remained of the shrinking food supply. The interloper should be eliminated immediately if he resisted deportation back over the bridge.

Satan resisted, vigorously. As Bartholomew flew at him with all the verve and fury of his forgotten youth, Satan charged without a moment's hesitation. Jezebel might have helped. But she lacked the wit to see that twenty meals in the future are better than one in the present —when it is not a question of actual starvation. Returning to her dinner, she let her mate take care of the enemy.

Bartholomew did his best. But his vision was not what it had been, and he misjudged his leap badly. Instead of landing squarely on Satan's head and shoulders as he had intended, he sailed clean over by a margin of at least two feet. Satan's accurate eye had foreseen what must happen. As Bartholomew sailed over his head like an eagle about to strike, Satan instantly put all the momentum of his irresistible charge into one magnificent leap. All of that leap was under the lunge of the three-foot dagger, which penetrated Bartholomew's back just above the pelvis. Satan staggered and all but lost his balance as Bartholomew lit and the dagger was disengaged by the momentum of the old fellow's leap. Quickly recovering, he wheeled about and landed on Bartholomew's stomach the instant the wounded reptile's shoulder struck the dirt.

Satan got much more than he had bargained for. If it had been one of his own kind he was trampling he need not have greatly feared his enemy's hind legs. Their talons might have scratched him severely, but they could not have slashed him within danger of his life. Bartholomew was badly wounded, but he had fallen into the deadliest of his fighting postures and the pain of his grievous hurt restored all the fury of his terrible prime. Before Satan could escape, his tail and legs were badly gashed. The wounds were not serious—except for the maddened reptile that had inflicted them. Their stinging pain sent all the hate and murder in Satan's great body surging to his heart.

Even Belshazzar could not have faced the maddened stabber with impunity as he now was. He waited till Bartholomew got to his feet, so he could be reached easily. The valiant old fighter put all his courage into a noble attempt at a sailing leap. But the spurting wound had already drained much of his vitality, and the muscles of his legs, stiffening with pain, refused to function. The intended leap was a mere flutter. It landed him squarely in front of Satan, within easy reach of the waiting devil's arm. To Satan's credit it should be stated that he put his opponent out of pain as speedily as was possible. Whether the stab was at random or calculated we could not decide. It pierced Bartholomew's heart.

Even the killing of her mate—if she was aware of it—failed to distract Jezebel from the serious business of feeding her starved body. She might herself be slain within the next three minutes, but she was not going to face eternity on an empty stomach. Only when Satan charged at her back after finishing Bartholomew did she turn her snarling head. Something in Satan's aspect must have told her it was time to be off. With one last snarl of fiendish hatred she abandoned her kill and raced down the ravine after the retreating refugees. This was her second blunder, as we were presently to see. Any retreat—and there were several open—other than down the ravine would have been less stupid.

Under the circumstances there was but one course open to Satan, and he promptly took it. His tribe and Jezebel's were evidently hereditary enemies. Their feud seemed irreconcilable. So long as one remained alive to compete for the food supply which Satan had so efficiently shepherded across the bridge, his own future was in danger. One opponent was disposed of; he must rout the other. With scarcely a passing glance at the tempting luxury all about him, Satan jerked his arms to the running balance and pelted down the ravine after Jezebel.

It seemed pertinent to explain here that Belshazzar almost certainly was Jezebel's son. The numerous close resemblances of scale pattern and other distinguishing marks establish the kinship beyond any reasonable doubt. This is the considered opinion of the experts on the great sauria.

The evidence regarding Bartholomew is less clear. The experts from the American Museum of Biological Science see much to substantiate Bartholomew's claim—if he would ever have made it—to be Belshazzar's father. Those from the corresponding British institution, on the other hand, fail to find indisputable evidence of any blood relationship between the two.

But to return to the record: pursuit of Jezebel and Satan down the green gloom of the ravine being beyond the powers of the analyser, the engineers canted forward and explored for its lower exit. This was found without difficulty, about fifteen miles in an airline from the entrance near the bridge. The exit was quite a respectable valley opening out on the gently sloping beach of the most beautiful lake we had ever seen. While waiting for Jezebel or the fleeing vegetarians to emerge we explored our perfect surroundings and silently estimated their potentialities of good or evil for those who had survived the discipline of the bridge.

To a casual inspection the spot was a nature lover's dream of heaven. No description of it could do it justice. I shall not attempt any, but merely catalogue the unmistakable evidences which at once caught our attention and seemed to prove that, whatever the super-structure of this thing of beauty might be, its foundations were probably sunk deep in a very fair copy of a mediaeval hell. The southern continent was about to part from its stricken neighbor slowly dying to the north, and this beautiful spot lay directly across one of the major planes of cleavage.

The four stupendous volcanoes, which we had seen from the dying continent only as faint patches of slightly deeper blue against the blue of the sky, loomed up bold and black, snow-capped and furiously fuming against the horizon to the south. An unscalable wall of sheer precipices, ten thousand feet or more in height, linked the smoking four with an impassable barrier.

Whatever came over the bridge would have to make a long detour to the west to pass that barrier and escape to the savannahs to the south. No browsing reptile would be tempted to make the long journey while hundreds of miles of luxuriant forests lay between it and a doubtful freedom. Nor could any flesh eater reconcile his cold-blooded body for perhaps years to the gloom of inhospitable forests where the herbage eaters were rarer than miracles. Only the ratlike, hairless mammals would make the journey, drawn ever southward by the promise of warmer lands which blew in every wind.

From the smoking cones our eyes dropped to the azure

expanse at our feet. This beautiful water had variety and character. Never had we seen such marvelous blues as those of the lazy whirlpools which dredged up the brilliant sands from the floor of the lake and spun them into lazy patterns over the surface. Nor had we ever seen greener and fresher islands than the gems which flashed and sparkled less than a mile from the shore, as the wind set all the fronds of their glossy tree ferns tossing. The slowly rising steam from the black rocks at the base of the nearest but enhanced the beauty of the slight violet haze over the whole island; the wind quickly blew it away. We were to see much of this island, the most beautiful of all.

Looking farther down the black shoreline we gradually picked out one promontory after another jutting far out into the blue. As on the lake by the valley of the flies, we soon identified these promontories as huge tongues of smoking slag being slowly pushed out into the water, and we wondered whether the new continent and the new race upon it, just starting its long climb up the slope of evolution, were to be plagued as the old had been by fire and water, by submersions and centuries of appalling earthquakes. If so, anything approaching the violence of what we had witnessed is still in the future of our race. The scurrying mammals escaped the outburst which we saw in the brewing. Whether their descendants, including ourselves, are to escape the next major revolution —should there ever be another of any magnitude—is a question which may be left to those who believe in the invincible supremacy of the human race. We who saw the passing of the reptiles are too chastened at present to rush into rash prophecies.

Just as the technicians began to get good results at the lower end of the ravine, the first of Satan's harassed herd staggered out.

The poor brute was on the point of collapse. After its heavy meal it should have had a fifteen-hour sleep; not a fifteen-mile race with the two devils. But it had beaten Jezebel. That for the moment was sufficient.

But it was only for the moment. The others—such as made the descent at all—were but a few hundred yards behind. Within ten minutes fifteen had blundered out on the slope leading to the lake.

Neither Jezebel nor Satan had yet emerged from the ravine. Sellar began to grow quite hopeful that one—he did not greatly care which—had murdered the other. As the minutes passed and still neither appeared, his optimism rose to ridiculous heights. Just as he was on the point of wagering two to one that the laggards had succeeded in assassinating one another, Jezebel scuttled from the ravine. To anticipate slightly, I may report here that she had not eliminated Satan. Her greater familiarity with the shrubbery of the ravine had enabled her to win the race by nearly ten minutes, in spite of Satan's incomparably higher class as a runner.

The next ten minutes were crucial.

It began with a nerve-shattering roar. Of course we heard nothing. But we easily inferred the cause from the effect. Our friend Belshazzar had been basking on a suspiciously warm outcrop of rock jutting far into the lake just opposite the opening of the ravine.

The hapless refugees were now nearly trapped between two brute facts. Behind them Jezebel cut off retreat up the ravine; in front of them the terrible Belshazzar, hungrier than a fasting monk, strode up the sloping beach to pick off whichever one might take his fancy. They did the only sensible thing. Without blundering the fifteen split into two groups. Seven went east, eight west. Belshazzar leapt with rage. For once in his life he ran—and how he ran. The eight were his. To our amazement he did not run *after* them, but *before*. From behind he might have leapt down the slope, forty feet if necessary, and have knocked two out with the mere impact of his terrible talons before the bunch could have time to scatter.

Jezebel, to our way of thinking, showed better strategy. Had she been thirty years younger her poor legs would have been equal to the twenty-foot leap which was all that separated her from the nearest of her seven. Drumming along at her hardest she let six go as they spread out like a fan, and pursued her victim to the very water's edge. Then we realized why Belshazzar's strategy was the superior, and began to guess why he happened to be sunning himself where and when he did.

Jezebel's awkward beast did not hesitate a second. Whether by instinct or from sheer fright it splashed straight into the water. Hearing the splash, Belshazzar involuntarily turned his head to see it. His too good memory had betrayed him. It was not the first he had heard, and all the chagrin of those other splashes lived again to taunt him with the remembrance of many good meals almost won and irretrievably lost. As his head turned and the great jaws gaped to hurl some deserved epithet at the blundersome Jezebel, his own eight scattered and raced around him to the water.

All fifteen now took to the water ungracefully but expertly and swam like hippopotamuses toward the green island.

To do Jezebel justice, it must be recorded that she did

her poor old best to retrieve her heartbreaking blunder. But she could not swim. Her kind had never mastered the simple trick, being desert born.

As her intended victim splashed and gurgled its breathless way out, she leapt a good twelve feet over the hateful water and landed squarely on the swimmer's exposed buttocks. Two talons even dug a considerable foothold. But it was no use. The water was rapidly deepening, and the swimmer submerged for a moment, hurling the terrified Jezebel flat on her back in the wet she detested. Having dumped its passenger, the ferry proceeded on its swift way toward the island, two dark streaks crimsoning its wake.

Jezebel crawled out, spluttering and swearing, to find Belshazzar towering over her like the day of judgment. To say that there was murder in his eye is putting it mildly. She saw as much as we did, if not more. Hating the water only less violently than she hated Belshazzar, she gave a half flop and splashed clumsily back to the limit of her depth. She dared go no farther. Belshazzar ramped along the water's edge, calling down all the floods of heaven to dump their deluges on Jezebel's stupid head. He dared not wade in and drown her himself, for he hated like sin to get his feet wet. Once he accidentally came down with one smashing foot in about six inches of water and splashed the other leg and his tail. His rage at the mishap was the worst exhibition of fury we had yet seen from him. It was as inconceivable for him to wade out to Jezebel as it would be for any man in his right mind to walk over ten yards of red-hot plowshares with his eternal salvation as the reward for impossible success.

How the contest would have ended had not Satan

intervened we cannot guess. Satan probably saved the day for poor old Jezebel. The uproar of Belshazzar's fury had reverberated far up the ravine, and Satan probably had mistaken the racket for old Jezebel's boastful challenge. Well, he was ready. Had he not recently slain her mate in a fair fight? He charged out of the ravine at top speed. Emerging onto the sloping beach he had difficulty in stopping himself in time.

It is extremely improbable that Satan remembered Belshazzar after nearly fifty years, in spite of the deep impression his rant must have made on his consciousness at the time. But whether Satan remembered Belshazzar or not, he recognized the devil when he saw him. With a scuffling slide he wheeled on the slope and raced back the way he had come.

Belshazzar immediately gave chase, marching up the slope with the lone, even stride we remembered so well.

Not till Belshazzar disappeared behind a shoulder of the ravine did Jezebel venture to crawl out of her hateful bath.

Four days later Belshazzar strode out into the arena before the bridgehead, masterful and full of meat. Jezebel was again on the point of starvation, but he paid not the slightest attention to her; the episode of the swimmer was ignored. In spite of his repletion he was chilled to the bone. The green gloom of the ferny jungles had penetrated to his very marrows and he lusted for the sun. Striding past Jezebel he made his swift way to the basalts of the bridge, now black and sultry as Tophet in the early afternoon blaze.

Selecting the hottest spot he squatted, flopped sideways, rolled over on his back and let the grateful, sizzling sun cook the vast expanse of his mountainous belly through and through. Presently he was fast asleep, his hindlegs trussed up like a roasting bird's, and his front talons resting lightly on his scaly chest. The enormous jaws gaped and he seemed to snore. Even in sleep he kept his head. The attitude of relaxed indolence into which he had flung himself was no brainless accident, but his most effective attitude of self-defense.

Satan did not appear to share Belshazzar's siesta. The technicians reported him patrolling the beach at the lower end of the ravine. Evidently he had guessed Belshazzar's secret. While his enemy slept he paced the volcanic outcrop in the foolishly optimistic hope that some rash swimmer from the island would join him for dinner.

Only an occasional "calf"—green at life and ignorant of the tradition of his family—was silly enough now to attempt the swim to the mainland. Occasionally a frantic "cow," with the dawnings of a maternal instinct just lightening her darkness as her whole race was about to be extinguished forever, would swim after her foolish child and endeavor to head it back to the island. On such occasions Belshazzar was happy for nearly a week: some of the mothers were of gigantic bulk.

Leaving the technicians to keep an eye on Satan, we concentrated on the starving Jezebel.

Hunger respects no law, human, natural or divine. So what Jezebel now attempted may be explained by an appeal to the old problem of the immovable body and the irresistible force. Belshazzar, snoring on his back on the sizzling rocks, was the immovable body. Jezebel foolishly solved the impossible problem by setting him in motion.

The sun was about to dip into the cold blue of the ocean when Jezebel stole up on the still snoring Belshazzar. She could stand the pangs of hunger no longer. What she now did was an act of blundering madness, no matter how ravenous she was. For some seconds she stood perfectly still, hunched together for the battle leap. Then she thought better—or worse—of her intention, and limply straightened up. Belshazzar's terrific feet were still curled over his stomach in the ideal defensive position. Old Jezebel might have had a chance had she sprung clear of the hind feet to land squarely on Belshazzar's throat. A young, agile reptile might have killed him before the talons had time to come into action. But not Jezebel. Her decision did her intelligence credit.

Had she turned her back on temptation then and there she might have faced her last sunset side by side with her great son. But she was hungry as hell. Like a poor infantile old woman she stood shilly-shallying, unable to make up her mind. The sun had set, and it was fast growing dusk. Belshazzar began to stir uneasily in the rapidly chilling air. His unconscious movement roused all of Jezebel's ebbing courage to a futile, utterly silly exhibition of ineffectual bravery.

Walking round to the sleeper's side she raised her left foot and held it indecisively for fully three seconds above the enormous paunch. If she meant anything by her absurd antics she should have got at it at once, instead of dilly-dallying like a nerveless craven. She finally half made up her mind, and immediately changed it when it was too late. The net result of her indecision was an irritating four-foot scratch, not deep enough to draw blood, across the tenderest region of Belshazzar's stomach.

In the rapidly failing light we lost the details of the sequel of Jezebel's rashness. Having attacked from the side she was clear of the first terrific slash, automatically delivered, of the murderous talons as Belshazzar's legs shot up, forward, and back, like released catapults. Already she was fleeing up the bridge toward the dying continent.

Belshazzar was not to be denied. He had been insulted; he would have his revenge.

He had it. Again, at the request of my collaborators, I suppress the scanty record caught before the darkness.

The sun rose red and angry over the deep waters of the channel at our left. We were on the basalt bridge, about ten miles from the shore of the southern continent.

The four stupendous cones to the south were in violent eruption. Even from our distance we clearly made out the torrents of lava rolling and tumbling their smoky rivers down to the lake.

Nature had decided to end an epoch. In this last outburst of a long revolution she wrote finis to the age-long epic of violence by severing the dying continent from its young sister to the south. The earth was exhausted and ripe for peace. But before peace could be established the very memory of old violence must be obliterated. We faced north to watch the end.

To give any adequate account of that last upheaval, which had been thousands of centuries in troubled preparation, would take a volume, and even then the story would not be half told—for no one could tell it. To be realized it must be seen in the records. By those living images any other restoration must be cold and trivial.

There is however one caution which must be repeated. The last upheavel of the revolution was no affair of a summer morning—as we humans think of summers and mornings. Before the last tremor of the final outburst died, the ratlike mammals had outgrown their insignificance, although man was still an undreamed-of possibility far in the misty future, and their race had acquired the beginnings of natural dignity.

From the records of the final upheaval I shall select only those fragments which relate to Belshazzar, without attempting more than a bare statement of the necessary facts.

We faced north on the shaking bridge. As the true violence began, a black monster about a quarter of a mile away leapt snarling to its feet, abandoning the remnants of its ghastly feast, and strode toward us. Knowing what he had done we had difficulty in calling him by his old name Belshazzar. But as no one could think of a more suitable appellation, we swallowed our pharisaical human feelings and remembered that he was a reptile. Nature perfected him ages before she ever thought of us, and if she gave him a different set of tabus and a tougher ethical hide than our own, it was not for us to criticize him. And as for brute nature herself, she may continue to soften as she gets her bloody hand used to decent material. Nevertheless it cost us something of an effort to follow Belshazzar's movements with sympathy.

A major shock struck the bridge just as Belshazzar decided it was time to break into a run. At the moment he was about a hundred yards north of us, coming down the basalt causeway full tilt. His jaws parted in a defiant snarl just as the chasm opened at his feet. If this was to be his end, then let it come, and be damned to it, to himself and to the whole world rising up against him. Never was a more perfect expression of contempt spat by any helpless creature at the tyrannical author of its darkened mind, its pain and its misery.

If this was not to be the end, he would not give in. To the last he would match strength against strength and what wits he had against blind chance. As the black mass beneath his feet heaved slowly over for the plunge to the sea, Belshazzar leapt like a gigantic bird. It was the leap of his life—nearly fifty feet. As he sailed over the chasm we thought he was done. But he was not. The rigid tail dipped slightly shifting the centre of gravity so the straightened legs advanced the necessary yard, and his talons grasped the nearer lip of the chasm. Instantly the tail smacked up hard against the back, and Belshazzar pitched forward to safety. In a flash he was on his feet, leaping and racing his way over the jarring bridge as it crumbled like sand and cascaded in black torrents into the foam.

The worst of the shock passed before Belshazzar reached the mainland. Having followed him into the ravine, and having seen him safely started on his descent to the beach, we went in search of Satan.

Satan was, so to speak, in heaven. The sublime spectacle of four volcanoes belching up fire and brimstone meant nothing to Satan. And as for the earthquake, he had positively revelled in it. But for that rough prank of nature he might still be patrolling the lava spit as hungry as the devil with not a meal in sight.

The first severe shock had jarred the island to its very roots. Every living creature on it rushed down to the water and plunged in. "The mainland—the mainland," might have been their cry had they been capable of reason. It certainly would endure longer than the island, already beginning to smoke in a hundred places. Old and young, those who could swim and those who forgot how in their terror, strong and weak, big and little, splashed pell mell for the pitching shore.

Satan received them, joyously, precipitately. Fear of a killer of their own race vanquished fear of the universal destroyer, and as the first victim fell, those who had reached the shore stampeded back into the boiling water. Two panic-stricken factions milled through one another in mid-channel. Soon they were exhausted. Many drowned; only those on the rim of the mob made their way around it and back to the shaking island, and only one floating fortress drifted shoreward and crawled out on the mainland.

Satan paid no attention to the newcomer. It was impregnable, and he had all he could do for the present to dispose of the weakling he had killed.

While waiting for Belshazzar to arrive we followed the progress of the eruptions. The lava had reached the forests, and to the murk of falling ashes was now added the pitchy smoke of blazing conifers. The visibility in our vicinity was still good, although the rocks were a sombre crimson and the vegetation almost black in the glare of a blood red sun.

I described the water of the lake as boiling, and to a certain extent this was literally true. Mud and sand were being churned up in prodigious quantities; great tracts of the surface of the water bubbled furiously, and steam drifted lazily from more than one expanse of comparative calm. Between us and the island however the water was still undisturbed, although as red and thick as paint.

Belshazzar arrived on the beach resolute and defiant. If nature chose to make a fool of herself by staging this ridiculous pantomime it was no concern of his. He had his own cattle to farm, and as long as he minded his own business he would continue to eat. Let the landscape play the fool if it likes; he had lived through almost as bad fifty years ago. In the hellish light his towering body glowed like a gigantic ember.

He strode down the beach toward his customary lookout. Suddenly he stopped, leaping with rage. Satan was defiling his favorite spot by celebrating some unclean rite of his own.

Satan looked up sharply. There was no mistaking that battle cry. Like a grotesque devil clambering out of the pit he pulled himself up by his hands, vaulted over a barrier of sombre red rock, and vanished in a flash of scarlet as the sun caught the lighter skin of his distended belly. He had dined long and completely, and now he was off. Belshazzar might have the uncracked skull and the three sharp baby horns if he cared for them.

Belshazzar did not; a greater prize was his for the taking. The bewildered tank which had floundered ashore, already demoralized by the earthquake, lost its head completely when it saw this dancing apparition going mad on the beach. The king and master of all devils had come in fire to judge the world.

As the awkward beast lumbered right about face and headed for the water, Belshazzar leapt upon his back, insane with rage. The racing feet sent sparks flying, but not even a minor injury was registered.

It was then that Belshazzar established his claim to intelligence beyond any reasonable shadow of a doubt. Noticing the swash of the waves, he ceased profitless ramping instantly and dashed for the rear end of the floating fortress. Twelve feet of water separated him from the shore. He could have made the leap without an effort, and for a moment the muscles of his legs tensed automatically. To escape the hated water was his natural impulse; his reaction was instinctive. Reason got the better of instinct—which is another way of saying that intelligence was born, if not already full grown but in abeyance. The muscles relaxed, Belshazzar wheeled about and strode to the forward end of the ferry, as it moved toward the island. Thirty feet from the shore he hunched down for an instant before he sailed like a bird high up to an overhanging ledge of black rock. In another instant he had crashed through the brake of tree ferns and vanished.

That last leap clinched his title to whatever Langtry claims in his behalf. For the shore at that point was precipitous, without an inch of beach. A landing for the floating tank at that spot was impossible. The bewildered creature lacked the wits or the intelligence to swim around half a mile till it found a beach. Turning tail as it crashed head on into the cliffs, it paddled frantically for the shore which it had left. We abandoned it there.

Forty-eight hours of the utmost violence obliterated the record in swirling clouds of crimson and black. An occasional spurt of clearer flame revealed splinters of red rock being thrust steaming up from the floor of the lake, only to vanish as if snatched down to the seething fires by invisible hands for more thorough smelting. Bridges were elaborated and destroyed in a second; the lake was twice drained for miles from the shore and twice refilled with clashing waters in less than an hour, and gradually more permanent structures began to emerge.

A smoking causeway united the island to the mainland, and seemed to survive the assaults of the earthquakes for several hours. At intervals all through the second night we caught flashes of this smoldering causeway still intact, but still too hot to bear a living foot. Then at the very peak of violence which within five minutes shattered the causeway and tilted the island crazily so that its whole western half was submerged, we saw Satan.

He was not on the causeway—its scorching rocks would have burned his feet to wisps in twenty yards—but far out in the water, galloping knee high parallel to the causeway. In the flash we caught of him he was running—or rather splashing—along the cooler floor of the lake, now elevated to within a yard or two of the surface by the upheaval of the causeway. The muscular arms swung at the running balance, and the long dagger flashed back and forth in the crimson light, redder than it had ever been in any of its hundreds of fights, fair or foul.

We had almost given up hope of getting a decipherable record when Sellar remembered that volcanic eruptions are usually accompanied by deluges of rain—for simple reasons that need not be gone into here. Our slogan became "Wait for the rain," while the engineers continued to run the specimens through the analyzer at half the natural rate.

As Sellar had anticipated, the deluge was not long

delayed. It registered in the record by a gradual strengthening of the light and a general sharpening of the image. Colors began to appear—muddied, it is true, owing to the superposition of the universal red—but still colors. At this point the specimens being analyzed exhibited serious defects (not yet remedied), so we cannot say how many hours or days of real time passed before the deluges cleared the atmosphere and the downpour finally ceased.

The air was as clear as glass. Lava had ceased temporarily to gush from the erupting cones, but they were still active. The lake was a slaty expanse of thick, bubbling mud broken by a confusion of jagged outcrops of black rock. The island had been all but submerged; a scant half acre of scorched greenery sloped steeply down to the boiling mud, and even this had been penetrated by the savage upthrust of a huge splinter of shattered rock as sharp as a trainload of scrap iron. Supporting the green slope an upturned wall of basalt leaned up at an angle of forty-five degrees from the bottom of the lake. This wall was one boundary of the fracture which had split the island in two; the rest of the island was sunk in the boiling mud. Only this scorched fragment remained of the reptiles' last refuge.

Knowing Belshazzar as we did we confidently expected to find him somewhere on that last fragment. His invincible resourcefulness surely had been able to overcome nature's hit or miss methods, and he could not have failed to find himself on the one scrap of the island, no matter how small, which had not been snatched into the boiling mud.

The causeway had long since disappeared. There was now no link with the mainland. Nevertheless we felt that

Belshazzar somehow would find a way to get ashore in the next outburst—whose signs were already evident in the fuming cones. They were streaming up again for a major eruption, and no doubt there would be sudden outcrops in the mud by which Belshazzar could leap ashore. Nothing could down him, we felt, not even the supreme anarchy to come.

The broken crest of the scorched greenery shook vigorously. We almost felt Belshazzar coming.

The ferns parted; a birdlike foot hesitated and advanced. Satan stepped out. To hoist himself up the last yard of the steep slope he grasped a jagged spear of the over-hanging rock by crooking the stubby fingers of his hand with the sound three-foot dagger, and pulled. His weight was too much for the fractured rock. The spear toppled. As he leapt back another loosened mass of rock shot after the spear, struck his hand, and broke the dagger off short.

"If he murdered Belshazzar," Sellar remarked, "it serves him right."

The words were barely uttered before Belshazzar appeared. He had heard his enemy, and no doubt had been stalking him. Limping badly he made his precarious way around the splinter, hugging the rock. Satan had disappeared into the tree ferns. Belshazzar did not pursue—he hated gloom. As if this were a normal sunny afternoon he clawed his way round to the front of the splinter where the sun was hottest, leaned his back against the rock, and eased himself into a sitting posture, letting his tail flop carelessly to the ground.

Leaning back, he stared at the sun and let its beneficent rays cook him through and through. His paunch, we noted without surprise, was distended to the natural limit.

Belshazzar cared not what nature might do; he would continue to live a normal happy life.

As his eyes closed and his enormous head nodded toward his shoulder, we noticed for the first time that he was badly wounded. The longest talon of his left foot was crushed. His days of leaping were over. Nature had got the better of him by one of her usual low subterfuges. Instead of killing him outright she had condemned him to death by starvation.

Was Belshazzar defeated? The drumtight expanse of his paunch shouted that he was not. So long as his unwilling ally Satan would continue to herd timid cattle into pens from which only the bravest might hope to escape, Belshazzar was not downhearted. Instead of moping over his crushed talon and the blank, black future, he snored like a Roman emperor after a debauch and put his trust in Satan. Should the worst come to the worst, Satan himself would provide at least one square meal. Belshazzar was still equal to the task of dressing the devil for dinner in spite of his injured foot.

Within ten minutes of sunset Satan put in his first appearance since losing his dagger. One glance at his sagging belly proved his hunger. Coming round the splinter from the back, he lost not a precious second.

This resolute devil was no shilly-shallying craven like the wretched Jezebel. Although one dagger was completely gone and the other was but a blunt stub, he charged. Even the charge was but a broken parody of what it might have been in a fair fight, as there was no take-off worth mentioning. Habit overmastered him, and he struck with all his strength at Belshazzar's throat —with the wrong thumb.

Belshazzar was now on his feet. Instinctively he tried to

spring, and failed. The injured foot collapsed. He lost his balance and crashed into the splintered rock. Satan was on him in a flash, stabbing blindly with both thumbs at Belshazzar's throat as a great slab of rock pinned the king of reptiles to the ground. The blunt stump of a dagger tore a great gash in Belshazzar's throat and the blood spurted like wine from a cask when the spigot is knocked out. As Satan leapt upon him, the trashing tail broke both the devil's legs and as he fell, came down in one terrific slash which broke his neck.

The sun set and the evening star stole out. Belshazzar raised his head. The last light died in his eyes as the head dropped back, the unconquerable jaws still wide in their last snarl of defiance.

# The Sands of Time

## by P. Schuyler Miller

A long shadow fell across the ledge. I laid down the curved blade with which I was chipping at the soft sandstone, and squinted up into the glare of the afternoon sun. A man was sitting on the edge of the pit, his legs dangling over the side. He raised a hand in salutation.

"Hi!"

He hunched forward to jump. My shout stopped him.

"Look out! You'll smash them!"

He peered down at me, considering the matter. He had no hat, and the sun made a halo of his blond, curly hair.

"They're fossils, aren't they?" he objected. "Fossils I've seen were stone, and stone is hard. What do you mean—I'll smash 'em?"

"I mean what I said. This sandstone is soft and the bones in it are softer. Also, they're old. Digging out dinosaurs is no pick-and-shovel job nowadays."

"Um-m-m." He rubbed his nose thoughtfully. "How old would you say they were?"

I got wearily to my feet and began to slap the dust out of my breeches. Evidently I was in for another siege of questions. He might be a reporter, or he might be any one of the twenty-odd farmers in the surrounding section. It would make a difference what I told him.

"Come on down here where we can talk," I invited. "We'll be more comfortable. There's a trail about a hundred yards up the draw."

"I'm all right." He leaned back on braced arms. "What is it? What did it look like?"

I know when I'm beaten. I leaned against the wall of the quarry, out of the sun, and began to fill my pipe. I waved the packet of tobacco courteously at him, but he shook his head.

"Thanks. Cigarette." He lighted one. "You're Professor Belden, aren't you? E. J. Belden. 'E' stands for Ephratah, or some such. Doesn't affect your digging any, though." He exhaled a cloud of smoke. "What's that thing you were using?"

I held it up. "It's a special knife for working out bones like these. The museum's model. When I was your age we used butcher knives and railroad spikes—anything we could get our hands on. There weren't any railroads out here then."

He nodded. "I know. My father dug for 'em. Hobby of his, for a while. Changed over to stamps when he lost his leg." Then, with an air of changing the subject, "That thing you're digging out—what did it look like? Alive, I mean."

I had about half of the skeleton worked out. I traced its outline for him with the knife. "There's the skull; there's the neck and spine, and what's left of the tail; this was its left foreleg. You can see the remains of the crest along the top of the skull, and the flat snout like a duck's beak. It's one of many species of trachodon—the duckbilled aquatic dinosaurs. They fed along the shore lines, on water plants and general browse, and some of them were bogged down and drowned."

"I get it. Big bruiser—little front legs and husky hind ones with a tail like a kangaroo. Sat on it when he got tired. Fin on his head like a fish, and a face like a duck. Did he have scales?"

"I doubt it," I told him. "More likely warts like a toad, or armor plates like an alligator. We've found skin impressions of some of this one's cousins, south of here, and that's what they were like."

He nodded again—that all-knowing nod that gets my eternal goat. He fumbled inside his coat and brought out a little leather folder or wallet, and leafed through its contents. He leaned forward and something white came scaling down at my feet.

"Like that?" he asked.

I picked it up. It was a photograph, enlarged from a miniature camera shot. It showed the edge of a reedy lake or river, with a narrow, sandy strip of beach and a background of feathery foliage that looked like tree ferns. Thigh-deep in the water, lush lily stalks trailing from its flat jaws, stood a replica of the creature whose skeleton was embedded in the rock at my feet—a trachodon. It was a perfect likeness—the heavy, frilled crest, and glistening skin with its uneven patches of dark tubercles, the small, webbed forepaws on skinny arms.

"Nice job," I admitted. "Is it one of Knight's new ones?"

"Knight?" He seemed puzzled. "Oh—the Museum of Natural History. No—I made it myself."

"You're to be congratulated," I assured him. "I don't know when I've seen a nicer model. What's it for—the movies?"

"Movies?" He sounded exasperated. "I'm not making movies. I made the picture—the photograph. Took it myself—here—or pretty close to here. The thing was alive, and is still for all I know. It chased me."

That was the last straw. "See here," I said, "If you're trying to talk me into backing some crazy publicity stunt, you can guess again. I wasn't born yesterday, and I cut my teeth on a lot harder and straighter science than your crazy newspaper syndicates dish out. I worked these beds before you were born, or your father, either, and there were no trachodons wandering around chasing smart photographers with the d.t.s, and no lakes or tree ferns for 'em to wander in. If you're after a testimonial for someone's model of Cretaceous fauna, say so. That is an excellent piece of work, and if you're responsible you have every right to be proud of it. Only stop this blither about photographing dinosaurs that have been fossils for sixty million years."

The fellow was stubborn. "It's no hoax," he insisted doggedly. "There's no newspaper involved and I'm not peddling dolls. I took that photograph. Your trachodon chased me and I ran. And I have more of the same to prove it! Here."

The folder landed with a thump at my feet. It was crammed with prints like the first—enlargements of Leica negatives—and for sheer realism I have never seen anything like them.

"I had thirty shots," he told me. "I used 'em all, and they were all beauties. And I can do it again!"

Those prints! I can see them now: landscapes that vanished from this planet millions of years before the first furry tree shrew scurried among the branches of the first temperate forests, and became the ancestor of mankind; monsters whose buried bones and fossil footprints are the only mementos of a race of giants vaster than any other creatures that ever walked the earth; there were more of the trachodons—a whole herd of them, it seemed, browsing along the shore of a lake or large river, and they had that individuality that marks the work of the true artist; they were Corythosaurs, like the one I was working on—one of the better-known genera of the great family of Trachodons. But the man who had restored them had used his imagination to show details of markings and fleshy structure that I was sure had never been shown by any recorded fossils.

Nor was that all. There were close-ups of plants—trees and low bushes—that were masterpieces of minute detail, even to the point of showing withered fronds, and the insects that walked and stalked and crawled over them. There were vistas of rank marshland scummed over with stringy algae and lush with tall grasses and taller reeds, among which saurian giants wallowed. There were two or three other varieties of trachodon that I could see, and a few smaller dinosaurs, with a massive bulk in what passed for the distance that might have been a Brontosaurus hangover from the Jurassic of a few million years before. I pointed to it.

"You slipped up there," I said. "We've found no traces of that creature so late in the Age of Reptiles. It's a very common mistake; every fantastic novelist makes it when he tries to write a time-traveling story. Tyrannosaurus eats Brontosaurus and is then gored to death by Triceratops. The trouble with it is that it couldn't happen."

The boy ground his cigarette butt into the sand. "I don't know about that," he said. "It was there—I photographed it—and that's all there was to it. Tyrannosaurus I didn't see—and I'm not sorry. I've read those yarns you're so supercilious about. Good stuff—they arouse your curiosity and make you think. Triceratops—if he's the chunky devil with three big horns sticking out of his head and snout—I got in profusion. You haven't come to him yet. Go down about three more."

I humored him. Sure enough, there was a vast expanse of low, rolling plains with some lumpy hills in the distance. The thing was planned very poorly—any student would have laid it out looking toward the typical Cretaceous forest, rather than away from it—but it had the same startling naturalness that the others had. And there were indeed Triceratops in plenty—a hundred or more, grazing stolidly in little family groups of three or four, on a rank prairie grass that grew in great tufts from the sandy soil.

I guffawed. "Who told you that was right?" I demanded. "Your stuff is good—the best I've ever seen—but it is careless slips like that that spoil everything for the real scientist. Reptiles never herd, and dinosaurs were nothing but overgrown reptiles. Go on—take your pictures to someone who has the time to be amused. I don't find them funny or even interesting."

I stuffed them into the folder and tossed it to him. He made no attempt to catch it. For a moment he sat staring down at me, then in a shower of sand he was beside me. One hob-nailed boot gouged viciously across the femur of my dinosaur and the other crashed down among its brittle ribs. I felt the blood go out of my face with anger, then come rushing back. If I had been twenty years younger I would have knocked him off his feet and dared him to come back for more. But he was as red as I.

"Damn it," he cried, "no bald-headed old fuzzy-wuzzy is going to call me a liar twice! You may know a lot about dead bones, but your education with regard to living things has been sadly neglected. So reptiles never herd? What about alligators? What about the Galápagos iguanas? What about snakes? Bah—you can't see any farther than your own nose and never will! When I show you photographs of living dinosaurs, taken with this very camera twenty-four hours ago, not more than three or four miles from where we're standing—well, it's high time you scrap your hide-bound, bone-dry theories and listen to a branch of science that's real and living, and always will be. I photographed those dinosaurs! I can do it again—any time I like. I will do it."

He stopped for breath. I simply looked at him. It's the best way, when some crank gets violent. He colored and grinned sheepishly, then picked up the wallet from where it had fallen at the base of the quarry cut. There was an inner compartment with a covering flap which I had not touched. He rummaged in it with a finger and thumb and brought out a scrap of leathery-looking stuff, porous and coated with a kind of shiny, dried mucus.

"Put a name to it," he demanded.

I turned it over in my palm and examined it carefully. It was a bit of eggshell—undoubtedly a reptilian egg, and a rather large one—but I could tell nothing more.

"It might be an alligator or crocodile egg, or it might

have been laid by one of the large oviparous snakes," I told him. "That would depend on where you found it. I suppose that you will claim that it is a dinosur egg—a fresh egg."

"I claim nothing," he retorted. "That's for you to say. You're the expert on dinosaurs, not I. But if you don't like that—what about this?"

He had on a hunting jacket and corduroy breeches like mine. From the big side pocket he drew two eggs about the length of my palm—misshapen and gray-white in color, with that leathery texture so characteristic of reptile eggs. He held them up between himself and the sun.

"This one's fresh," he said. "The sand was still moist around the nest. This other is from the place where I got the shell. There's something in it. If you want to, you can open it."

I took it. It was heavy and somewhat discolored at the larger end, where something had pierced the shell. As he had said, there was evidently something inside. I hesitated. I felt that I would be losing face if I took him at his word to open it. And yet—

I squatted down and, laying the egg on a block of sandstone beside the weird, crested skull of the Corythosaur, I ripped its leathery shell from end to end.

The stench nearly felled me. The inside was a mass of greenish-yellow matter such as only a very long-dead egg can create. The embryo was well advanced, and as I poked around in the noisome mess it began to take definite form. I dropped the knife and with my fingers wiped away the last of the putrid ooze from the twisted, jellylike thing that remained. I rose slowly to my feet and looked him squarely in the eye.

"Where did you get that egg?"

He smiled—that maddening, slow smile. "I told you," he said. "I found it over there, a mile or so, beyond the belt of jungle that fringes the marshes. There were dozens of them—mounds like those that turtles make, in the warm sand. I opened two. One was fresh; the other was full of broken shells—and this." He eyed me quizzically. "And what does the great Professor Belden make of it?"

What he said had given me an idea. "Turtles," I mused aloud. "It could be a turtle—some rare species—maybe a mutation or freak that never developed far enough to really take shape. It must be!"

He sounded weary. "Yes," he said flatly, "it could be a turtle. It isn't but that doesn't matter to you. Those photographs could be fakes, and none-too-clever fakes at that. They show things that couldn't happen—that your damned dry-bone science says are wrong. All right —you've got me. It's your round. But I'm coming back, and I'm coming to bring proof that will convince you and every other stiffnecked old fuzz-buzz in the world that I, Terence Michael Aloysius Donovan, have stepped over the traces into the middle of the Cretaceous era and lived there, comfortably and happily, sixty million years before I was born!"

He walked away. I heard his footsteps receding up the draw, and the rattle of small stones as he climbed to the level of the prairie. I stood staring down at the greenish mess that was frying in the hot sun on the bright-red sandstone. It could have been a turtle, malformed in the embryo so that its carapace formed a sort of rudimentary, flaring shield behind the beaked skull. Or it could be—something else.

If it was that something, all the sanity and logic had gone out of the world, and a boy's mad, pseudoscientific dream became a reality that could not possibly be real. Paradox within paradox—contradiction upon contradiction. I gathered up my tools and started back for camp.

During the days that followed we worked out the skeleton of the Corythosaur and swathed it in plaster-soaked burlap for its long journey by wagon, truck and train back to the museum. I had perhaps a week left to use as I saw fit. But somehow, try as I would, I could not forget the young, blond figure of Terry Donovan, and the two strange eggs that he had pulled out of his pocket.

About a mile up the draw from our camp I found the remains of what had been a beach in Cretaceous times. Where it had not weathered away, every ripple mark and worm burrow was intact. There were tracks—remarkable fine ones—of which any museum would be proud. Dinosaurs, big and little, had come this way, millions of years ago, and left the mark of their passing in the moist sand, to be buried and preserved to arouse the apish curiosity of a race whose tiny, hairy ancestors were still scrambling on all fours.

Beyond the beach had been marshes and a quicksand. Crumbling white bones protruded from the stone in incalculable profusion, massed and jumbled into a tangle that would require years of careful study to unravel. I stood with a bit of crumbling bone in my hand, staring at the mottled rock. A step sounded on the talus below me. It was Donovan.

Some of the cocksure exuberance had gone out of him. He was thinner, and his face was covered with a stubbly growth of beard. He wore shorts and a tattered shirt, and his left arm was strapped to his side with bands of some gleaming metallic cloth. Dangling from the fingers of his good hand was the strangest bird I have ever seen.

He flung it down at my feet. It was purplish-black with a naked red head and wattled neck. Its tail was feathered as a sumac is leafed, with stubby feathers sprouting in pairs from a naked, ratty shaft. Its wings had little three-fingered hands at the joints. And its head was long and narrow, like a lizard's snout, with great, round, lidless eyes and a mouthful of tiny yellow teeth.

I looked from the bird to him. There was no smile on his lips now. He was staring at the footprints on the rock.

"So you've found the beach." His voice was a weary monotone.

"It was a sort of sandy spit, between the marshes and the sea, where they came to feed and be fed on. Dog eat dog. Sometimes they would blunder into the quicksands and flounder and bleat until they drowned. You see—I was there. That bird was there—alive when those dead, crumbling bones were alive—not only in the same geological age but in the same year, the same month—the same day! You've got proof now—proof that you can't talk away! Examine it. Cut it up. Do anything you want with it. But by the powers, this time you've got to believe me! This time you've got to help!"

I stooped and picked the thing up by its long scaly legs. No bird like it had lived, or could have lived, on this planet for millions of years. I thought of those thirty photographs of the incredible—of the eggs he had had, one of them fresh, one with an embryo that might, conceivably, have been an unknown genus of turtle.

"All right," I said. "I'll come. What do you want?"

He lived three miles away across the open prairie. The

house was a modernistic metal box set among towering cottonwoods at the edge of a small reservoir. A power house at the dam furnished light and electricity—all that he needed to bring civilized comfort out of the desert.

One wing of the house was windowless and sheer-walled, with blower vents at intervals on the sloping roof. A laboratory, I guessed. Donovan unlocked a steel door in the wall and pushed it open. I stepped past him into the room.

It was bare. A flat-topped desk stood in the corner near the main house, with a shelf of books over it. A big switchboard covered the opposite wall, flanked by two huge D.C. generators. There were cupboards and a long worktable littered with small apparatus. But a good half of the room was empty save for the machine that squatted in the middle of the concrete floor.

It was like a round lead egg, ten feet high and half as broad. It was set in a cradle of steel girders, raised on massive insulators. Part of it stood open like a door, revealing the inside—a chamber barely large enough to hold a man, with a host of dials and switches set in an insulated panel in the leaden wall, and a flat Bakelite floor. Heavy cables came out of that floor to the instrument board, and two huge, copper bus bars were clamped to the steel base. The laboratory was filled with the drone of the generators, charging some hidden battery, and there was a faint tang of ozone in the air.

Donovan shut and locked the door. "That's the Egg," he said. "I'll show it to you later, after you've heard me out. Will you help me with this arm of mine, first?"

I cut the shirt away and unwrapped the metallic gauze that held the arm tight against his body. Both bones of the forearm were splintered and the flesh gashed as though by jagged knives. The wound had been cleaned, and treated with some bright-green antiseptic whose odor I did not recognize. The bleeding had stopped, and there was none of the inflammation that I should have expected.

He answered my unspoken question. "She fixed it up—Lana. One of your little playmates—the kind I didn't see the first time—wanted to eat me." He was rummaging in the bottom drawer of the desk. "There's no clean cloth here," he said. "I haven't time to look in the house. You'll have to use that again."

"Look here," I protested, "you can't let a wound like that go untreated. It's serious. You must have a doctor."

He shook his head. "No time. It would take a doctor two hours to get out here from town. He'd need another hour, or more, to fool around with me. In just forty minutes my accumulators will be charged to capacity, and in forty-one I'll be gone—back there. Make a couple of splints out of that orange crate in the corner and tie me up again. It'll do—for as long as I'll be needing it."

I split the thin boards and made splints, made sure that the bones were set properly and bound them tightly with the strange silvery cloth, then looped the loose ends in a sling around his neck. I went into the house to get him clean clothes. When I returned he was stripped, scrubbing himself at the laboratory sink. I helped him clamber into underwear, a shirt and breeches, pull on high-top shoes. I plugged in an electric razor and sat watching him as he ran it over his angular jaw.

He was grinning now. "You're all right, Professor," he told me. "Not a question out of you, and I'll bet you've been on edge all the while. Well—I'll tell you everything. Then you can take it or leave it.

"Look there on the bench behind you—that coiled

spring. It's a helix—a spiral made up of two-dimensional cross sections twisted in a third dimension. If you make two marks on it, you can go from one to the other by traveling along the spring, round and round for about six inches. Or you can cut across from one spiral to the next. Suppose your two marks come right together—so. They're two inches apart, along the spring—and no distance at all if you cut across.

"So much for that. You know Einstein's picture of the universe—space and time tied up together in some kind of four-dimensional continuum that's warped and bent in all sorts of weird ways by the presence of matter. Maybe closed and maybe not. Maybe expanding like a balloon and maybe shrinking like a melting hailstone. Well—I know what that shape is. I've proved it. It's spiraled like that spring—spiraled in time!

"See what that means? Look—I'll show you. This first scratch, here on the spring, is today—now. Here will be tomorrow, a little further along the wire. Here's next year. And here is some still later time, one full turn of the coil away, directly above the first mark.

"Now watch. I can go from today to tomorrow—to next year—like this by traveling with time along the spring. That's what the world is doing. Only by the laws of physics—entropy and all that—there's no going back. It's one-way traffic. And you can't get ahead any faster than time wants to take you. That's if you follow the spring. But you can cut across!

"Look—here are the two marks I just made, now and two years from now. They're two inches apart, along the coiled wire, but when you compress the spring they are together—nothing between them but the surface of the two coils. You can stretch a bridge across from one to the other, so to speak, and walk across—into a time two years from now. Or you can go the other way, two years into the past.

"That's all there is to it. Time is coiled like a spring. Some other age in earth's history lies next to ours, separated only by an intangible boundary, a focus of forces that keeps us from seeing into it and falling into it. Past time—present time—future time, side by side. Only it's not two years, or three, or a hundred. It's sixty million years from now to then, the long way around!

"I said you could get from one coil of time to the next one if you built a bridge across. I built that bridge—the Egg. I set up a field of forces in it—no matter how—that dissolve the invisible barrier between our time and the next. I give it an electromagnetic shove that sends it in the right direction, forward or back. And I land sixty million years in the past, in the age of dinosaurs."

He paused, as if to give me a chance to challenge him. I didn't try. I am no physicist, and if it was as he said—if time was really a spiral, with adjacent coils lying side by side, and if his leaden Egg could bridge the gap between —then the pictures and the eggs and the bird were possible things. And they were more than possible. I had seen them.

"You can see that the usual paradoxes don't come in at all," Donovan went on. "About killing your grandfather, and being two places at once—that kind of thing. The time screw has a sixty-million-year pitch. You can slide from coil to coil, sixty million years at a time, but you can't cover any shorter distance without living it. If I go back or ahead sixty million years, and live there four days,

I'll get back here next Tuesday, four days from now. As for going ahead and learning all the scientific wonders of the future, then coming back to change the destiny of humanity, sixty million years is a long time. I doubt that there'll be anything human living then. And if there is—if I do learn their secrets and come back—it will be because their future civilization was built on the fact that I did so. Screwy as it sounds, that's how it is."

He stopped and sat staring at the dull-gray mass of the Egg. He was looking back sixty million years, into an age when giant dinosaurs ruled the earth. He was watching herds of Triceratops grazing on the Cretaceous prairie —seeing unsuspected survivors of the genus that produced Brontosaurus and his kin, wallowing in some protected swamp—seeing rat-tailed, purple-black Archaeopteryx squawking in the tree ferns. And he was seeing more!

"I'll tell you the whole story," he said. "You can believe it or not, as you like. Then I'll go back. After that—well, maybe you'll write the end, and maybe not. Sixty million years is a long time!"

He told me: how he hit on his theory of spiraled time; how he monkeyed around with the mathematics of the thing until it hung together—built little models of machines that swooped into nothingness and disappeared; how he made the Egg, big enough to hold a man, yet not too big for his generators to provide the power to lift it and him across the boundary between the coils of time—and back again; how he stepped out of the close, cramped chamber of the Egg into a world of steaming swamps and desert plains, sixty million years before mankind!

That was when he took the pictures. It was when the

Corythosaur chased him, bleating and bellowing like a monster cow, when he disturbed its feeding. He lost it among the tree ferns, and wandered warily through the bizarre, luxurious jungle, batting at great mosquitoes the size of horseflies and ducking when giant dragonflies zoomed down and seized them in midair. He watched a small hornless dinosaur scratch a hole in the warm sand at the edge of the jungle and ponderously lay a clutch of twenty eggs. When she had waddled away, he took one—the fresh one he had shown me—and scratched out another from a nest that had already hatched. He had photographs—he had specimens—and the sun was getting low. Some of the noises from the salt marshes along the seashore were not very reassuring. So he came back. And I laughed at him and his proofs, and called him a crazy fake!

He went back. He had a rifle along this time—a huge thing that his father had used on elephants in Africa. I don't know what he expected to do with it. Shoot a Triceratops, maybe—since I wouldn't accept his photographs—and hack off its ungainly, three-horned head for a trophy. He could never have brought it back, of course, because it was a tight enough squeeze as it was to get himself and the big rifle into the Egg. He had food and water in a pack—he didn't much like the look of the water that he had found "over there"—and he was in a mood to stay until he found something that I and every one like me would have to accept.

Inland, the ground rose to a range of low hills along the horizon. Back there, he reasoned, there would be creatures a little smaller than the things he had seen buoying up their massive hulks in the sea and marshes. So, shutting the door of the Egg and heaping cycad fronds over it to hide it from inquisitive dinosaurs, he set out across the plain toward the west.

The Triceratops herds paid not the slightest attention to him. He doubted that they could see him unless he came very close, and then they ignored him. They were herbivorous, and anything his size could not be an enemy. Only once, when he practically fell over a tiny, eight-foot calf napping in the tall grass, did one of the old ones emit a snuffling, hissing roar and come trotting toward him with its three sharp spikes lowered and its little eyes red.

There were many small dinosaurs, light and fleet of foot, that were not so unconcerned with his passage. Some of them were big enough to make him feel distinctly uneasy, and he fired his first shot in self-defense when a creature the size of an ostrich leaned forward and came streaking at him with obviously malicious intent. He blew its head off at twenty paces, and had to duck the body that came clawing and scampering after him. It blundered on in a straight line, and when it finally collapsed he cooked and ate it over a fire of dead grass. It tasted like iguana, he said, and added that iguana tasted a lot like chicken.

Finally, he found a stream running down from the hills and took to its bed for greater safety. It was dry, but in the baked mud were the tracks of things that he hadn't seen and didn't want to see. He guessed, from my description, that they had been made by Tyrannosaurus or something equally big and dangerous.

Incidentally, I have forgotten the most important thing of all. Remember that Donovan's dominating idea was to prove to me, and to the world, that he had been in the Cretaceous and hobnobbed with its flora and fauna. He was a physicist by inclination, and had the physicist's flair for ingenious proofs. Before leaving, he loaded a lead cube with three quartz quills of pure radium chloride that he had been using in a previous experiment, and locked the whole thing up in a steel box. He had money to burn, and besides, he expected to get them back.

The first thing he did when he stepped out of the Egg on that fateful second trip was to dig a deep hole in the packed sand of the beach, well above high tide, and bury the box. He had seen the fossil tracks and ripple marks in the sandstone near his house, and guessed rightly enough that they dated from some time near the age to which he had penetrated. If I, or someone equally trustworthy, were to dig that box up one time coil later, he would not only have produced some very pretty proof that he had traveled in time—his name and the date were inside the tube—but an analysis of the radium, and an estimate of how much of it had turned into lead, would show how many years had elapsed since he buried it. In one fell swoop he would prove his claim, and give the world two very fundamental bits of scientific information: an exact date for the Cretaceous period, and the "distance" between successive coils in the spiral of time.

The stream bed finally petered out in a gully choked with boulders. The terrain was utterly arid and desolate, and he began to think that he had better turn back. There was nothing living to be seen, except for some small mammals like brown mice that got into his pack the first night and ate the bread he was carrying. He pegged a rock at them, but they vanished among the boulders, and an elephant gun was no good for anything their size. He wished he had a mousetrap. Mice were something that he could take back in his pocket.

The morning of the second day some birds flew by overhead. They were different from the one he killed later—more like sea gulls—and he got the idea that beyond the hills, in the direction they were flying, there would be either more wooded lowland or an arm of the sea. As it turned out, he was right.

The hills were the summit of a ridge like the spine of Italy, jutting south into the Cretaceous sea. The sea had been higher once, covering the sandy waste where the Triceratops herds now browsed, and there was a long line of eroded limestone cliffs, full of the black holes of wave-worn caves. From their base he looked back over the desert plain with its fringe of jungle along the shore of the sea. Something was swimming in schools, far out toward the horizon—something as big as whales, he thought—but he had forgotten to bring glasses and he could not tell what they were. He set about finding a way to climb the escarpment.

Right there was where he made his first big mistake. He might have known that what goes up has to come down again on the other side. The smart thing to do would have been to follow the line of the cliffs until he got into the other valley, or whatever lay beyond. Instead, he slung his gun around his neck and climbed.

The summit of the cliffs was a plateau, hollowed out by centuries of erosion into a basin full of gaudy spires of rock with the green stain of vegetation around their bases. There was evidently water and there might be animals that he could photograph or kill. Anything he found up here, he decided, would be pretty small.

He had forgotten the caves. They were high-arched, wave-eaten tunnels that extended far back into the cliffs, and from the lay of the land it was probable that they opened on the inside as well. Besides, whatever had lived on the plateau when it was at sea level had presumably been raised with it and might still be in residence. Whether it had wandered in from outside, or belonged there, it might be hungry—very hungry. It was.

There was a hiss that raised the short hair all along his spine. The mice that he had shied rocks at had heard such hisses and passed the fear of them down to their descendants, who eventually became his remote ancestors. And they had cause for fear! The thing that lurched out of the rocky maze, while it didn't top him by more than six feet and had teeth that were only eight inches long, was big enough to swallow him in three quick gulps, gun and all.

He ran. He ran like a rabbit. He doubled into crannies that the thing couldn't cram into and scrambled up spires of crumbling rock that a monkey would have found difficult, but it knew short cuts and it was downwind from him, and it thundered along behind with very few yards to spare. Suddenly he popped out of a long, winding corridor onto a bare ledge with a sheer drop to a steaming, stinking morass alive with things like crocodiles, only bigger. At the cliff's edge the thing was waiting for him.

One leap and it was between him and the crevice. He backed toward the cliff, raising his rifle slowly. It sat watching him for a moment, then raised its massive tail, teetered forward on its huge hind legs, and came running at him with its tiny foreclaws pumping like a sprinter's fists.

He threw up the gun and fired. The bullet plowed into its throat and a jet of smoking blood sprayed him as its groping claws knocked the rifle from his grasp. Its hideous jaws closed on his upflung left arm, grinding the bones until he screamed. It jerked him up, dangling by his broken arm, ten feet in the air; then the idea of death hit it and it rolled over and lay twitching on the blood-soaked rock. Its jaws sagged open, and with what strength he had left Donovan dragged himself out of range of its jerking claws. He pulled himself up with his back against a rock and stared into the face of a second monster!

This was the one that had trailed him. The thing that had actually tasted him was a competitor. It came striding out of the shadowy gorge, the sun playing on its bronzed armor, and stopped to sniff at the thing Donovan had killed. It rolled the huge carcass over and tore out the belly, then straightened up with great gouts of bloody flesh dribbling from its jaws, and looked Donovan in the eye. Inch by inch, he tried to wedge himself into the crack between the boulders against which he lay. Then it stepped over its deceased relative and towered above him. Its grinning mask swooped down and its foul breath was in his face.

Then it was gone!

It wasn't a dream. There were the rocks—there was the carcass of the other beast—but it was gone! Vanished! In its place a wisp of bluish vapor was dissipating slowly in the sunlight. Vapor—and a voice! A woman's voice, in an unknown tongue.

She stood at the edge of the rocks. She was as tall as he, with very white skin and very black hair, dressed in shining metal cloth that was wound around her like bandage, leaving her arms and one white leg free. She was made like a woman and she spoke like a woman, in a voice that thrilled him in spite of the sickening pain in his arm. She had a little black cylinder in her hand, with a narrowed muzzle and a grip for her fingers, and she was pointing it at him. She spoke again, imperiously, questioning him. He grinned, tried to drag himself to his feet, and passed out cold.

It was two days before he came to. He figured that out later. It was night. He was in a tent somewhere near the sea, for he could hear it pounding on hard-packed sands. Above its roar there were other noises of the night; mutterings and rumblings of great reptiles, very far away, and now and then a hissing scream of rage. They sounded unreal. He seemed to be floating in a silvery mist, with the pain in his wounded arm throb, throb, throbbing to the rhythm of the sea.

Then he saw that the light was moonlight, and the silver the sheen of the woman's garment. She sat at his feet, in the opening of the tent, with the moonlight falling on her hair. It was coiled like a coronet about her head, and he remembered thinking that she must be a queen in some magic land, like the ones in fairy tales.

Someone moved, and he saw that there were others —men—crouching behind a breastwork of stone. They had cylinders like the one the woman had carried, and other weapons on tripods like parabolic microphones— great, polished reflectors of energy. The wall seemed more for concealment than protection, for he remembered the blasting power of the little cylinder and knew that no mere heap of rock could withstand it long. Unless, of course, they were fighting some foe who lacked their science. A foe native to this Cretaceous age—hairy, savage men with stones and clubs.

Realization struck him. There were no men in the Cretaceous. The only mammals were the mouselike marsupials that had robbed his pack. Then—who was the woman and how had she come here? Who were the men who guarded her? Were they—could they be—travelers in time like himself?

He sat up with a jerk that made his head swim. There was a shimmering, flowing movement in the moonlight and a small, soft hand was pressed over his mouth, an arm was about his shoulders, easing him back among the cushions. He called out and one of the men rose and came into the tent. He was tall, nearly seven feet, with silvery white hair and a queer-shaped skull. He stared expressionlessly down at Donovan, questioning the woman in that same strange tongue. She answered him, and Donovan felt with a thrill that she seemed worried. The other shrugged—that is, he made a queer, quick gesture with his hands that passed for a shrug—and turned away. Before Donovan knew what was happening, the woman gathered him up in her arms like a babe and started for the door of the tent.

Terry Donovan is over six feet tall and weighs two hundred pounds. He stiffened like a naughty child. It caught her off guard and they went down with a thud, the woman underneath. It knocked the wind out of her, and Donovan's arm began to throb furiously, but he scrambled to his feet, and with his good hand helped her to rise. They stood eyeing each other like sparring cats, and then Terry laughed.

It was a hearty Irish guffaw that broke the tension, but it brought hell down on them. Something spanged on the barricade and went whining over their heads. Something else came arching and went through the moonlight and fell at their feet—a metal ball the size of his head, whirring like a clock about to strike.

Donovan moved like greased lightning. He scooped the thing up with his good hand and lobbed it high and wide in the direction from which it came, then grabbed the woman and ducked. It burst in midair with a blast of white flame that would have licked them off the face of the earth in a twinkling—and there was no sound, no explosion such as a normal bomb should make! There was no bark of rifles off there in the darkness, though slugs were thudding into the barricade and screaming overhead with unpleasant regularity. The tent was in ribbons, and seeing no reason why it should make a better target than need be, he kicked the pole out from under it and brought it down in a billowing heap.

That made a difference, and he saw why. The material of the tent was evanescent, hard to see. It did something to the light that fell on it, distorted it, acting as a camouflage. But where bullets had torn its fabric a line of glowing green sparks shone in the night.

The enemy had lost their target, but they had the range. A bullet whined evilly past Donovan's ear as he dropped behind the shelter of the wall. His groping hand found a familiar shape—his rifle. The cartridge belt was with it. He tucked the butt between his knees and made sure that it was loaded, then rose cautiously and peeped over the barricade.

Hot lead sprayed his cheek as a bullet pinged on the stone beside him. There was a cry from the woman. She had dropped to her knees beside the tent, and he could see that the ricochet had cut her arm. The sight of blood on her white skin sent a burning fury surging through him. He lunged awkwardly to his feet, resting the rifle on top of the wall, and peered into the darkness.

Five hundred yards away was the jungle, a wall of utter blackness out of which those silent missiles came. Nothing was visible against its shadows—or was that a lighter spot that slipped from tree to tree at the very edge of the moonlight? Donovan's cheek nestled against the stock of his gun and his eyes strained to catch that flicker of gray in the blackness. It came—the gun roared—and out of the night rang a scream of pain. A hit!

Twice before sunup he fired at fleeting shadows, without result. Beside him, the oldest of the four men —the one he had seen first—was dressing the woman's wound. It was only a scratch, but Donovan reasoned that in this age of virulent life forms, it was wise to take every precaution. There might be germs that no one had even heard of lurking everywhere. The others were about his own age, or seemed to be, with the same queer heads and white hair as their companion's. They seemed utterly disinterested in him and what he was doing.

As the first rays of the sun began to brighten the sky behind them, Donovan took stock of the situation. Their little fortress was perched on a point of rock overlooking the sea, with the plateau behind it. Salt marshes ran inland as far as he could see, edged with heavy jungle. And in No Man's Land between the two was the queerest ship he had ever seen.

It was of metal, cigar-shaped, with the gaping mouths of rocket jets fore and after and a row of staring portholes. It was as big as a large ocean vessel and it answered his question about these men whose cause he was championing. They had come from space—from another world!

Bodies were strewn in the open space between the ship and the barricade. One lay huddled against a huge boulder, a young fellow, barely out of his teens as we would gauge it. Donovan's gaze wandered away, then flashed back. The man had moved!

Donovan turned eagerly to the others. They stared at him, blank-faced. He seized the nearest man by the shoulder and pointed. A cold light came into the other's eyes, and Donovan saw his companions edging toward him, their hands on the stubby cylinders of their weapons. He swore. Damn dummies! He flung the rifle down at the woman's sandaled feet and leaped to the top of the wall. As he stood there he was a perfect target, but no shot came. Then he was among the scattered rocks, zigzagging toward the wounded man. A moment later he slid safely into the niche behind the boulder, and lifted the other into a sitting position against his knee. He had been creased—an ugly furrow plowed along his scalp—but he seemed otherwise intact.

Donovan got his good shoulder under the man's armpit and lifted him bodily. From the hill behind the barricade a shot screamed past his head. Before he could drop to safety a second slug whacked into the body of the man in his arms, and the youth's slim form slumped in death.

Donovan laid him gently down in the shelter of the boulder. He wondered whether this would be the beginning of the end. Under fire from both sides, the little fortress could not hold out for long. A puff of vapor on the hillside told him why the fire was not being returned. The damned cylinders had no range. That was why the enemy was using bullets—air guns, or whatever the things were. All the more reason why he should save his skin while the saving was good. He ducked behind the rock, then straightened up and streaked for the shelter of the trees.

Bullets sang around him and glanced whistling from the rocks. One whipped the sleeve that hung loose at his side and another grooved the leather of his high-top boots. All came from behind—from the hill above the camp—and as he gained the safety of the forest he turned and saw the foe for the first time.

They were deployed in a long line across the top of the ridge behind the camp. They had weapons like fat-barreled rifles, with some bulky contraption at the breach. As he watched they rose and came stalking down the hillside, firing as they came.

They were black, but without the heavy features of a Negro. Their hair was as yellow as corn, and they wore shorts and tunics of copper-colored material. Donovan saw that they were maneuvering toward a spur from which they could fire down into the little fortress and pick off its defenders one by one. With the men at the barricade gone, they would be coming after him. If he started now, he might make his way through the jungle to a point where he could cut back across the hills and reach the Egg. He had a fifty-fifty chance of making it. Only—there was the woman. It was murder to leave her, and suicide to stay.

Fate answered for him. From the barricade he heard the roar of his rifle and saw one of the blacks spin and fall in a heap. The others stood startled, then raced for cover. Before they reached it, two more were down, and Donovan saw the woman's sleek black head thrust above the top of the rocky wall with the rifle butt tucked in the hollow of her shoulder.

That settled it. No one with her gumption was going to say that Terry Donovan had run out on her. Cautiously, he stuck his head out of the undergrowth and looked to left and right. A hundred feet from him one of the blacks lay half in and half out of the forest. One of the outlandish-looking rifles was beside him. Donovan pulled his head back and began to pry his way through the thick undergrowth.

The Donovan luck is famous. The gun was intact, and with it was a belt case crammed with little metal cubes that had the look of ammunition. He poked the heavy barrel into the air and pushed the button that was set in the butt. There was a crackling whisper, barely audible, and a slug went tearing through the fronds above him. He tried again, and an empty cube popped out into his palm. He examined it carefully. There was a sliding cover that had to be removed before the mechanism of the gun could get at the bullets it contained. He slipped in one of the loaded cubes and tried again. A second shot went whistling into space. Then, tucking the gun under his arm, he set out on a flanking trip of his own.

He knew the range of the weapon he was carrying, if not its nature, and he knew how to use it. He knew that if he could swing far around to the east, along the sea, he might come up on the ridge behind the blacks and catch them by surprise. Then if the gang in the fort would lend a hand, the war was as good as over.

It was easier said than done. A man with one mangled arm strapped to his side, and a twenty-pound rifle in his good hand, is not the world's best mountaineer. He worked his way through the jungle into the lee of the dunes that lay between the cliffs and the beach, then ran like blue blazes until he was out of sight of the whole fracas, cut back inland, took his lip in his teeth, and began to climb.

There were places where he balanced on spires the size and sharpness of a needle, or so he said. There were places where he prayed hard and trod on thin air. Somehow he made it and stuck his head out from behind a crimson crag to look down on a very pretty scene.

The ten remaining blacks were holed up on the crest of the ridge. They were within range of the camp, but they didn't dare get up and shoot because of whoever was using the rifle. That "whoever"—the woman, as Donovan had suspected—was out of sight and stalking them from the north just as he was doing from the south. The fighting blood of his Irish ancestors sizzled in his veins. He slid the misshapen muzzle of his weapon out over the top of the rock and settled its butt in the crook of his good arm. He swiveled it around until it pointed in the direction of two of the blacks who were sheltering under the same shallow ledge. Then he jammed down the button and held on.

The thing worked like a machine gun and kicked like one. Before it lashed itself out of his grip one of the foemen was dead, two were flopping about like fish out of water, and the rest were in full flight. As they sprang to their feet the woman blazed away at them with the elephant gun. Then the men from the barricade were swarming over the rock wall, cylinders in hand, and mowing the survivors down in a succession of tiny puffs of blue smoke. In a moment it was over.

Donovan made his way slowly down the hillside. The

woman was coming to meet him. She was younger than he had thought—a lot younger—but her youth did not soften her. He thought that she might still be a better man than he, if it came to a test. She greeted him in her soft tongue, and held out the rifle. He took it, and as he touched the cold metal a terrific jolt of static electricity knocked him from his feet.

He scrambled up ruefully. The woman had not fallen, but her eyes blazed with fury. Then she saw that he had not acted intentionally, and smiled. Donovan saw now why the blacks wore metal suits. Their weapons built up a static charge with each shot, and unless the gunner was well grounded it would accumulate until it jumped to the nearest conductor. His rubber soled shoes had insulated him, and the charge built up on him until he touched the barrel of the rifle, whereupon it grounded through the steel and the woman's silvery gown.

They went down the hillside together. Donovan had given the woman the gun he had salvaged, and she was examining it carefully. She called out to the men, who stood waiting for them, and they began to search the bodies of the blacks for ammunition. Half an hour later they were standing on the beach in the shadow of the great rocket. The men had carried their equipment from the camp and stowed it away, while Donovan and the woman stood outside bossing the job. That is, she bossed while he watched. Then he recalled who and where he was. Helping these people out in their little feud was one thing, but going off with them, Heaven knew where, was another. He reached down and took the woman's hand.

"I've got to be going," he said.

Of course, she didn't understand a word he said. She

frowned and asked some question in her own tongue. He grinned. He was no better at languages than she. He pointed to himself, then up the beach to the east where the Egg should be. He saluted cheerfully and started to walk away. She cried out sharply and in an instant all four men were on him.

He brought up the rifle barrel in a one-handed swing that dropped the first man in his tracks. The gun went spinning out of his hand, but before the others could reach him he had vaulted the man's body and caught the woman to him in a savage, one-arm hug that made her gasp for breath. The men stopped, their ray guns drawn. One second more and he would have been a haze of exploded atoms, but none of them dared fire with the woman in the way. Over the top of her sleek head he stared into their cold, hard eyes. Human they might be, but there was blessed little of the milk of human kindness in the way they looked at him.

"Drop those guns," he ordered, "or I'll break her damned neck!" None of them moved. "You heard me!" he barked. "Drop 'em!"

They understood his tone. Three tapering cylinders thudded on the sand. He thrust the woman forward with the full weight of his body and trod them into the sand.

"Get back," he commanded. "Go on. Scram!"

They went. Releasing the woman, he leaped back and snatched up the weapon she had dropped. He poked its muzzle at her slender waist and fitted his fingers cozily about the stock. He jerked his head back, away from the ship.

"You're coming with me," he said.

She stared inscrutably at him for a moment, then without a word, walked past him and set off up the beach.

Donovan followed her. A moment later the dunes had hidden the ship and the three men who stood beside it.

Then began a journey every step of which was a puzzle. The girl—for she was really little more—made no attempt to escape. After the first mile Donovan thrust the ray gun into his belt and caught up with her. Hours passed, and still they were slogging wearily along under the escarpment. In spite of the almost miraculous speed with which it was healing, the strain and activity of the past few hours had started his arm throbbing like a toothache. It made him grumpy, and he had fallen behind when a drumming roar made him look up.

It was the rocket ship. It was flying high, but as he looked it swooped down on them with incredible speed. A thousand feet above it leveled off and a shaft of violet light stabbed down, missing the girl by a scant ten feet. Where it hit the sand was a molten pool, and she was running for her life, zigzagging like a frightened rabbit, streaking for the shelter of the cliffs. With a shout, Donovan raced after her.

A mile ahead the ship zoomed and came roaring back at him. A black hole opened in the face of the cliff. The girl vanished in its shadows, and as the thunder of the rocket sounded unbearably loud in his ears, Donovan dived after her. The ray slashed across the rock above his head and droplets of molten magma seared his back. The girl was crouching against the wall of the cave. When she saw him she plunged into the blackness beyond.

He had had enough of hide and seek. He wanted a show-down and he wanted it now. With a shout, he leaped after the girl's receding figure and caught her by the shoulder, spinning her around.

Instantly he felt like an utter fool. He could say nothing

that she could understand. The whole damned affair was beyond understanding. He had strong-armed her into coming with him—and her own men had tried to burn her down. Her—not him. Somehow, by something he had done, he had put her in danger of her life from the only people in the entire universe who had anything in common with her. He couldn't leave her alone in a wilderness full of hungry dinosaurs, with a gang of gunmen on her trail, and he couldn't take her with him. The Egg would barely hold one. He was in a spot, and there was nothing he could do about it.

There was the sound of footsteps on the gravel behind them. In the dim light he saw the girl's eyes go wide. He wheeled. Two men were silhouetted against the mouth of the cave. One of them held a ray gun. He raised it slowly.

Donovan's shoulder flung the girl against the wall. His hand flicked past his waist and held the gun. Twice it blazed and the men were gone in a puff of sparkling smoke. But in that instant, before they were swept out of existence, their guns had exploded in a misdirected burst of energy that brought the roof crashing down in a thundering avalanche, sealing the cave from wall to wall.

The shock flung Donovan to the ground. His wounded arm smashed brutally into the wall and a wave of agony left him white and faint. The echoes of that stupendous crash died away slowly in the black recesses of the cave. Then there was utter silence.

Something stirred beside him. A small, soft hand touched his face, found his shoulder, his hand. The girl's voice murmured, pleading. There was something she wanted—something he must do. He got painfully to his feet and awaited her next move. She gently detached the ray gun from his fingers, and before he knew it he was being hustled through utter darkness into the depths of the cave.

He did a lot of thinking on that journey through blackness. He put two and two together and got five or six different answers. Some of them hung together to make sense out of nightmare.

First, the girl herself. The rocket, and Donovan's faith in a science that he was proving fallible, told him that she must have come from another planet. Her unusual strength might mean that she was from some larger planet, or even some star. At any rate, she was human and she was somebody of importance.

Donovan mulled over that for a while. Two races, from the same or different planets, were thirsting for each other's blood. It might be politics that egged them on, or it might be racial trouble or religion. Nothing else would account for the fury with which they were exterminating each other. The girl had apparently taken refuge with her bodyguard on this empty planet. Possession of her was important. She might be a deposed queen or princess —and the blacks were on her trail. They found her and laid siege—whereupon Terry Donovan of 1937 A.D. came barging into the picture.

That was where the complications began. The girl, reconnoitering, had saved him from the dinosaur which was eating him. Any one would have done as much. She lugged him back to camp—Donovan flushed at the thought of the undignified appearance he must have made—and they patched him up with their miraculous green ointment. Then the scrap began, and he did his part to bring them out on top. Did it damn well, if any one was asking. Donovan didn't belong to their gang and didn't want to, so when they started for home he did likewise. Only it didn't work out that way.

She had ordered her men to jump him. She wanted to hang on to him, whether for romantic reasons, which was doubtful, or because she needed another fighting man. They didn't get very far with their attempt to gang up on him. That was where the worst of the trouble began.

Grabbing her as he had had been a mistake. Somehow that act of touching her—of doing physical violence to her person—made a difference. It was as though she were a goddess who lost divinity through his violence, or a priestess who was contaminated by his touch. She recognized that fact. She knew then that she would have short shrift at the hands of her own men if she stayed with them. So she came along. Strangely enough, the men did not follow for some time. It was not until they returned to the rocket, until they received orders from whoever was in that rocket, that they tried to kill her.

Whoever was in the rocket! The thought opened new possibilities. A priest, enforcing the taboos of his god. A politician, playing party policy. A traitor, serving the interests of the blacks. None of these did much to explain the girl's own attitude, nor the reason why this assumed potentate, if he was in the rocket during the battle, had done nothing to bring one side or the other to victory. It didn't explain why hours had passed before the pursuit began. And nothing told him what he was going to do with her when they reached the Egg. If they ever did.

The cave floor had been rising for some time when Donovan saw a gleam of light ahead. At once the girl's pace quickened, and she dropped his arm. How, he wondered, had she been able to traverse that pitch-black labyrinth so surely and quickly? Could she see in the dark, or judge her way with some strange sixth sense? It added one more puzzle to the mysteries surrounding her.

He could have danced for joy when they came out into the light. They had passed under the ridge and come out at the foot of the cliffs which he had climbed hours before. The whole landscape was familiar: the gullies in the barren plain, the fringe of swamp and jungle, and the reefs over which the oily sea was breaking. There, a few miles to the north, the Egg was hidden. There was safety—home—for one.

She seemed to know what he was thinking. She laid a reassuring hand on his arm and smiled up at him. This was his party from now on. Then she saw the pain in his eyes. His arm had taken more punishment than most men could have stood and stayed alive. Her nimble fingers peeled away the dressing and gently probed the wound to test the position of the broken bones. Evidently everything was to her liking, for she smiled reassuringly and opened a pouch at her waist, from which she took a little jar of bright-green ointment and smeared it liberally on the wound. It burned like fire, then a sensuous sort of glow crept through his arm and side, deadening the pain. She wadded the dirty bandages into a ball and threw them away. Then, before Donovan knew what was happening, she had ripped a length of the metallic-looking fabric from her skirt and was binding the arm tightly to his side.

Stepping back, she regarded him with satisfaction, then turned her attention to the gun she had taken from him. A lip of the firing button and an empty cartridge cube popped out into her palm. She looked at him and he at her. It was all the weapon they had, and it was empty. Donovan shrugged. Nothing much mattered anyway. With an answering grimace she sent it spinning away among the rocks. Side by side, they set off toward the coast and the Egg.

It was the sky that Donovan feared now. Dinosaurs they could outwit or outrun. He thought he could even fight one of the little ones, with her to cheer him on. But heat rays shot at them from the sky, with no cover within miles, was something else again. Strangely enough, the girl seemed to be enjoying herself. Her voice was a joy to hear, even if it didn't make sense, and Donovan thought that he got the drift of her comments on some of the ungainly monstrosities that blemished the Cretaceous landscape.

Donovan had no desire to be in the jungle at night, so they took their time. He had matches, which she examined with curiosity, and they slept, back to back, beside a fire of grass and twigs in the lee of a big boulder. There was nothing to eat, but it didn't seem to matter. A sort of silent partnership had been arrived at, and Donovan, at least, was basking in its friendly atmosphere.

Every road has its ending. Noon found them standing beside the leaden hulk of the Egg, face to face with reality. One of them, and only one, could make the journey back. The Egg would not hold two, nor was there power enough in its accumulators to carry more than one back through the barrier between time coils. If the girl were to go, she would find herself alone in a world unutterably remote from her own, friendless and unable to understand or to make herself understood. If Donovan returned, he must leave her here alone in the Cretaceous jungle, with no food, no means of protection from man or beast, and no knowledge of what might be happening sixty million years later which would seal her fate for good.

There was only one answer. Her hand went to his arm and pushed him gently toward the open door of the Egg. He, and he alone, could get the help which they must have and return to find her. In six hours at the outside the Egg should be ready to make its return trip. In that six hours Donovan could find me, or some other friend, and enlist my aid!

Fortune played into his hands. There was a patter of footsteps among the fallen fronds, and a small dinosaur appeared, the body of a bird in its jaws. With a whoop, Donovan sprang at it. It dropped the bird and disappeared. The creature was not dead, but Donovan wrung its scrawny neck. Here was proof that must convince me of the truth of his story that would bring me to their aid!

He stepped into the machine. As the door swung shut, he saw the girl raise her hand in farewell. When it opened again, he stepped out on the concrete floor of his own laboratory, sixty million years later.

His first thought was for the generators that would recharge the batteries of the Egg. Then, from the house and the laboratory, he collected the things that he would need: guns, food, water, clothing. Finally, he set out to fetch me.

He sat there, his broken arm strapped to his side with that queer metallic cloth, the torn flesh painted with some aromatic green ointment. A revolver in its holster lay on the desk at his elbow; a rifle leaned against the heap of duffel on the floor of the Egg. What did it all mean? Was it part of some incredibly elaborate hoax, planned for some inconceivable purpose? Or—fantastic as it seemed—was it truth?

"I'm leaving in ten minutes," he said. "The batteries are charged."

"What can I do?" I asked. "I'm no mechanic—no physicist."

"I'll send her back in the Egg," he told me. "I'll show you how to charge it—it's perfectly simple—and when it's ready you will send it back, empty, for me. If there is any delay, make her comfortable until I come."

I noted carefully everything he did, every setting of every piece of apparatus, just as he showed them to me. Then, just four hours after he threw that incredible bird down at my feet, I watched the leaden door of the Egg swing shut. The hum of the generators rose to an ugly whine. A black veil seemed to envelop the huge machine —a network of emptiness which ran together and coalesced into a hole into which I gazed for interminable distances. Then it was gone. The room was empty. I touched the switch that stopped the generators.

The Egg did not return—not on that day, nor the next, nor even while I waited there. Finally, I came away. I have told his story—my story before—but they laugh as I did. Only there is one thing that no one knows.

This year there were new funds for excavation. I am still senior paleontologist at the museum, and in spite of the veiled smiles that are beginning to follow me, I was chosen to continue my work of previous seasons. I knew from the beginning what I would do. The executors of Donovan's estate gave me permission to trace the line of

the ancient Cretaceous beach that ran across his property.
I had a word picture of that other world as he had seen it,
and a penciled sketch, scrawled on the back of an
envelope as he talked. I knew where he had buried the
cube of radium. And it might be that this beach of fossil
sands, preserved almost since the beginning of time, was
the same one in which Terry Donovan had scooped a hole
and buried a leaden cube, sealed in a steel box.

I have not found the box. If it is there, it is buried under
tons of rock that will require months of labor and
thousands of dollars to remove. We have uncovered a
section of the beach in whose petrified sands every mark
made in that ancient day is as sharp and clear as though it
were made yesterday; the ripples of the receding tide
—the tracks of sea worms crawling in the shallow
water—the trails of the small reptiles that fed on the
flotsam and jetsam of the water's edge.

Two lines of footprints come down across the wet sands
of that Cretaceous beach, side by side. Together they
cross the forty-foot slab of sandstone which I have
uncovered, and vanish where the rising tide has filled
them. They are prints of a small, queerly made sandal and
a rubber-soled hiking boot—of a man and a girl.

A third line of tracks crosses the Cretaceous sands and
overlies those others—huge, splayed, three-toed, like the
prints of some gigantic bird. Sixty million years ago,
mighty Tyrannosaurus and his smaller cousins made such
tracks. The print of one great paw covers both the girl's
footprints as she stands for a moment, motionless, beside
the man. They, too, vanish at the water's edge.

That is all, but for one thing: an inch or two beyond the
point where the tracks vanish, where the lapping waters

have smoothed the sand, there is a strange mark. The grains of sand are fused, melted together in a kind of funnel of greenish glass that reminds me of the fulgurites that one often finds where lightning has struck iron-bearing sand, or where some high-voltage cable has grounded. It is smoother and more regular than any fulgurite that I have ever seen.

Two years ago I saw Terry Donovan step into the leaden Egg that stood in its cradle on the floor of his laboratory, and vanish with it into nothingness. He has not returned. The tracks which I have described, imprinted in the sands of a Cretaceous beach, are very plain, but workmen are the only people besides myself who have seen them. They see no resemblance to human footprints in the blurred hollows in the stone. They know, for I have told them again and again during the years that I have worked with them, that there were no human beings on the earth sixty million years ago. Science says—and is not science always right?—that only the great dinosaurs of the Cretaceous age left their fossil footprints in the sands of time.

# A Sound of Thunder

## by Ray Bradbury

The sign on the wall seemed to quaver under a film of sliding warm water. Eckels felt his eyelids blink over his stare, and the sign blurred in this momentary darkness:

TIME SAFARI, INC.
SAFARIS TO ANY YEAR IN THE PAST.
YOU NAME THE ANIMAL.
WE TAKE YOU THERE.
YOU SHOOT IT.

A warm phlegm gathered in Eckels' throat; he swallowed and pushed it down. The muscles around his mouth formed a smile as he put his hand slowly out upon the air, and in that hand waved a check for ten thousand dollars to the man behind the desk.

"Does this safari guarantee I come back alive?"

"We guarantee nothing," said the official, "except the dinosaurs." He turned. "This is Mr. Travis, your Safari Guide in the Past. He'll tell you what and where to shoot. If he says no shooting, no shooting. If you disobey instructions, there's a stiff penalty of another ten thousand dollars, plus possible government action, on your return."

Eckels glanced across the vast office at a mass and tangle, a snaking and humming of wires and steel boxes, at an aurora that flickered now orange, now silver, now blue. There was a sound like a gigantic bonfire burning all of Time, all the years and all the parchment calendars, all the hours piled high and set aflame.

A touch of the hand and this burning would, on the instant, beautifully reverse itself. Eckels remembered the wording in the advertisements to the letter. Out of chars and ashes, out of dust and coals, like golden salamanders, the old years, the green years, might leap; roses sweeten the air, white hair turn Irish-black, wrinkles vanish; all, everything fly back to seed, flee death, rush down to their beginnings, suns rise in western skies and set in glorious easts, moons eat themselves opposite to the custom, all and everything cupping one in another like Chinese boxes, rabbits into hats, all and everything returning to the fresh death, the seed death, the green death, to the time before the beginning. A touch of a hand might do it, the merest touch of a hand.

"Hell and damn," Eckels breathed, the light of the Machine on his thin face. "A real Time Machine." He shook his head. "Makes you think. If the election had gone badly yesterday, I might be here now running away from the results. Thank God Keith won. He'll make a fine President of the United States."

"Yes," said the man behind the desk. "We're lucky. If Deutscher had gotten in, we'd have the worst kind of dictatorship. There's an anti-everything man for you, a militarist, anti-Christ, anti-human, anti-intellectual. People called us up, you know, joking but not joking. Said if Deutscher became President they wanted to go live in 1492. Of course it's not our business to conduct Escapes, but to form Safaris. Anyway, Keith's President now. All you got to worry about is—"

"Shooting my dinosaur," Eckels finished it for him.

"A *Tyrannosaurus rex*. The Thunder Lizard, the damnedest monster in history. Sign this release. Anything happens to you, we're not responsible. Those dinosaurs are hungry."

Eckels flushed angrily. "Trying to scare me!"

"Frankly, yes. We don't want anyone going who'll panic at the first shot. Six Safari leaders were killed last year, and a dozen hunters. We're here to give you the damnedest thrill a *real* hunter ever asked for. Traveling you back sixty million years to bag the biggest damned game in all Time. Your personal check's still there. Tear it up."

Mr. Eckels looked at the check for a long time. His fingers twitched.

"Good luck," said the man behind the desk. "Mr. Travis, he's all yours."

They moved silently across the room, taking their guns with them, toward the Machine, toward the silver metal and the roaring light.

First a day and then a night and then a day and then a night, then it was day-night-day-night-day. A week, a month, a year, a decade! A.D. 2055. A.D. 2019. 1999! 1957! Gone! The Machine roared.

They put on their oxygen helmets and tested the intercoms.

Eckels swayed on the padded seat, his face pale, his jaw stiff. He felt the trembling in his arms and he looked down and found his hands tight on the new rifle. There were four other men in the Machine. Travis, the Safari Leader, his assistant, Lesperance, and two other hunters, Billings and Kramer. They sat looking at each other, and the years blazed around them.

"Can these guns get a dinosaur cold?" Eckels felt his mouth saying.

"If you hit them right," said Travis on the helmet radio. "Some dinosaurs have two brains, one in the head, another far down the spinal column. We stay away from those. That's stretching luck. Put your first two shots into the eyes, if you can, blind them, and go back into the brain."

The Machine howled. Time was a film run backward. Suns fled and ten million moons fled after them. "Good God," said Eckels. "Every hunter that ever lived would envy us today. This makes Africa seem like Illinois."

The Machine slowed; its scream fell to a murmur. The Machine stopped.

The sun stopped in the sky.

The fog that had enveloped the Machine blew away and they were in an old time, a very old time indeed, three hunters and two Safari Heads with their blue metal guns across their knees.

"Christ isn't born yet," said Travis. "Moses has not gone to the mountain to talk with God. The Pyramids are still in the earth, waiting to be cut out and put up. *Remember* that. Alexander, Caesar, Napoleon, Hitler —none of them exists."

The men nodded.

"That"—Mr. Travis pointed—"is the jungle of sixty

million two thousand and fifty-five years before President Keith."

He indicated a metal path that struck off into green wilderness, over steaming swamp, among giant ferns and palms.

"And that," he said, "is the Path, laid by Time Safari for your use. It floats six inches above the earth. Doesn't touch so much as one grass blade, flower, or tree. It's an anti-gravity metal. Its purpose is to keep you from touching this world of the past in any way. Stay on the Path. Don't go off it. I repeat. *Don't go off.* For *any* reason! If you fall off, there's a penalty. And don't shoot any animal we don't okay."

"Why?" asked Eckels.

They sat in the ancient wilderness. Far birds' cries blew on a wind, and the smell of tar and an old salt sea, moist grasses, and flowers the color of blood.

"We don't want to change the Future. We don't belong here in the Past. The government doesn't *like* us here. We have to pay big graft to keep our franchise. A Time Machine is damn finicky business. Not knowing it, we might kill an important animal, a small bird, a roach, a flower even, thus destroying an important link in a growing species."

"That's not clear," said Eckels.

"All right," Travis continued, "say we accidentally kill one mouse here. That means all the future families of this one particular mouse are destroyed, right?"

"Right."

"And all the families of the families of the families of that one mouse! With a stamp of your foot, you annihilate first one, then a dozen, then a thousand, a million, a *billion* possible mice!"

"So they're dead," said Eckels. "So what?"

"So what?" Travis snorted quietly. "Well, what about the foxes that'll need those mice to survive? For want of ten mice, a fox dies. For want of ten foxes, a lion starves. For want of a lion, all manner of insects, vultures, infinite billions of life forms are thrown into chaos and destruction. Eventually it all boils down to this: fifty-nine million years later, a cave man, one of a dozen on the *entire world,* goes hunting wild boar or saber-tooth tiger for food. But you, friend, have *stepped* on all the tigers in that region. By stepping on *one* single mouse. So the cave man starves. And the cave man, please note, is not just *any* expendable man, no! He is an *entire future nation.* From his loins would have sprung ten sons. From *their* loins one hundred sons, and thus onward to a civilization. Destroy this one man, and you destroy a race, a people, an entire history of life. It is comparable to slaying some of Adam's grandchildren. The stomp of your foot, on one mouse, could start an earthquake, the effects of which could shake our earth and destinies down through Time, to their very foundations. With the death of that one cave man, a billion others yet unborn are throttled in the womb. Perhaps Rome never rises on its seven hills. Perhaps Europe is forever a dark forest, and only Asia waxes healthy and teeming. Step on a mouse and you crush the Pyramids. Step on a mouse and you leave your print, like a Grand Canyon across Eternity. Queen Elizabeth might never be born, Washington might not cross the Delaware, there might never be a United States at all. So be careful. Stay on the Path. *Never* step off!"

"I see," said Eckels. "Then it wouldn't pay for us even to touch the *grass*?"

"Correct. Crushing certain plants could add up infinitesimally. A little error here would multiply in sixty million years, all out of proportion. Of course maybe our theory is wrong. Maybe Time *can't* be changed by us. Or maybe it can be changed only in little subtle ways. A dead mouse here makes an insect imbalance there, a population disproportion later, a bad harvest further on, a depression, mass starvation, and finally, a change in *social* temperament in far-flung countries. Something much more subtle, like that. Perhaps only a soft breath, a whisper, a hair, pollen on the air, such a slight, slight change that unless you looked close you wouldn't see it. Who knows? Who really can say he knows? We don't know. We're guessing. But until we do know for certain whether our messing around in Time *can* make a big roar or a little rustle in history, we're being damned careful. This Machine, this Path, your clothing and bodies, were sterilized, as you know, before the journey. We wear these oxygen helmets so we can't introduce our bacteria into an ancient atmosphere."

"How do we know which animals to shoot?"

"They're marked with red paint," said Travis. "Today, before our journey, we sent Lesperance here back with the Machine. He came to this particular era and followed certain animals."

"Studying them?"

"Right," said Lesperance. "I track them through their entire existence, noting which of them live longest. Very few. How many times they mate. Not often. Life's short. When I find one that's going to die when a tree falls on him, or one that drowns in a tar pit, I note the exact hour, minute, and second. I shoot a paint bomb. It leaves a red patch on his hide. We can't miss it. Then I correlate our arrival in the Past so that we meet the Monster not

more than two minutes before he would have died anyway. This way, we kill only animals with no future, that
are never going to mate again. You see how *careful* we
are?"

"But if you came back this morning in Time," said
Eckels eagerly, "you must've bumped into *us,* our Safari!
How did it turn out? Was it successful? Did all of us get
through—alive?"

Travis and Lesperance gave each other a look.

"That'd be a paradox," said the latter. "Time doesn't
permit that sort of mess—a man meeting himself. When
such occasions threaten, Time steps aside. Like an
airplane hitting an air pocket. You felt the Machine jump
just before we stopped? That was us passing ourselves on
the way back to the Future. We saw nothing. There's no
way of telling *if* this expedition was a success, *if* we got our
monster, or whether all of us—meaning *you,* Mr. Eckels
—got out alive."

Eckels smiled palely.

"Cut that," said Travis sharply. "Everyone on his
feet!"

They were ready to leave the Machine.

The jungle was high and the jungle was broad and the
jungle was the entire world forever and forever. Sounds
like music and sounds like flying tents filled the sky, and
those were pterodactyls soaring with cavernous gray
wings, gigantic bats out of a delirium and a night fever.
Eckels, balanced on the narrow Path, aimed his rifle
playfully.

"Stop that!" said Travis. "Don't even aim for fun,
damn it! If your gun should go off—"

Eckels flushed. "Where's our *Tyrannosaurus?*"

Lesperance checked his wrist watch. "Up ahead. We'll bisect his trail in sixty seconds. Look for the red paint, for Christ's sake. Don't shoot till we give the word. Stay on the Path. *Stay on the Path!*"

They moved forward in the wind of morning.

"Strange," murmured Eckels. "Up ahead, sixty million years, Election Day over. Keith made President. Everyone celebrating. And here we are, a million years lost, and they don't exist. The things we worried about for months, a lifetime, not even born or thought about yet."

"Safety catches off, everyone!" ordered Travis. "You, first shot, Eckels. Second, Billings. Third, Kramer."

"I've hunted tiger, wild boar, buffalo, elephant, but Jesus, this is *it,*" said Eckels. "I'm shaking like a kid."

"Ah," said Travis.

Everyone stopped.

Travis raised his hand. "Ahead," he whispered. "In the mist. There he is. There's His Royal Majesty now."

The jungle was wide and full of twitterings, rustlings, murmurs, and sighs.

Suddenly it all ceased, as if someone had shut a door.

Silence.

A sound of thunder.

Out of the mist, one hundred yards away, came *Tyrannosaurus rex.*

"Jesus God," whispered Eckels.

"Sh!"

It came on great oiled, resilient, striding legs. It towered thirty feet above half of the trees, a great evil god, folding its delicate watchmaker's claws close to its oily reptilian chest. Each lower leg was a piston, a thousand pounds of white bone, sunk in thick ropes of muscle, sheathed over in a gleam of pebbled skin like the mail of a terrible warrior. Each thigh was a ton of meat, ivory, and steel mesh. And from the great breathing cage of the upper body those two delicate arms dangled out front, arms with hands which might pick up and examine men like toys, while the snake neck coiled. And the head itself, a ton of sculptured stone, lifted easily upon the sky. Its mouth gaped, exposing a fence of teeth like daggers. Its eyes rolled, ostrich eggs, empty of all expression save hunger. It closed its mouth in a death grin. It ran, its pelvic bones crushing aside trees and bushes, its taloned feet clawing damp earth, leaving prints six inches deep wherever it settled its weight. It ran with a gliding ballet step, far too poised and balanced for its ten tons. It moved into a sunlit arena warily, its beautifully reptile hands feeling the air.

"My God!" Eckels twitched his mouth. "It could reach up and grab the moon."

"Sh!" Travis jerked angrily. "He hasn't seen us yet."

"It can't be killed." Eckels pronounced this verdict quietly, as if there could be no argument. He had weighed the evidence and this was his considered opinion. The rifle in his hands seemed a cap gun. "We were fools to come. This is impossible."

"Shut up!" hissed Travis.

"Nightmare."

"Turn around." commanded Travis. "Walk quietly to the Machine. We'll remit one half your fee."

"I didn't realize it would be this *big*," said Eckels. "I miscalculated, that's all. And now I want out."

"It *sees* us!"

"There's the red paint on its chest!"

The Thunder Lizard raised itself. Its armored flesh glittered like a thousand green coins. The coins, crusted with slime, steamed. In the slime, tiny insects wriggled, so that the entire body seemed to twitch and undulate, even while the monster itself did not move. It exhaled. The stink of raw flesh blew down the wilderness.

"Get me out of here," said Eckels. "It was never like this before. I was always sure I'd come through alive. I had good guides, good safaris, and safety. This time, I figured wrong. I've met my match and admit it. This is too much for me to get hold of."

"Don't run," said Lesperance. "Turn around. Hide in the Machine."

"Yes." Eckels seemed to be numb. He looked at his feet as if trying to make them move. He gave a grunt of helplessness.

"Eckels!"

He took a few steps, blinking, shuffling.

"Not *that* way!"

The Monster, at the first motion, lunged forward with a terrible scream. It covered one hundred yards in four seconds. The rifles jerked up and blazed fire. A windstorm from the beast's mouth engulfed them in the stench of slime and old blood. The Monster roared, teeth glittering with sun.

Eckels, not looking back, walked blindly to the edge of the Path, his gun limp in his arms, stepped off the Path, and walked, not knowing it, in the jungle. His feet sank into green moss. His legs moved him, and he felt alone and remote from the events behind.

The rifles cracked again. Their sound was lost in shriek

and lizard thunder. The great lever of the reptile's tail swung up, lashed sideways. Trees exploded in clouds of leaf and branch. The Monster twitched its jeweler's hands down to fondle at the men, to twist them in half, to crush them like berries, to cram them into its teeth and its screaming throat. Its boulder-stone eyes leveled with the men. They saw themselves mirrored. They fired at the metallic eyelids and the blazing black iris.

Like a stone idol, like a mountain avalanche, *Tyrannosaurus* fell. Thundering, it clutched trees, pulled them with it. It wrenched and tore the metal Path. The men flung themselves back and away. The body hit, ten tons of cold flesh and stone. The guns fired. The Monster lashed its armored tail, twitched its snake jaws, and lay still. A fount of blood spurted from its throat. Somewhere inside, a sac of fluids burst. Sickening gushes drenched the hunters. They stood, red and glistening.

The thunder faded.

The jungle was silent. After the avalanche, a green peace. After the nightmare, morning.

Billings and Kramer sat on the pathway and threw up. Travis and Lesperance stood with smoking rifles, cursing steadily.

In the Time Machine, on his face, Eckels lay shivering. He had found his way back to the Path, climbed into the Machine.

Travis came walking, glanced at Eckels, took cotton gauze from a metal box, and returned to the others, who were sitting on the Path.

"Clean up."

They wiped the blood from their helmets. They began to curse too. The Monster lay, a hill of solid flesh. Within, you could hear the sighs and murmurs as the farthest chambers of it died, the organs malfunctioning, liquids running a final instant from pocket to sac to spleen, everything shutting off, closing up forever. It was like standing by a wrecked locomotive or a steam shovel at quitting time, all valves being released or levered tight. Bones cracked: the tonnage of its own flesh, off balance, dead weight, snapped the delicate forearms, caught underneath. The meat settled, quivering.

Another cracking sound. Overhead, a gigantic tree branch broke from its heavy mooring, fell. It crashed upon the dead beast with finality.

"There." Lesperance checked his watch. "Right on time. That's the giant tree that was scheduled to fall and kill this animal originally." He glanced at the two hunters. "You want the trophy picture?"

"What?"

"We can't take a trophy back to the Future. The body has to stay right here where it would have died originally, so the insects, birds, and bacteria can get at it, as they were intended to. Everything in balance. The body stays. But we *can* take a picture of you standing near it."

The two men tried to think, but gave up, shaking their heads.

They let themselves be led along the metal Path. They sank wearily into the Machine cushions. They gazed back at the ruined Monster, the stagnating mound, where already strange reptilian birds and golden insects were busy at the steaming armor.

A sound on the floor of the Time Machine stiffened them. Eckels sat there, shivering.

"I'm sorry," he said at last.

"Get up!" cried Travis.

Eckels got up.

"Go out on that Path alone," said Travis. He had his rifle pointed. "You're not coming back in the Machine. We're leaving you here!"

Lesperance seized Travis' arm. "Wait—"

"Stay out of this!" Travis shook his hand away. "This son of a bitch nearly killed us. But it isn't *that* so much. Hell, no. It's his *shoes!* Look at them! He ran off the Path. My God, that *ruins* us! Christ knows how much we'll forfeit! Tens of thousands of dollars of insurance! We guarantee no one leaves the Path. He left it. Oh, the damn fool! I'll have to report to the government. They might revoke our license to travel. God knows *what* he's done to Time, to History!"

"Take it easy, all he did was kick up some dirt."

"How do we *know?*" cried Travis. "We don't know anything! It's all a damn mystery! Get out there, Eckels!"

Eckels fumbled his shirt. "I'll pay anything. A hundred thousand dollars!"

Travis glared at Eckels' checkbook and spat. "Go out there. The Monster's next to the Path. Stick your arms up to your elbows in his mouth. Then you can come back with us."

"That's unreasonable!"

"The Monster's dead, you yellow bastard. The bullets! The bullets can't be left behind. They don't belong in the Past; they might change something. Here's my knife. Dig them out!"

The jungle was alive again, full of the old tremorings and bird cries. Eckels turned slowly to regard that primeval garbage dump, that hill of nightmares and terror. After a long time, like a sleepwalker, he shuffled out along the Path.

He returned, shuddering, five minutes later, his arms

soaked and red to the elbows. He held out his hands. Each held a number of steel bullets. Then he fell. He lay where he fell, not moving.

"You didn't have to make him do that," said Lesperance.

"Didn't I? It's too early to tell." Travis nudged the still body. "He'll live. Next time he won't go hunting game like this. Okay." He jerked his thumb wearily at Lesperance. "Switch on. Let's go home."

1492. 1776. 1812.

They cleaned their hands and faces. They changed their caking shirts and pants. Eckels was up and around again, not speaking. Travis glared at him for a full ten minutes.

"Don't look at me," cried Eckels. "I haven't done anything."

"Who can tell?"

"Just ran off the Path, that's all, a little mud on my shoes—what do you want me to do—get down and pray?"

"We might need it. I'm warning you, Eckels, I might kill you yet. I've got my gun ready."

"I'm innocent. I've done nothing!"

1999. 2000. 2055.

The Machine stopped.

"Get out," said Travis.

The room was there as they had left it. But not the same as they had left it. The same man sat behind the same desk. But the same man did not quite sit behind the same desk.

Travis looked around swiftly. "Everything okay here?" he snapped.

"Fine. Welcome home!"

Travis did not relax. He seemed to be looking at the very atoms of the air itself, at the way the sun poured through the one high window.

"Okay, Eckels, get out. Don't ever come back."

Eckels could not move.

"You heard me," said Travis. "What're you *staring* at?"

Eckels stood smelling of the air, and there was a thing to the air, a chemical taint so subtle, so slight, that only a faint cry of his subliminal senses warned him it was there. The colors, white, gray, blue, orange, in the wall, in the furniture, in the sky beyond the window, were . . . were . . . And there was a *feel*. His flesh twitched. His hands twitched. He stood drinking the oddness with the pores of his body. Somewhere, someone must have been screaming one of those whistles that only a dog can hear. His body screamed silence in return. Beyond this room, beyond this wall, beyond this man who was not quite the same man seated at this desk that was not quite the same desk . . . lay an entire world of streets and people. What sort of world it was now, there was no telling. He could feel them moving there, beyond the walls, almost, like so many chess pieces blown in a dry wind. . . .

But the immediate thing was the sign painted on the office wall, the same sign he had read earlier today on first entering.

Somehow, the sign had changed:

TYME SEFARI INC.

SEFARIS TU ANY YEER EN THE PAST.

YU NAIM THE ANIMALL.

WEE TAEK YU THAIR.

YU SHOOT ITT.

Eckels felt himself fall into a chair. He fumbled crazily at the thick slime on his boots. He held up a clod of dirt, trembling. "No, it *can't* be. Not a *little* thing like that. No!"

Embedded in the mud, glistening green and gold and black, was a butterfly, very beautiful, and very dead.

"Not a little thing like *that!* Not a butterfly!" cried Eckels.

It fell to the floor, an exquisite thing, a small thing that could upset balances and knock down a line of small dominoes and then big dominoes and then gigantic dominoes, all down the years across Time. Eckels' mind whirled. It *couldn't* change things. Killing one butterfly couldn't be *that* important! Could it?

His face was cold. His mouth trembled, asking: "Who —who won the presidential election yesterday?"

The man behind the desk laughed. "You joking? You know damn well. Deutscher, of course! Who else? Not that damn weakling Keith. We got an iron man now, a man with guts, by God!" The official stopped. "What's wrong?"

Eckels moaned. He dropped to his knees. He scrabbled at the golden butterfly with shaking fingers. "Can't we," he pleaded to the world, to himself, to the officials, to the Machine, "can't we take it *back,* can't we *make* it alive again? Can't we start over? Can't we—"

He did not move. Eyes shut, he waited, shivering. He heard Travis breathe loud in the room: he heard Travis shift his rifle, click the safety catch, and raise the weapon.

There was a sound of thunder.

# Poor Little Warrior!

## by Brian W. Aldiss

Claude Ford knew exactly how it was to hunt a brontosaurus. You crawled heedlessly through the mud among the willows, through the little primitive flowers with petals as green and brown as a football field, through the beauty-lotion mud. You peered out at the creature sprawling among the reeds, its body as graceful as a sock full of sand. There it lay, letting the gravity cuddle it nappy-damp to the marsh, running its big rabbit-hole nostrils a foot above the grass in a sweeping semicircle, in a snoring search for more sausagy reeds. It was beautiful: here horror had reached its limits, come full circle and finally disappeared up its own sphincter. Its eyes gleamed with the liveliness of a week-dead corpse's big toe, and its compost breath and the fur in its crude aural cavities were particularly to be recommended to anyone who might otherwise have felt inclined to speak lovingly of the work of Mother Nature.

But as you, little mammal with opposed digit and .65 self-loading, semi-automatic, dual-barrelled, digitally computed, telescopically sighted, rustless, high-powered rifle gripped in your otherwise-defenseless paws, slide along under the bygone willows, what primarily attracts you is the thunder lizard's hide. It gives off a smell as deeply resonant as the bass note of a piano. It makes the elephant's epidermis look like a sheet of crinkled lavatory paper. It is gray as the Viking seas, daft-deep as cathedral foundations. What contact possible to bone could allay the fever of that flesh? Over it scamper—you can see them from here!—the little brown lice that live in those gray walls and canyons, gay as ghosts, cruel as crabs. If one of them jumped on you, it would very likely break your back. And when one of those parasites stops to cock its leg against one of the bronto's vertebrae, you can see it carries in its turn its own crop of easy-livers, each as big as a lobster, for you're near now, oh, so near that you can hear the monster's primitive heart-organ knocking, as the ventricle keeps miraculous time with the auricle.

Time for listening to the oracle is past: you're beyond the stage for omens, you're now headed in for the kill, yours or his; superstition has had its little day for today, from now on only this windy nerve of yours, this shaky conglomeration of muscle entangled untraceably beneath the sweat-shiny carapace of skin, this bloody little urge to slay the dragon, is going to answer all your orisons.

You could shoot now. Just wait till that tiny steam-shovel head pauses once again to gulp down a quarry-load of bullrushes, and with one inexpressibly vulgar bang you can show the whole indifferent Jurassic world that it's standing looking down the business end of evolution's six-shooter. You know why you pause, even as you pretend not to know why you pause; that old worm conscience, long as a baseball pitch, long-lived as a tortoise, is at work; through every sense it slides, more monstrous than the serpent. Through the passions: saying here is a sitting duck, O Englishman! Through the intelligence: whispering that boredom, the kite-hawk who never feeds, will settle again when the task is done. Through the nerves: sneering that when the adrenalin currents cease to flow the vomiting begins. Through the maestro behind the retina: plausibly forcing the beauty of the view upon you.

Spare us that poor old slipper-slopper of a word, *beauty;* holy mom, is this a travelogue, or are we out of it? *"Perched now on this titanic creature's back, we see a round dozen—and, folks, let me stress that round—of gaudily plumaged birds, exhibiting between them all the colour you might expect to find on lovely, fabled Copacabana Beach. They're so round because they feed from the droppings that fall from the rich man's table. Watch this lovely shot now! See the bronto's tail lift. . . . Oh, lovely, yep, a couple of hayricks-full at least emerging from his nether end. That sure was a beauty, folks, delivered straight from consumer to consumer. The birds are fighting over it now. Hey, you, there's enough to go round, and anyhow, you're round enough already. . . . And nothing to do now but hop back up onto the old rump steak and wait for the next round. And now as the sun sinks in the Jurassic West, we say 'Fare well on that diet' . . ."*

No, you're procrastinating, and that's a life work. Shoot the beast and put it out of your agony. Taking your courage in your hands, you raise it to shoulder level and squint down its sights. There is a terrible report; you are half stunned. Shakily, you look about you. The monster still munches, relieved to have broken enough wind to unbecalm the Ancient Mariner.

Angered (or is it some subtler emotion?), you now burst from the bushes and confront it, and this exposed condition is typical of the straits into which your consideration for yourself and others continually pitches you. Consideration? Or again something subtler? Why should you be confused just because you come from a confused civilisation? But that's a point to deal with later, if there is a later, as these two hog-wallow eyes pupilling you all over from spitting distance tend to dispute. Let it not be by jaws alone, O monster, but also by huge hooves and, if convenient to yourself, by mountainous rollings upon me! Let death be a saga, sagacious, Beowulfate.

Quarter of a mile distant is the sound of a dozen hippos springing boisterously in gymslips from the ancestral mud, and next second a walloping great tail as long as Sunday and as thick as Saturday night comes slicing over your head. You duck as duck you must, but the beast missed you anyway because it so happens that its coordination is no better than yours would be if you had to wave the Woolworth Building at a tarsier. This done, it seems to feel it has done its duty by itself. It forgets you. You just wish you could forget yourself as easily; that was, after all, the reason you had to come the long way here. *Get Away from It All,* said the time-travel brochure, which meant for you getting away from Claude Ford, a husbandman as futile as his name with a terrible wife called Maude. Maude and Claude Ford. Who could not adjust to themselves, to each other, or to the world they were born in. It was the best reason in the as-it-is-at-present-constituted world for coming back here to shoot giant saurians—if you were fool enough to think that one hundred and fifty million years either way made an ounce of difference to the muddle of thoughts in a man's cerebral vortex.

You try and stop your silly, slobbering thoughts, but they have never really stopped since the coca-collaborating days of your growing up; God, if adolescence did not exist it would be unnecessary to invent it! Slightly, it steadies you to look again on the enormous bulk of this tyrant vegetarian into whose presence you charged with such a mixed death-life wish, charged with all the emotion the human orga(ni)sm is capable of. This time the bogeyman is real, Claude, just as you wanted it to be, and this time you really have to face up to it before it turns and faces you again. And so again you lift Ole Equaliser, waiting till you can spot the vulnerable spot.

The bright birds sway, the lice scamper like dogs, the marsh groans, as bronto sways over and sends his little cranium snaking down under the bile-bright water in a forage for roughage. You watch this; you have never been so jittery before in all your jittered life, and you are counting on this catharsis wringing the last drop of acid fear out of your system for ever. Okay, you keep saying to yourself insanely over and over, your million-dollar twenty-second-century education going for nothing, okay, okay. And as you say it for the umpteenth time, the crazy head comes back out of the water like a renegade express and gazes in your direction.

Grazes in your direction. For as the champing jaw with its big blunt molars like concrete posts works up and down, you see the swamp water course out over rimless lips, lipless rims, splashing your feet and sousing the ground. Reed and root, stalk and stem, leaf and loam, all are intermittently visible in that masticating maw and, struggling, straggling or tossed among them, minnows, tiny crustaceans, frogs—all destined in that awful, jaw-full movement to turn into bowel movement. And as the glump-glump-glumping takes place, above it the slime-resistant eyes again survey you.

*These beasts live up to two hundred years,* says the time-travel brochure, and this beast has obviously tried to live up to that, for its gaze is centuries old, full of decades upon decades of wallowing in its heavyweight thoughtlessness until it has grown wise on twitterpatedness. For you it is like looking into a disturbing misty pool; it gives you a psychic shock. You fire off both barrels at your own reflection. Bang-bang, the dumdums, big as paw-paws, go.

With no indecision, those century-old lights, dim and sacred, go out. These cloisters are closed till Judgment Day. Your reflection is torn and bloodied from them for ever. Over their ravaged panes nictitating membranes slide slowly upwards, like dirty sheets covering a cadaver. The jaw continues to munch slowly, as slowly the head sinks down. Slowly, a squeeze of cold reptile blood toothpastes down the wrinkled flank of one cheek. Everything is slow, a creepy Secondary Era slowness like the drip of water, and you know that if you had been in charge of creation you would have found some medium less heart-breaking than Time to stage it all in.

Never mind! Quaff down your beakers, lords. Claude Ford has slain a harmless creature. Long live Claude the Clawed!

You watch breathless as the head touches the ground, the long laugh of neck touches the ground, the jaws close for good. You watch and wait for something else to happen, but nothing ever does. Nothing ever would. You could stand here watching for a hundred and fifty million years, Lord Claude, and nothing would ever happen here again. Gradually your bronto's mighty carcass, picked loving clean by predators, would sink into the slime, carried by its own weight deeper; then the waters would rise, and old conqueror Sea come in with the leisurely air of a card-sharp dealing the boys a bad hand. Silt and sediment would filter down over the mighty grave, a slow rain with centuries to rain in. Old bronto's bed might be raised up and then down again perhaps half a dozen times, gently enough not to disturb him, although by now the sedimentary rocks would be forming thick around him. Finally, when he was wrapped in a tomb finer than any Indian rajah ever boasted, the powers of the Earth would raise him high on their shoulders until, sleeping still, bronto would lie in a brow of the Rockies high above the waters of the Pacific. But little any of that would count with you, Claude the Sword; once the midget maggot of life is dead in the creature's skull, the rest is no concern of yours.

You have no emotion now. You are just faintly put out. You expected dramatic thrashing of the ground, or bellowing; on the other hand, you are glad the thing did not appear to suffer. You are like all cruel men, sentimental; you are like all sentimental men, squeamish. You tuck the gun under your arm and walk round the dinosaur to view your victory.

You prowl past the ungainly hooves, round the septic white of the cliff of belly, beyond the glistening and how-thought-provoking cavern of the cloaca, finally posing beneath the switch-back sweep of tail-to-rump. Now your disappointment is as crisp and obvious as a visiting card: the giant is not half as big as you thought it was. It is not one half as large, for example, as the image of you and Maude is in your mind. Poor little warrior, science will never invent anything to assist the titanic death you want in the contraterrene caverns of your fee-fi-fo fumblingly fearful id!

Nothing is left to you now but to slink back to your time-mobile with a belly full of anticlimax. See, the bright dung-consuming birds have already cottoned on to the true state of affairs; one by one, they gather up their hunched wings and fly disconsolately off across the swamp to other hosts. They know when a good thing turns bad, and do not wait for the vultures to drive them off; all hope abandon, ye who entrail here. You also turn away.

You turn, but you pause. Nothing is left but to go back, no, but 2181 A.D. is not just the home date; it is Maude. It is Claude. It is the whole awful, hopeless, endless business of trying to adjust to an overcomplex environment, of trying to turn yourself into a cog. Your escape from it into *the Grand Simplicities of the Jurassic,* to quote the brochure again, was only a partial escape, now over.

So you pause, and as you pause, something lands socko on your back, pitching you face forward into tasty mud. You struggle and scream as lobster claws tear at your neck and throat. You try to pick up the rifle but cannot, so in agony you roll over, and next second the crab-thing is greedying it on your chest. You wrench at its shell, but it giggles and pecks your fingers off. You forgot when you killed the bronto that its parasites would leave it, and that to a little shrimp like you they would be a deal more dangerous than their host.

You do your best, kicking for at least three minutes. By the end of that time there is a whole pack of the creatures on you. Already they are picking your carcass loving clean. You're going to like it up there on top of the Rockies; you won't feel a thing.

# The Wings of a Bat

## by Paul Ash

I do *not* like pterodactyls. No doubt they have their good points; the evening flight over Lake Possible lends a picturesque touch to the Cretaceous sunset, and breast of young *Pteranodon,* suitably marinated, makes a passable roast. But as a result of personal and unfortunate experience I have taken a dislike to them, and nobody can claim they haven't heard me mention the fact—nobody, that is, at Indication One. And this means the whole —human—population of the world at the present date.

I am employed by the Mining and Processing Branch of Cretaceous Minerals, Inc., as a doctor—my contract says so. Of course, with a total planetary population of twenty-eight, there is not a great amount of doctoring to be done. I understand that the original staff list of Indication One did not call for a doctor; the Board intended to have all members of the team take a hypnocourse in nursing so that, if necessary, they could take care of each other. Yaro Land, the mining boss, knocked that idea on the head. He said he wasn't going to have his staff tinkering with each other, and that if anyone got injured or sick, in the absence of proper medical attention, he would displace them right back to 2071.

The Board amended its calculations and advertised for: Doctor, qualified; no dependents; willing to travel; Midget Preferred.

Time Displacement is expensive even now—or perhaps I should say, even *then*—even, that is, in the year when I was recruited, fifty-three years after I was born and somewhere between 100 and 110 million years after the date at which I am writing this.

When Dr. Winton Boatrace first displaced a milligram of matter it went back twenty-four hours, and the experiment cost him 272 credits for power alone. C.M. Inc.'s engineers can do better than that, but even so, the power to displace the average staff member costs about Cr.500.000, give or take Cr.100.000—or thereabouts. It's not the date that counts—Displacement is a threshold effect, and it takes no more *power* to get to the Middle Cretaceous than to the middle of last week—it's the weight. I suppose someone in Personnel did read my diploma and references, but their most important checking was done with a pair of scales. I weighed forty-one kilograms, and got the job. Except for Henry, I'm the smallest man here.

Yaro Land is the biggest—five foot seven, and stocky. I imagine the Board couldn't get first-class knowledge of sea-mining, combined with all-round engineering experience, plus administrative ability—and the sheer guts to make the first Displacement of all, not knowing whether he might find himself in the ocean or right in front of a Tyrannosaur—in a smaller package.

As a matter of fact, the details of my qualifications

weren't that important. Diploma or no, there are not so many things I could do that anyone else on the team couldn't do almost as well. They've all been trained in the first-aid treatment of injuries, from a sprained pinkie to a fractured skull. The deep freeze contains a billion units of Unimycin, the latest, safest, most powerful antibiotic on the market, in self-injecting ampoules. And if anyone needs major surgery or really elaborate nursing, he'll *still* have to go back to 2071—or, to be quite accurate, 2071 plus however much time he's spent at Indication One. But, if anyone gets moderately sick—the kind of condition that cures itself in a week or two, provided someone feeds the patient nourishing meals and keeps him from getting out of bed—I'm at hand.

No doubt any member of the team could do that, too. The weak point in the Board's original plan was that it provided no spare wheels at all—for nursing, or anything else. Even the most skilled specialist sometimes needs a third hand, or an eye on dials somewhere at the back of his head. So it's also in my contract that I lend a hand—or eye, or foot—as and when required. I don't mind, even though I'm seldom trusted with anything that could not be done just as well by one of these dexterous little egg-eating dinosaurs, if you caught it and trained it young. I still have a good deal of free time; among other things I edit and print our weekly newspaper—with a great deal of interference from the subscribers and contributors. Within reason, I'll do anything that's asked . . . bring in the tapes from the meteorology station, watch dials on the mineralometer, cook supper. But I will *not* act as veterinary surgeon to stray items of the Cretaceous fauna. It isn't reasonable, it isn't in my contract, and one must draw the line somewhere.

I hold surgery every morning; that is, I sit in my office, and anyone who feels like it drops in for a chat. Mostly they come to complain about the cuts in their last literary effort. If anyone has any symptoms they care to discuss I'm there to listen and help. That Unimycin has been burning a hole in the deep freeze for over a year.

When Henry came in I was polishing up my editorial for the next issue, and I took the opportunity to read him part of it. He seemed restless, but I paid no attention; he usually is. Too much thyroid, I suspect. Also, we have different ideas on literary style. It was Henry who got the name of the paper, *Weekly Bulletin of the Indication One Branch of Cretaceous Minerals, Inc.*—which at least had the merit of accuracy—shortened to *The Chalk Age Gazette*. The switch, admittedly, was carried by the unanimous vote of the subscribers and contributors—the Editor abstaining—but it was Henry's idea.

Halfway through my third paragraph he interrupted.

"Doc, it's *suffering!* Please!"

"Henry," I said, "I am accustomed to criticism. Lack of appreciation I have grown to expect. But downright abuse, combined with atrocious grammar—"

He pointed a quivering finger at my blotter.

"But it's sick!"

I began to suspect that I had here the first case of delusional insanity in the Middle Cretaceous—which would, of course, be the earliest on record. I looked at the blotter. On it—put there by Henry, presumably, while I thought he was listening—was a lumpish something which seemed to be wrapped in large, withered leaves. I took it to be crude tobacco—the plant grows like a weed in this climate, but nobody has managed a satisfactory cure

—and poked it experimentally with the tip of my pen.

Henry groaned—loudly. I looked up in astonishment, whereupon the pen jerked violently against my hand and was twitched away.

I looked down. The lump on my botter had expanded to twice its previous size, revealing that the "leaves" were broad leathery wrinkled wings. A bloodshot little eye had opened in the middle. It had produced from somewhere a sharp, swordlike beak about seven inches long, and with this, and a set of bony fingers, like a spider's legs, it was trying to dismember the pen.

I said: "Get that creature out of here!"

"But, Doc," protested Henry, "she's *sick!* and she's only a baby!"

I valued that pen. Pouncing, I attempted to get it back. The "baby's" grip tightened: pen, pterosaur, and blotter slid towards me as a unit. The head drew back, preparing for a thrust. I reversed direction hastily and shoved the whole outfit to the other side of the desk.

"Henry, I will *not* have pterodactyls in my office! Take it away!"

I maintain that my attitude was not unreasonable, or even unkind. I knew no more about the treatment of sick pterodactyls than Henry did—if anything, less. And, as I said, I dislike them. I had a very nasty experience once with a pterodactyl, and, if Henry doesn't know that, he ought to: he's heard the story often enough.

It happened when I was out on Lake Possible, fishing, in a glass-fiber dinghy—about six weeks after my Displacement—at the end of a beautiful day.

That lake! C.M. Inc.'s engineers claim that they

understand Dr. Boatrace's Theorems of Temporal Displacement—if "understand" is the word, when you have to plod through three brand-new systems of calculus before you can even begin—but they don't pretend to know how he made his map of Indication One.

So far as I can see, getting a fix on a section of past time is like casting a line over weeds; you can be pretty sure the hook will catch *somewhere,* but how far away depends not only on the length of your line but also on the current, the distribution of weeds, and how hard and fast you reel in. Boatrace's "hook" was the gadget he called his Minimal Temporal Trace: I gather he was pretty sure he could displace it to somewhere in the Middle or Upper Cretaceous, and so he did, but there's still a slight uncertainty about the exact date—a factor of ten million years or so.

Once the Trace was fixed he could displace other items to the same point—like sliding a ring along your snagged line. I understand that—I think. What I don't see, and neither does anyone else, is how the Trace—a bit of metal and crystal no bigger than the top of my thumb—could send back and tell him what kind of place it had landed in.

Well, there it is. I'm told he used to displace one, and shut himself up for several hours, then come out and displace another. One day, he came out with a penciled map that looked as though Baby had got hold of the telephone pad, and told them he'd found what he wanted and they could dust off the big machine—the one built to displace a man.

Yaro, who's not afraid to use a dirty word when there's no other that fits, told me once he reckoned the old man was using some form of Psi technique. Boatrace knew what he wanted—the ideal setup for sea-mining, a medium-sized island with strong deep-water currents close by—and he just went on casting until the "feel" of the line told him that this time he was into a fish instead of a snag.

Another thing I'll never understand is why Yaro was willing to make that first Displacement, with only Boatrace's map as evidence that he'd find solid ground at the Exit Point. It's just a faint wavering oval, about twice as long as it is wide, with a scribble underneath that reads—I'm told—"*First Indication of Desires . . .*" Not even his daughter can decipher the final word. There's just one feature marked; a clear, hard-edged circle, near one end, about half the width of the oval. It looks as though he put a semi-credit on the paper and ran the pencil around it. By some freak the label he wrote on is quite legible, even to me: "*Aq. p . . . ? Lake, possibly??*"

As a drawing of a natural feature, it's about as convincing as a monocle on an amoeba. Well, I'm a respectable matter-fearing materialist, but if Boatrace was really using Psi . . . No. As a member in good standing of the WMA I prefer to assume he was using something else. (The principle of hyperdimensic transductility, perhaps, or a couple of patent double million magnifying gas microscopes of extra power.) But Lake Possible is a flooded caldera; seen from above—from the island's central peak, for instance—it forms an unbelievably perfect ring.

Seen from dinghy level, that afternoon, it looked like the best fishing water I'd ever seen. Great clumsy twelve-inch insects, something like a dragonfly, were blundering into the wavelets, and big fat red-lipped fishes—a kind of coelacanth—were popping up to take them all around the boat. The only trouble was that they didn't see the desirability of any lure in my book.

I didn't really care; it was such a perfect day. The air was warm, but crisp, not steamy; there was just enough wind to dry the sweat on my face. However, our cook-housekeeper wanted to try her hand at fish chowder and I'd promised to bring in the raw materials. So an hour before sunset I decided to try trolling from a moving boat. I fixed a couple of rods, one with a minnow, one with a spoon, and hoisted the sail.

Close-hauled, the boat moved through the water at just the proper speed. I sat back, with half an eye on the rods and another half on the sail, leaving one to enjoy the general peacefulness of the scene. Then, after about ten minutes, I glanced over my shoulder, and the devil was after me.

Well, what would *you* have thought? Bat wings, twenty feet across—rolling eyeballs. China white and black—a scarlet devil's grin and a horn on its head.

I let out a yell, and ducked. The sail flapped once; I automatically tightened the sheet and the rough feel of it brought me back to my senses—or I thought it did. The actual effect was to make me assume I'd had a brief hallucination; I simply could not have seen what I thought I had.

I screwed up my courage to look back—and there it was, huge, hideous, and three-dimensional, as I remembered it. Like the boat, it was headed into the wind. There was a single row of bony struts along the front of each wing, and the great leathery membrane was ballooning like a spinnaker behind. It wasn't Old Nick, of course.

However, I did not feel that much better when I realized that I was being followed by a Pteranodon.

I'd seen them often enough at a distance, planing slowly around the circle of the cliffs; or out at sea, skimming along with those incredible beaks half open, just above the surface of the waves. That had not prepared me for the sheer *monstrosity* of the creature riding the wind behind me, twenty feet away. It looked big enough to carry me off and feed me to its young.

The beak was foreshortened, of course, since I was seeing it head-on; it was also half agape, so that I saw the bright-red lining of the mouth. The "horn" was that great sloping bony crest that continues the line of the beak back over the shoulders, which was foreshortened, too, when I first caught sight of it.

I couldn't cram on more sail—I had only a little balanced lug—but I could get the wind behind me by heading in to the nearer shore. However, if I did that straightaway I would wind up at the base of a two-hundred-foot cliff. I would have to hold on for a quarter of a mile, then run for Landing Gap.

May I never have such a sail again. I tried to keep my mind on flag, sheet and tiller, but I couldn't refrain, any more than Lot's wife could, from looking back. Once when I glanced over my shoulder I found that frightful thing wagging its head at me—left, right, left, right, showing off the two-foot length of beak and the bright-blue streaks on the side of the crest.

When I headed in to the Gap I hoped the wind would bother it, blowing directly from behind it, but it wheeled along with the boat and just flattened out a little, holding station without so much as a flap. Aerodynamically, those things aren't primitive; they're the culmination of seventy million years of evolution. The air is their home. I was in such a lather that I didn't think at all about shedding way from the boat. I left the sail full until I heard the keel grate on the shingle. I had just enough sense, then, to let the sheet go, but it was too late. The mast was just a little pole of green wood—there had been no time to season it, even Yaro had been less than a year at Indication One—and it snapped clean in two. Down came the sail on top of me as I sprawled on the bottom of the boat, and by the time I mustered up enough spunk to crawl out from under, the *Pteranodon* had gone.

That's why I don't like pterodactyls—pterosaurs —pteranodons—in the Cretaceous all three words come to the same thing. If the little fluttering *Pterodactylus* was still around, or even the hen-sized *Rhamphorhynchus*, I might be able to regard them as fellow-creatures, but they both died out at the end of the Jurassic. The creature Henry had dumped on my desk was another *Pteranodon*. It was a very young one, admittedly, about the size of a pigeon apart from those shrouding wings, and with only a faint ridge to mark the incipient crest. Nevertheless its beak was quite large enough to do damage.

"Doc, she's *sick*," Henry told me in accents of maudlin reproach. "I found her on the roof this morning . . . she must have lost her mammy during the night. Did you, Fiona?" He spread his hands in a protective gesture over the leathery bundle, removing them just in time to avoid a fast jab.

Pteranodons are viviparous, bearing one young at a time. After birth the infant clings head-down to the lower part of the mother's belly, held in place partly by her feet, partly by its own and by the four unmodified "fingers" projecting from the second joint of the wing. I had no idea how big they were when they first ventured on independent flight.

I looked up at Henry in an incredulous double-take. "*What* did you call her?" Hastily I recollected myself. "Never mind. Get her out of here."

Henry is not quite twenty, and it has never seriously occurred to him that anybody might disagree with him, fundamentally, over anything that really *mattered* . . . such as the right-to-life—and hence to medical assistance —of a sick infant reptile of repulsive appearance and dubious disposition. He thought I was simply acting crusty and middle-aged for the fun of being a "character," and hadn't time to humor me.

"I think the trouble is exhaustion," he said earnestly. "It's been blowing half a gale for three days, so probably her mother couldn't get fish for her. Are you hungry, Fiona?"

"Henry!" Yaro loomed in the doorway, monumentally disapproving. "We wait for you!"

"Bettertryheronfishdocthere'ssomeinthiscanI'llbeback assoonaspossiblebegoodnowFiona," said Henry on his way to the door, and was gone.

I had drawn the line at acting as vet but Henry's assumption that all good men came to the aid of the party was a powerful eraser. Besides, it's very difficult deliberately to let an animal starve. I couldn't even make believe that I was too busy. Yaro's team were busy assembling and testing a cadmium extraction unit, which is not a job for unskilled labor, and the other specialists were immersed in their various routines. Even Elsa was doing the week's baking—not quite like Mother's, but you'd never think the base was carbohydrate extracted from pulped water-weed—and the kitchen was out of bounds until she finished.

Fiona had found my "In" tray and was squatting in it, tented in her wings. The pen lay on the desk, slobbered but undamaged. I rolled it cautiously towards me with a ruler and she opened her mouth—the lining was shell-pink, not the adult scarlet—and hissed faintly, but seemed to lack energy for anything else. I got out a pair of heavy gauntlets, made from the belly-leather of a sea-crocodile, and a pair of long bone forceps and opened Henry's can. It contained pieces of steamed fish left from dinner the night before.

How do you persuade a ptcrodactyl to open its jaws? I hesitated to use force—the bones looked fragile. I tried tapping the tip of her beak with a morsel of fish, held in the forceps. She retreated promptly to the farthest confines of the "In" tray and pulled her wings over her head. I spread several choice fragments on a small dish and put them in front of her. Fiona inspected them with a red-rimmed eye, then, deciding they were harmless, paid no further heed to them. I tried hissing, while waving the forceps under her beak; I even picked up bits of fish in my gloved fingers and thrust them upon her. No good. She hid inside her capacious wings and this time showed no sign of coming out. I removed some bits of fish from my chair and sat down to think things out.

Fish-eating birds, I seemed to remember, did not simply drop bits of fish for their offspring to pick up; they stuck food right down their throat. Which meant that the beak had to be open. Vague recollections of high-school biology indicated that the opening of the beak was often a reflex response to the sight of the mother—or father —bearing supplies. No, not even that. A dummy with just a few parental features would often set off the response.

Wildly I thought about draping myself in a tarpaulin to suggest wings. But in all probability the essential feature was the beak, from which, after all, the food would come. I considered ways and means of constructing one before I remembered that there were a couple of Pteranodon heads, dried and mounted, on the common-room wall. We did not hunt for amusement, but we had tested the edibility and other useful characteristics of every species on the island and somebody with baronial instincts had imposed this form of decoration. Elsa was always wanting to get rid of the trophies, but so far as I remembered they were still in place.

They were. I unhooked the larger one and brought it back to the office. It had been varnished, and kept its color quite well; even the eye, thanks to the bony ring in the sclerotic, was still quite lifelike. I got a bit of fish ready, worked my hand into the skull, and hissed to attract attention.

Fiona drew back the edge of her wing and peered at me suspiciously from one half-open eye. Then her wings shut down as abruptly as an umbrella and she was shuffling towards the head, beak gaping and neck outstretched. I pushed the bit of fish to the back of her throat.

Fiona closed her beak thoughtfully, and I whipped the head out of sight. The underside of her baggy throat heaved once, twice, and I thought she was swallowing. Then she stretched forward, shook her head up and down a few times, and opened her beak. The bit of fish fell out.

I rushed off to the kitchen and begged a raw fish from Elsa. This time I thought I'd got it; for about ten minutes Fiona gaped obediently at the dried head and then I thrust the fish into her beak. I saw it go down, until there was a distinct bulge under her sternum and she was weighed down in front. Apparently she would have gone on feeding forever, but I called a halt at that point, not knowing how to cope with indigestion in a pterodactyl. I left her, as I thought, digesting. About an hour later I heard a faint rhythmic gasping, and looking up from the proofs I was correcting I saw Fiona, beak downwards, regurgitating the lot.

The fragments were unchanged; no sign of digestion. Perhaps parent pteranodons pre-digested food for their young. By this time my blood was up; I didn't intend to let this infuriating creature die if I could help it. I had no pepsin in stock, but Elsa had brought some pawpaw seeds with her, and while the resulting trees had not yet born ripe fruit, there were plenty of leaves. I knew these could be used as tenderizers; they might do the trick. I sneaked into the kitchen garden and removed a few; wrapped the remainder of the fish in them, and left them for an hour in the sun.

Henry came in as I was shoveling the messy, part-digested result into Fiona's beak, and was, I am glad to say, impressed. He removed Fiona, the In-tray, the forceps, and what was left of the fish, and I cleaned up the office and myself and went to lunch.

I felt distinctly pleased with myself, which was tempting Fate, of course, and I should have known better. The staff abounded in amateur naturalists, many of them with strongly developed maternal—or paternal—instincts. I had a pretty picture of myself advising and directing them in the care and feeding of the young *Pteranodon*. What I had forgotten, of course, was that, however pleased they might be to baby-sit with Fiona, their professional schedules would make it impossible for them to do so during working hours.

There was great competition to take care of her once work was over; but *Pteranodon,* like most reptiles, is a strictly diurnal creature. Half an hour after sunset, which in those latitudes occurred every day at 18:15 hours, Fiona was asleep. At least I didn't have to get up and feed her at dawn. Half the camp took turns at keeping her overnight, until nearly every cabin had acquired a faint lingering stink of predigested fish. Henry, with one person chosen by rota for the privilege, looked after her during luncheon break. But from 8:00 till 12:30, 14:00 till 17:30 hours, she was mine, all mine.

You may wonder why, feeling as I did, I allowed myself to get stuck with the brute. The explanation, though complicated, can be given in one word: Morale. It's a tricky thing in any community. When twenty-nine people make up the total population of the world and will for the next nine years, it's the most important thing of all. It was outrageous of Henry to foist his beastly protegée on me, but then Henry, as I have mentioned, was quite incapable of seeing the matter in that light. A Henry who knew and accepted the fact that some men just don't care to act as foster-fathers to the strayed young of other classes of vertebrates would be someone quite different from the Henry I knew. And sudden personality changes are upsetting in a small community. Or to put it another way, we all had to depend on each other for things far outside the services we had contracted to supply, and anything that upset that dependence—reasonable or not—was dangerous and bad. Or, to put it in the simplest way possible, I simply hadn't the moral courage to refuse.

Fiona ate voraciously and grew at an inordinate rate —she must have put on about two ounces a day. At the end of two weeks she weighed four pounds, with a wing-span of more than eight feet, and I began to think, hopefully, that any day now she would start flying and be able to fend for herself. My hopes took a severe setback when someone pointed out that, for all we knew to the contrary, she had no inborn instincts in that direction and would have to be *taught* to fly. Several people tried it; they took her out into the clearing around the cabins, perched her on rocks, trees, or roofs, withdrew to a distance, waved pieces of fish, and called her to come. Fiona, after gaping hopefully for some minutes—she had now learned to open her beak at the sight of a human being—usually turned her back on them and signified disapproval in a vulgar but unmistakable manner. To some extent I sympathized. After all, none of her would-be-instructors was able to fly.

Quite by accident, this time, I solved the problem myself. A small outdoor shelter had been constructed for Fiona alongside my office. Three weeks after her arrival I had given her the second feed of the day and returned to the office to read some manuscripts. It was becoming increasingly difficult to get people to write anything except nature notes, a development which had started with Fiona's arrival. I had just unearthed a perfunctory review on the latest batch of books—C.M. Inc. sent us a dozen, on micro-microfilm, once a month—when I heard an irritable hiss, and there was Fiona shuffling through the door.

She made straight for the desk, gave an inefficient-looking hop and caught the raised edge at the back with the fingers of one wing. With a prodigious effort she got a grip with the other "hand," and there she hung, feet scuffling at the smooth surface, waving her beak angrily at me over the top until I came out of my stupefaction and got to my feet. This seemed to stimulate her. She brought up one hind foot, took a grip on the raised edge, and heaved up and forward. A moment's confused and indescribable activity and she landed with a flop on my pile of manuscripts.

Half of them shot off the desk, but she caught the top one in her foot and began methodically ripping it to pieces. I seized a towel which was hanging over the back of my chair—I needed a shower every time I fed her—and flapped it angrily.

"Go away, Fiona! Shoo—!"

Fiona unfolded her wings and flapped vigorously back, sending the remainder of the papers flying.

Idiotically, I flapped again. Fiona drew herself up, raised her wings as high as she could, ran at me over the blotter—and took off.

I, of course, knew that she *ought* to be able to fly, but I doubt whether she had ever suspected the fact. Anyway, there was no room to do it in the office. She sailed straight into the wall and was knocked out.

For the rest of the morning she was punch-drunk, but I

had discovered how to teach her to fly. She simply needed a stimulus; the sight of something that flapped. In nature, no doubt, it would have been a parent's wings, unfolding and limbering up, but the towel was a sufficient substitute. In a couple of days Fiona was flying from the top of the computer building right across the clearing—a distance of a hundred yards. In a week she had discovered how to use a thermal and would spiral effortlessly in the updraft over the sun-warmed rooms; and come down only to be fed.

That was the snag. Fiona had no idea of fishing for her own food. Taken to the lake, she would fly there for a while, but every time she got hungry she wheeled and planed unerringly for home. We tried throwing fish to her, to teach her to feed on the wing. If it fell on the ground, she landed and picked it up. If it fell in the water she squalked angrily, landed, and opened her beak to show us where it ought to have gone.

"The trouble is," Henry informed me accusingly. "Fiona doesn't know she's a *Pteranodon*. She probably thinks she's a human being." He reflected. "Or perhaps she thinks pteranodons look like you."

It seemed improbable to me, but various works on animal behavior seemed to agree with him. A bird—and pterodactyls are more similar to birds than to any other Tertiary group—reared in captivity tends to direct many of its instinctive activities towards people, rather than its own species. Konrad Lorenz was fed on caterpillars by a pet raven; and there are numerous sad cases of geese and peacocks and other large birds which fell in love with their keepers and tried to lure them on to the nest. Henry and I were almost equally disquieted by what we read; Henry on behalf of Fiona's psyche and future sex life, I because I was beginning to doubt whether I would ever be free again.

In the end, by simply throwing her fish into a small pool—dead at first, later on alive—I taught Fiona to take food from water. It was not at all the same thing as fishing on the wing, but it was the best I could do. Then Henry and I took her out on Lake Possible one evening, in the dinghy, and marooned her on a rock.

We rigged the sail to cover the boat, and, when she was not looking, crawled underneath it and hid. Presently we heard indignant hissings and the gulping squawk that indicated she wanted to be fed. Then there was a scrabbing on the side of the boat and a weight descended on the canvas covering my back.

I kept as still as I could while Fiona shuffled around on my shoulder blades and finally came to rest on the back of my head. I wanted nothing to distract her at the critical moment, which must—I thought, resolutely stifling discomfort as sharp claws probed the crevice between my ear and my skull—come soon. Ten minutes later we heard a series of rustling flaps; the pteranodons on their homeward flight dipping down to inspect Fiona, and rising again as they made for the caves and ledges of the cliffs. I began to think that we were on a fruitless errand; then I felt Fiona's grip tighten on my occipital bones and heard her wings flap once. Then nothing for a moment; until there was one last swooping rush above me—a belated member of the flock—and my face was pushed down on the thwart as Fiona took off.

We waited until full dark, not to risk distracting her; then rowed to shore and plodded home. Henry seemed rather dispirited and I felt that a show of pleasure would be out of place. As we parted on the way to our respective cabins he looked back over his shoulder.

"Cheer up, Doc," he said. "at least we know that *she* knows the way home."

I gave him a cold look—wasted, of course, in the darkness—and went off to shower and change. I slept badly that night; waking three or four times from a doze, in the belief that I had heard the click of claws on the fiberglass roof. In the morning I opened the door cautiously, half expecting twenty pounds of young *Pteranodon* to come plummeting down with an urgent squawk, demanding to be fed. But no. Fiona's favorite roosts and perches were still clearly marked, both to the eye and the olfactory sense, but they were all vacant Fiona, it appeared, had left us for good.

The details of the mining operations are not, for the most part, relevant to this story, and some of them—for instance, the reason why it's economically practical to carry out the process in the Cretaceous, although sea-mining in the twenty-first century pays no Displacement costs—form part of a very big industrial secret. So I'll just say that the extraction units consist of gently tapering tunnels about fifty feet long, constructed of hoops and slats, and lined with plastic-coated cloth. They're not heavy, in fact they are amazingly fragile for the work they have to do, but they're unwieldy. When a whole battery of tunnels is complete, they are lashed side by side into rafts, towed out to sea, stacked one raft on top of another, and sunk in water deep enough to put them safely below the turbulence zone. The units float at first, but after an hour's soaking they lose buoyancy. That's the moment when you maneuver the next raft over the top and get them bolted together; then the next, and so on. The timing's tricky, and the whole operation calls for a flat calm—twelve hours of it.

The first battery—thirty-five units—was ready for assembly just about two years after I arrived at Indication One. Yaro was closer to the jitters than I'd ever have thought he could be. Those units represented two years of hard work for all concerned—even me. The assembly and sinking *had* to go right. This was the test. Of course, since all the basic manufactures—aluminum, fiberglass, cloth, plastic—had been set up, it would only take three months to produce the next battery. If anything went wrong with this one, morale would take a terrible beating and the whole project would be set back far more than three months. Besides, he needed to make tests, check that the thing really did work as it should—it would take most of a year to be certain of that.

We waited out three days of light winds and loppetty little waves—some people wanted to take a chance on them, but Yaro was taking no risks with this first batch of babies—and then on the fourth morning I woke to a flat, oppressive stillness and thought: This is it.

Everyone else thought so, too. Breakfast arrived half an hour early and found everyone present, except for half a dozen who'd grabbed themselves sandwiches and gone to start the units on their way to the beach. At least, I hadn't noticed that anyone else was missing, until Yaro wanted to ask Linda McDonough a question and then found that she wasn't there.

Linda is our astronomer; she also took a six months' cram course in meteorology before being displaced. If you wonder why a mining company needs an astronomer —enough to pay Cr.500,000 just for her fare—I have to say that that's part of the industrial secret aforesaid. The reasons why we need a meterologist are obvious; we needed her particularly that morning and she was missing.

One of the girls went to her cabin, and came back in a hurry for me. I went—in fact, I ran; not that Linda sounded dangerously sick, but it was the first call for my professional services in over a month.

I found Linda half-dressed and very cross with herself for oversleeping; she was also feverish, puffy, and covered with an irritating rash.

She admitted having been slightly off-color for several days. It was plainly an allergy of some sort. I was planning scratch tests, and had just realized the interesting possibilities—she hadn't been affected by any of the common allergens in the twenty-first Century, such as eggs, or shellfish, or pollen, but proteins, as well as physical structure, can undergo a lot of evolution in a hundred million years—when Linda gave me details. For the last few days, since she'd done all the calculations she could on the data available and further observation had been impossible owing to overcast, she'd been helping to apply plastic to the filter-cloths for the extraction units. She began to feel seedy the following day.

That left nothing to investigate, except which of the plastics caused the trouble. There are several in use here, all with molecules so complex they're halfway to being alive; the whole extraction process depends on their peculiar properties. I had to admit, though, that the question was of purely academic interest. Standard anti-allergen treatment would clear up the trouble and she'd have to stay away from the filters, whichever plastic she was allergic to. Linda said that she wasn't going to be scratched to bits simply in the name of medical science—a deplorable attitude and an extreme overstatement—and we were still arguing when Yaro arrived, wanting to know whether the calm would last out the day, or not.

Linda tottered over to her desk and found the latest computer-digest of the meteorology data. Her eyes were watering and she obviously found it hard to concentrate. After several minutes she announced that there had been a slight, steady drop in the barometer readings for two days, which probably meant a blow coming up; it might be today or it might be tomorrow, but without last night's data tapes she couldn't be sure.

I thought Yaro was about to explode. It was very unlike him—or very unlike anything I knew of him so far—but the situation was clearly getting on nerves he had never realized he possessed.

"I'll go and get the new tapes," promised Linda feverishly, reaching for her clothes. "I'll be able to tell you in an hour or so."

"You're not going anywhere," I told her. "*I'll* fetch the tapes. I've done it before."

"But if I go I can get a direct reading on the barometer and call Yaro on the radio and—"

"Young lady," I said, "that meteorology diploma has gone to your head. I was reading barometers before you were born."

"*Why* I permitted that station to be set up on a hill top two miles away . . ." came in a threatening background rumble. I knew that the site had been chosen, with his approval, for several excellent reasons, and that Linda had suggested asking for a few duplicate instruments to be kept in the settlement—but that, on grounds of Displacement costs, Yaro had turned her down.

Plodding up the way to the Peak, with the two-way radio strapped to my back, I found myself thinking: *The calm before the storm.* In our weather-controlled society the cliché has lost all contact with its real meaning. I simply didn't know whether it applied to this situation, or not. There had been quite a number of gales in the two years I had spent at Indication One; I seemed to remember that there *had* been an interval of calm before most of them, but how long it lasted, and whether calm was *always* followed by a storm, I simply could not decide. There seemed, now, an ominous heaviness in the air. I was not sure that I had noticed it before Linda mentioned the drop in barometric pressure.

Yaro's dilemma was plain. If he called off the assembly of the battery today and there was no storm—or if it held off for twelve hours—he would have wasted the best opportunity he was likely to have for at least a week, and probably more. It would give his reputation a heavy knock, which was important; faith in Yaro's judgment was a very vital factor in general *morale*. In some ways it might be worse than losing part of the battery in an unexpected storm that could be written off as bad luck. Holding things up unnecessarily might be considered old-maidish.

I came out on the first ridge, high enough to see over the rise on the other side of the settlement, and caught a glimpse of the sea. It was so smooth it didn't even sparkle, though that might have been partly due to the haze of overcast. There were no distinct clouds; I found I didn't care for the look of the sky.

A long train of light, big-wheeled carts was assembling at the edge of the settlements. There were caves —pumice—in the hillside and we used them for storage and for working on rainy days—mostly we worked out of doors. At the moment those precious extractor units could be wheeled back under cover in ten minutes or less, but once they'd been taken down to the beach it would need an hour. If they'd been unloaded from the carriers—

I dropped that line of thought and pressed on. The path led through a stand of cycads in a sheltered dip, then out onto bare rock, where it was marked only by cairns. One of the things one misses in this era is grass, also heather, gorse, bracken—cover-plants in general. I had been walking rapidly for twenty minutes, most of it uphill, and was sweating freely, but I was pleased to note that my respiration was steady and undistressed. Two years ago I'd have been panting after half as much exercise.

The Met station was on top of a bluff; the shortest way up to it involved leaving the path and climbing twenty feet of rock-face. It was easy enough in daylight, broken into convenient ledges. I knew that Linda used the path only after sunset or when her hands were full.

I had just got up onto the first ledge and was reaching for a handhold when two things happened simultaneously. The radio receiver gave a loud click, indicating that someone had turned on a transmitter, and a huge triangular shadow slid suddenly down the rocks and away over my head.

For a moment I simply froze; then I got a grip on a knob of rock and turned my head very carefully to look behind me.

Yaro's voice said sharply, "Doctor, have you read the barometer?"

His voice seemed to come from my shoulder blades, which was one minor element in my confusion—I kept wanting to get round and see where it was coming from. However, my attention had already been split three ways. Part for his question—by no means the biggest part. Another—even smaller—for an unexpected glimpse of the sea, with a dull steely shine to it now and a dark purple line on the horizon that had not been there before. But the largest—paralyzingly large—fragment was taken up with the full-grown *Pteranodon* that was just wheeling to pass over me again.

"Doctor, answer, please. What is the pressure?"

I said, "I can't—" Then, at the top of my voice, "*Go away!*"

The *Pteranodon* was circling in a tighter curve than I would have believed possible for those twenty-foot wings. It was going to brush right over my scalp if it didn't hit me in the face. I flattened against the rocks. There was a thump above me and the brief rattle of a pebble, dislodged. I squeezed a glance past the rock-face an inch from my eyeballs, and saw the *Pteranodon* sitting on the ledge above me, huddled in its wings.

"Doctor, what is wrong? Did you fall just then? Are you hurt?"

I managed a rather croaky "*No.*" Then, coming to my senses, with a rush, "I haven't got to the Met station yet. I just started the final climb, but there's a *Pteranodon* in the way!"

"A what?"

"It's sitting on a ledge above me. Maybe it's got a nest here or something. I'll go round by the path; I'll be there in ten minutes. Don't worry, I'll get that reading." An idea which had been nagging away at the back of my brain suddenly surged to the front. "Yaro! Don't let the carriers move any farther! There's a storm coming up over the sea, I *saw* it!"

Yaro said sharply, "I am looking at the sea. I see nothing."

"I'm higher up than you, I can see farther. Over the horizon, a dark line. I think it's getting closer. Put those units under cover. If it comes up fast you won't—"

"Calm yourself, they have not started the journey. This storm, how sure are you that it approaches us?"

That was a nasty one. The situation did not exactly make for accurate judgment, even if I'd had any experience on which to base one. That dark line might not be a storm at all. It was not as though I spent much of my time gazing out to sea; for all I knew the horizon might have a thick purple border every second day.

I didn't want to be responsible for holding up the job, possibly for nothing. The answer, of course, was to get those barometric records as quickly as I could. I looked up at the *Pteranodon* and yelled, *"Shoo!"*

By way of answer the creature unfolded its wings halfway and leaned forward over the ledge, and I stepped backwards into the air and dropped four feet onto a rock.

It was a flat rock, and by some miracle I didn't tumble backwards and break the radio; I managed a flop forwards and landed on all fours. I scrambled away crab-fashion, got to my feet, and ran. Fifty yards round the base of the bluff would bring me to a relatively gentle slope, and another hundred yards up that was the Met station. The first stretch was flat, in the sense that it wasn't rising, but it was far from smooth. I was panting hard, now, and my

legs were only half under control, but I had almost
reached the beginning of the slope when there was a
*swoosh!* A vast canopy of wings slid over me, dipped into
a curtain, and then suddenly shut down into a shape no
bigger than a two-year-old.

It had a beak, though. I stopped, and backed away. I
was vaguely conscious of Yaro shouting to somebody
—not me—he was calling someone to take over the radio.
I sidled slowly along a wall of rock, keeping an eye on the
enemy, remembering that presently I would come to a
sort of niche or alcove about six feet wide. If I wasn't
careful I could get backed into it and be trapped—

"Hey! Doc!" It was Henry, sounding excited. "What's
wrong? Yaro said you were having trouble with a
*Pteranodon.* Is it Fiona?"

As though stimulated by the sound of his voice the
creature half unfolded itself, then shut down tight and
waddled a few steps after me.

"*Now* look what you'd done," I muttered crossly.
"Don't *shout.*"

Henry obediently lowered his voice. "What's happening? What's she doing? *Is* it Fiona, Doc?"

With difficulty I kept my voice down to an infuriated
whisper. "How would I know?"

It was nine months since I'd last seen Fiona. It was
almost as long since I'd even thought of her. This creature
was about twice as large as she'd been when I loosed her.
Would Fiona be full grown now? I hadn't the slightest
idea. Nor did I find it even faintly reassuring that this
creature *might* be my former acquaintance. Even when
we were closest she had had no inhibitions about taking a
peck at me.

The *Pteranodon*—Fiona or not—repeated its performance, opening, shutting, and coming a few steps closer. I backed, and found the rock curving away into the alcove. I hastily abandoned my hold on it and took two steps rapidly backwards, intending to get past the gap and have my back to solid stone once more.

With an angry-sounding squawk, the *Pteranodon* jumped. I did a complicated and ungainly dancestep that took me backwards and sideways—into the alcove. Then my foot slipped and I landed with a bone-shaking thump on hard dampish mud.

The reptile took a little run at me, folding its wings the while. I flopped wildly away from it on elbows and bottom until I hit my head on a rock. I was at the back of the alcove. Being unable to retreat farther, I sat up—there was just room to do so without braining myself on the overhang, and shrank into the smallest possible space; knees up, head down, arms folded over it to protect my eyes. There was a rustle and a hiss like a gas-leak, but no savage thrust. Instead, after a minute or so, I felt a sharp but not unfriendly nudge; I became conscious of a strong dry musky odor; and peeking cautiously under my folded arms I found the *Pteranodon* sitting quietly beside me.

Henry was uttering questions and exhortations in a steady, whispered string.

"Shut up!" I breathed back. "No, I'm not hurt. I'm in a sort of shallow cave. The brute's right here alongside, if I try to escape it'll probably attack."

"Doc, listen, this is important. It *must* be Fiona. It's like we said, she thinks she's human, or maybe she thinks you're a *Pteranodon*. What was she doing before? How did she get you into the cave?"

"For God's sake!" I whispered fiercely. "Forget your blasted nature notes! I can't get to the Met station. Tell Yaro I'm dead *certain* there's a storm coming, and I'll take the responsibility if I'm wrong . . . No, don't say that, just tell him I'm *sure*."

I felt my voice weaken on the last word. I still wasn't sure—and there was no way for me to take the responsibility for the decision. The team would still blame Yaro for trusting me if I turned out to be wrong.

Henry was still whispering. "Doc, did she keep opening and shutting her wings? Shutting them *right* down, as though she wanted to take up as little space as possible? And did she chase you into the cave? Did she—"

"Yes!" I screamed—so far as one can scream in a whisper. "Yes, she did! And now that you've proved how much you know about pteranodons, will you get your alleged mind off your hobby and on to your job? Will you tell Yaro—"

"Doc, it's all *right*. Yaro decided five minutes ago to put everything under cover; it's being done right now. The cabins were battened down before he called you, just in case. You don't have to worry. We can see the storm from here, now; the sky's changing. There's a sort of dark edge sliding up to it. It'll be overhead in two minutes. But listen, that opening and shutting the wings—that's the Wind Dance. I mean that's what the old pteranodons do to warn the young ones there's a blow coming and to get under cover. George and I saw them at it three or four times, and there was *always* a high wind afterwards. Maybe they see it coming from high up, like you did. Fiona was trying to warn you, that's all."

I was just preparing a comment when I heard the storm break.

It hit the settlement thirty seconds before reaching the Peak, so that I heard the rising howl twice over—once on the radio, once, incomparably louder, right overhead. Fiona also heard the transmitted sound of it and huddled even tighter into her wings. I saw the nictitating membrane slide over her eyeball—and then the wind came.

It whipped past the cave mouth with a noise like torn silk, carrying a mass of leaves and twigs ripped from the cycads a quarter of a mile away. It must have torn the trees bare in its first rush. One moment the air outside seemed solid with flying greenery, the next it had gone past, still in one mass—except for a small part that eddied into the cave and whirled round us before it was snatched out again.

The cave was about six feet deep; it kept us out of the path of the storm, but the stray tendrils that reached in the mouth of it were enough to pluck violently at my hair and clothes—and Fiona's wings. I saw her quiver at the first tug of it, and put an arm across in front of her. Henry was yelling something about adaptive behavior, the one really dangerous enemy of pteranodons being a really strong wind. I heard the words *ritual behavior* and *adaptation* emerging above the transmitted noise—Henry was indoors, of course. They were vaguely familiar to me from the reams of notes which he and several others, apparently mistaking the *Gazette* for *The Journal of Animal Behavior* and undeterred by previous rejections, were always sending in. Then, incredibly, the noise began to increase, to a level where not even Henry could compete. Battered by sheer volume of sound even more than by the searching fingers of the wind, I crouched dazedly at the back of the cave. I was vaguely aware of pressure as Fiona shoved in behind me—having done her bit by getting me under cover, she was now capitalizing on it. Then I ceased, really, to be aware of anything outside the small tight-packed huddle of my own body.

After the wind, rain. How long either of them lasted I had no idea. Suddenly the howling died, and a moment later the floor of the cave was swamped; its mouth was curtained with a waterfall, and my already-deafened ears were assaulted by the drumming of water on naked rock. That didn't stop all at once; the rain eased off slowly, so that I was barely conscious that the noise decreased.

Then something moved beside me. Fiona pushed out from behind my back and waddled, squelching, to the cave mouth. She sat there for a minute or two, folding and unfolding her wings in an irritable manner. Then she waddled outside. Six feet away was a boulder; she scrambled up on to it, stretched to her full height, and began limbering up—shaking, flapping, jumping up and down.

I watched, without really taking it in. I hadn't moved; I didn't think I *could* move; I was stiff, soaked, and too numb to be really aware of it. Then I noticed Yaro. He was talking to me, from a little way off—quietly, insistently. I realized suddenly that he'd been talking for quite a while, but I hadn't paid attention to him.

I said, "Sorry, Yaro. What did you say?"

That at least was the idea. It was kind of creaky and not, I gather, very audible, but it was speech of sorts.

There was a wild shout: "He answered!" It didn't sound like Yaro at all. I mean, it was his voice, all right, but completely out of character; positively excited.

I said, "Sorry; must have dropped off."

"Dropped off!" He sounded rather wild and positively hilarious. I began to feel something must be *really* out of key. "Caught out of doors in a hurricane, he drops off! Doc, you found some shelter? You are not hurt?"

Now he mentioned it, I wasn't sure. I tried to unfold myself and investigate, but my hands were locked around my knees and I seemed to have lost the combination; also I had stiffened in one piece. I couldn't figure out how to get undone. Then I realized that the view had altered outside. Something was missing.

"She's gone," I said. "Fiona. She's gone."

I managed to start moving after a while. I didn't get very far, though. They came to fetch me as fast as they could; nearly every man in the team. There were all sorts of new gulleys in the way; a couple of temporary rivers several feet deep; tree trunks and boulder scattered in all directions. I could have walked, though; there was no need to carry me. But they did, taking turns until I came out of my daze sufficiently to rebel. I got back to the settlement walking on my own feet.

The damage was surprisingly small. Linda says we caught just the fringe of a hurricane, or maybe a typhoon—the Met station was blown right off the bluff, so she didn't get the records to see how it developed. The units, and all the more important machinery, had been moved into the caves and the entrance blocked. Only one cabin blew away. They're domes of fiberglass, securely anchored six feet down; nothing for the wind to catch hold of, provided the windows and doors are properly closed. It was three weeks before the extraction units could be assembled, but when the weather finally quieted it was done without a single hitch.

There's been a lot of nonsense about the whole affair. Maybe Fiona saved my life; I don't know. I imagine one glance at the barometer would have been enough for me; I'd have run for shelter, and I might have reached it—there are lots of caves. But it's certainly nonsense to say that her warning saved the whole of Indication One. Yaro had given the orders to batten down before he knew anything about the Wind Dance; in fact I heard Henry and George explaining it to him next day, with pantomime—very odd they looked. And, if she'd only let me get to the Met station, the figures would have warned him a lot more convincingly than anything else could.

But there it is—nearly everyone is firmly convinced that Henry's stray baby grew up to save the settlement, and, of course, me. It creates a sort of moral climate which is irresistible. I no longer dare to turn down contributions on natural history, and the name of the paper has been changed to *The Chalk Age Gazette and Pterodactyl-Watchers' Guide.*

# The Runners

## by Bob Buckley

I've discovered that I'm not that fond of dinosaurs. The big ones smell bad and haven't the wits of an insect, while the smaller beasts, though brighter, would just as soon chomp off an arm as grin at you. And I've never seen one of them grin. Not yet.

But there we were, right down among them . . . hell revisited. That's what Rogers calls the place.

I stood on the dry clay bank and looked out to sea. The sun was warm, but none of us wore much more than shorts, and a wide-brimmed hat was keeping my brain uncooked. Below me was a river. A broad expanse of bluish-brown water, unnamed, widening here at its mouth where it emptied into the sea. The Rockies should have been there, not a horizon-to-horizon body of water dotted with islands. But they weren't. They wouldn't appear until much later.

The waves were stained brown for some distance out. The channel carried a lot of sediment down from the arid highlands that began where the shoreline forests thinned, and a considerable delta had been built up. Mangrove-like trees covered the sandbanks and provided nesting sites for the thousands of shrieking sea birds that seemed to rise into the dark sky like towers of white smoke whenever a pteranodon sailed majestically past. I think they're pteranodons. James disagrees. I guess he should know. He's one of the paleontologists.

Just visible above the curve of the purple-misted horizon was the snow-capped cone of a volcano. It's a big one. Rogers has named it Feathertop, for the cumulus plume that sweeps off its eastern ridge. It's as good a name as any other, and I've marked it as such on the map we're preparing.

Beyond Feathertop are more volcanoes, and the rugged coastline of Cordilleran North America. One day it would all be California and the other West Coast states, including the long, dry finger of Baha. In this time, though, it was a gigantic island continent.

Presently, our method of dropping back to the Mesozoic Era is classified. And in such an unofficial accounting such as this, I doubt my explanation of the physics involved would make much sense, anyway. I'll leave it only to say that we didn't use a time machine. Our vehicle was a very ordinary pressure-resistant freight shuttle with a high thrust kicker installed on her stern. An automated fuel barge had accompanied us. We had left it parked in synchronous orbit over Cratonic North America, which is the landmass that lies East of the Sundance Sea and joins with Europe.

Getting back, according to the physicists, would be much trickier than our arrival. But the pay was indecently high, and the computers said it was possible, so we went.

The first crew that dropped back did so by accident.

They had been gone so long that they had actually developed a taste for dried lizard meat. But they got back. And they hadn't the least conception of the behavior of the Jovian Twist Effect.

It was our task to map the terrain, and document the interval of temporal transfer.

Our crew was small by necessity. Rogers was the geologist, and Jack and James were paleontologists. I was the pilot. But before going for an advanced degree at the Astronautics Academy, I had majored in Animal Behavior. And I had another hat to wear, as well. I was also the camp astronomer.

All this just to determine what year it was!

We were completely on our own. No calm banter with Mission Control. No encouraging messages from the girl friends. We were the only primates on all of Mesozoic Earth. I guess we should have felt proud, or scared if we were smart. But, mostly, we were too busy to feel anything but tired.

I had set the shuttle down on a lofty plateau of Precambrian basalt that reared out of the continental platform like a giant's black bench. Sixty million years later it wouldn't be there. Erosion would have spread it out across the surrounding valleys as a fine, dark sand.

There wasn't much growing on it. Some crevices had captured a few scanty drifts of soil, and here and there groves of cycads had taken roost. Some were huge, and even the little ones looked ancient.

James told us they were related to the Dioön, a genus living only in eastern Mexico in our time.

We soon discovered that they had spines which raised welts whenever they stabbed the skin as we unloaded the copter from the shuttle's hold. After we had finished, and I was examining the shuttle's air cushion landing gear for damage, James strolled up with some kind of pterodactyl flopping limply in his hands. He was examining it with a delighted, though slightly bemused expression on his face.

"Well," I asked, "what is it?"

On the long trip out we had argued extensively about how closely twentieth-century reconstructions would match reality. I personally doubted that we would recognize much of anything. The very nature of fossilization tends to destroy the various epidermal embellishments that make living animals so unique.

Now, seeing James and his puzzlement, I couldn't stop myself from grinning.

The creature was light tan in color. Its body, head and wings were covered with a very fine fur almost like felt. The jaws were long and toothy and protected by a beak of horn. The right wing was torn.

I took James' prize away. The corpse was still warm. I palpated the body and discovered a crop with what felt like a small lizard secreted within. There were other features, too.

"It's a male," I told him.

"How do you know that?" he demanded.

I flicked the bright-red, partially inflated wattles that depended from the underside of the throat.

"This is a display organ. Since your pterodactyl filled a bird-like niche in this environment, it's reasonable for us to assign bird-like behaviors to it. If you'll look around, I think you'll discover a nest with a female brooding young. I doubt infant pterodactyls could maintain their body heat any more than young birds can."

James took back his once-living fossil and gave me a puzzled, somewhat wounded look. He didn't say anything, but later I noticed him wandering about the plateau peering behind each clump of rocks. He never told me if he found a nest, though.

That afternoon, with Jack assigned to monitor us from the bridge of the shuttle, we left the plateau behind and followed the sea coast north. This was the first of our scouting trips. We hoped to compile enough data to allow us to date this time. The data was to consist of the animal life.

Rogers piloted. I was the spotter, and James sat beside me with a microfile on his lap. Its memory was stuffed with the reconstructions and skeletal overlays of every life form discovered to have existed in the Mesozoic. By keeping a tally on the identified genera we would develop a fauna which could be related to a sedimentary unit. This would give us a crude date, a period within the broad outline of the Jurassic, or Cretaceous. Later, I would use astronomy to provide us with the fine tuning.

Rogers flew low over the beach, startling small plesiosaurs who fled back into the surf with many a hump and tumble. These were juveniles. James wasn't prepared to identify them.

I think he was hedging. He was too fascinated with watching them to consult the file.

The beach curved. White sand was replaced with a low ground cover. Bushes, small trees. Here and there we saw animals, but only their backs and heads and necks. It wasn't good enough to make an identification.

James began to look unhappy.

We crossed a shallow bay. A mosasaur rolled below us

and sounded again. That provided a small clue. Mosasaurs were monitors who adapted to live in the open sea. They were late to develop. But this one vanished before James could find it on the file.

It began to look as though the only way we might make a positive identification would be to catch one of the beasts and X-ray it, comparing its skeleton with the fossils in the file.

When I said this aloud James got an odd gleam in his eye. I knew at once I had made a serious mistake. I didn't want to see the three of us wrestling with six tons of angry dinosaur. I explained the difficulties of such a feat in great detail.

"We have our guns," James countered.

By "guns," James meant tranquilizers. We were to avoid killing anything. This was common sense. Of course, the dinosaurs were a dead line, without descendents. But the experts didn't want to take chances. What if Great Uncle Harry were to vanish? And so on.

The tranq guns were bulky and badly balanced. But they used an electronic sight that couldn't miss, and a micro-computer to optically weigh, type, and select the proper dosage and formula of tranquilizer for a target.

Knowing this, James was all ready to start hunting.

Rogers came to our rescue by explaining that the carrying capacity of our copter was limited. The telling point came when he said he was turning inland. The upland environments were known to be the habitats of ceratopsians. These giant grazers were well documented across the Upper Mesozoic.

Rogers gained altitude and we whirred off toward what would one day be Montana.

Eventually the sea faltered at our left, giving way to saltflats and badlands. There were brackish swamps in the valleys, and a lot of bones gleaming whitely on the islands. But apart from some yellowish, sickly reeds, nothing grew there. It was a dead land. Even so, James wanted to land for a brief exploration.

Rogers refused and pointed to a scaly lump sheltering behind an eroded outcrop of limestone.

It was a carnosaur. Young, only slightly larger than the copter, scrawny as death, and sleeping. Times had been bad for the beast. Its hide was tawny brown in color, with streaks of green. This might have been pigmentation, or some exotic disease. He lacked the funny ridges on his spine that the movie monsters had. But he did have a brightly colored dewlap crumpled under his throat.

"Probably a male," I told James.

He sighed. Images were fleeting across the screen of the microfile.

About that time the flesh-eating dinosaur woke up. He raised his head slowly and peered about the raw landscape with rheumy, bloodshot eyes. He looked like all the hangovers in the world rolled into one thundering head-ache.

I guessed that his good living had dried up a long time ago, and now even the dregs were gone. If we had passed this way one week later the scavengers would have been exploring his bones.

Awkwardly, using his forelegs as props, he pushed himself up into a standing position, his long tail thrust stiffly out behind, like the balancing pole of a wire walker. Snorting, he took a couple of shambling steps toward the copter. Our downblast was kicking up a miniature gale. It blew dust and rattled the reeds in their beds of dried mud.

Nothing like us had ever appeared in his world before. But movement had always equated itself with food and he was hungry enough to eat whatever came within reach of his jaws.

Meanwhile, James had stopped fiddling with the controls of the microfile.

"I'm going to say it's a variety of dryptosaur. It's certainly not an allosaur, or ceratosaur. Of course, the juvenile characteristics confuse the issue. We only have adults in the record."

"Dryptosaurs are Upper Cretaceous, aren't they?"

"This might be a stem form. He's pretty generalized. Might predate Tyrannosaurus."

As the carnosaur neared, Rogers lifted the copter higher.

"Why don't we try to lead him out of this death trap?" he asked.

"That's manipulation, and we're to leave the environment alone as much as possible. If this beast starved to death in this swamp, we can't change it."

"Sounds hardhearted," Rogers countered. Then he laughed softly. "Of course, that ol' boy doesn't look much like a saint. Maybe this is his reckoning."

So saying, he swung the copter around and took us off toward some low hills that rose on the horizon.

I took some holo shots of the puzzled carnosaur and promptly forgot him.

He didn't forget us, though.

The hills were shrouded by a dense growth of conifers. We could see oaks in the valleys, and a few palms, and laurel. Here and there were glades filled with viburnum and draped with the sprawling vines of the wild grape. It was all very inviting. Homey looking, in an exotic sort of way. Man had never touched this land with either plow or foot. It was totally unspoiled.

Rogers put us down in a meadow carpeted with a plant that resembled grass, but wasn't.

I opened the door. The breeze that puffed in was chill. It brought with it the scent of invisible dogwoods and the sough of the pines.

James pointed abruptly.

"Upper Cretaceous. No doubt about it, now. There's a hadrosaur."

We looked to where his hand was aimed.

The dinosaur was a big one, over forty feet long.

Hadrosaurs were bipedal vegetarians. As we watched, this one moved its dull gray mass out into the open. The head was flattened, and this variety lacked the characteristic crest. It was chewing on a pine bough. The hind limbs were large and muscular, the tail equally so, and flattened like the blade of an oar. While we observed, fascinated, it tore down another limb and ran it slowly through its great, broad beak, machining off the needles. The skin was smooth, but pebbled with tiny scales. While the predominant color was gray, the belly was light tan. But it might have been mud.

James had been busy with the file.

"That's an Anatosaurus. They were widespread throughout western America. This one is an adult."

He slung the file over his shoulder on its strap and reached for a tranq gun.

"Let's go out."

"It might not be safe," I said doubtfully.

"You didn't come over a billion miles and seventy million years to hide in a helicopter, did you, Bill?"

He had me there.

We left Rogers with the copter. Someone had to guard our only means of rapid flight. I took another of the guns, and we wandered out into the meadow.

This was going to be our first face-to-face encounter. The behavior of the dinosaurs was pretty much of a mystery to us. All we knew was what we had seen so far, and what the ancient trackways had provided, which was damned little. Considering the tiny brains and massive bodies, though, there had to be a sizeable instinctual component to everything they did. That meant rigid behavior patterns. They didn't have enough brain for "reason," or much information storage.

I told James to keep behind me and we started out toward the forest and the hadrosaur. The "grass" smelled sweet as we pushed through it. Some clumps were knee-high, with spires of narrow seedcases. Sometimes we saw movements across the meadow as unseen inhabitants of the grassy sea scurried out of our way.

The hadrosaur had watched us dismount with one large eye. It also whiffed the air, but we were downwind. It maintained a calm attitude until we were fifty feet away. Then it stopped chewing. It didn't take a Lorenz to guess that it was about to react to our presence.

I took James' shoulder and held it. He stopped.

For a long time the only movement was the wind swaying the trees.

Then, quite suddenly, the dinosaur bolted. It ran with incredible swiftness considering the overgrown nature of the forest. Mostly, it "bulled" its way through like a two-legged bulldozer. We lost sight of it, but we could hear it crashing through the underbrush. Then came a splash and quiet.

"Must be a lake over the next rise," James speculated.

"Hadrosaurs used rivers and lakes as hiding places from the carnosaurs. That's the theory, anyway. Maybe we just proved it. Do you think it took us for baby carnosaurs?"

"I hope not," I muttered. I thought it was a rather depressing comparison.

James gazed around the clearing. The sun was low and beginning to gild the treetops with the ruddy tones of sunset.

"We'd better find a safe place to camp. It's getting late."

I didn't argue the point.

On the way back to the copter, I tripped over something lying embedded in the root-bound soil. It was the femur of a medium-sized dinosaur, very long and delicate, almost like a bird.

James was delighted with my find. He tore up the grass in great clumps and found more bones. We were standing over the resting place of a disarticulated skeleton. Most of the remains were badly chewed. But I found a skull in a good state of preservation. Unfortunately, the braincase was broken away, but what remained was high-domed and the eye-sockets faced forward. This, and the teeth said that their owner had been a hunter.

James carried everything worth saving back to the copter in triumph. It was as though he were bearing the crown jewels of ancient England. He was in his glory. Amid all the manisfestations of dinosaurian life he had found some bones. He was the paleontologist's paleontologist. I guess old habits never die.

We examined the bones while Rogers took the copter up to find us a "safe harbor."

James consulted the file briefly. He seemed to know just what he was looking for. He pronounced the bones as belonging to the genus Stenonychosaurus. This was a small theropod related to the giant Tyrannosaurus, but only distantly. They had had close relatives in Central Asia. It was guessed that they were nocturnal foragers, probably feeding off small mammals and newly hatched dinosaurs. Previously they had been known only from the Oldman formation of Alberta. Remains were rare. But that was probably because they didn't fossilize well. The bones we had discovered would not have been preserved. Eventually they would have become one with the soil.

There was a lake beyond the hill, as James had guessed. It was large, irregular in shape, and broken by several small, sandy islands. Rogers selected one well out in the middle as our landing site and camp. The water wasn't too deep for a carnosaur to wade, but I doubted that any would try. The hadrosaurs seemed to feel that the area was safe, and that was reason enough for us. They should know.

The big dinosaurs stayed in the forest long after sundown. We could hear them feeding noisily far into the night as we broke open our ration packs and set them heating. When we were finished, watches had to be set. I took the third by choice. The copter carried a radio link and I could use the relay in the shuttle to interrogate the astronomical computer on board the orbiting barge. It was busy mapping the Cretaceous firmament for us.

After James woke me I spent some time stomping around the soft sand of the island shore to make sure that nothing dangerous was sneaking up on us. There wasn't, so I started my work.

A little before dawn something hooted in the forest. I was busy examining a star chart and didn't take much notice. After a while, though, I abruptly realized that there wasn't a hadrosaur to be heard in the forest. They had abandoned their feeding binge.

Gazing across the lake, I saw a number of dim shapes studding the water's surface like Egyptian statues. The hadrosaurs had joined us in the water.

A chill unrelated to the cool wind blowing out of the north ran up my spine and stopped in the vicinity of my neck.

I fumbled with the big flashlight strapped to my belt and shone it out across the water. The beam was like a spear of lightning. Everything it touched stood out in stark, silent relief as I moved it along the far shore.

The carnosaur's eyes flashed scarlet as the beam hit him. It was our old hungry friend from the drying swamp. He must have been half dead after traveling all that way in only one day, but he was a persistent devil, to be sure. And he had found himself a young hadrosaur.

He raised his dripping, gore-splattered muzzle from his kill. He had to be dazzled by the glare of my light, but it seemed as though he were grinning at me. Then, with the single-mindedness born of hunger, he went back to his feeding. There was a lot of lost time to make up for.

At first light he was still there. Belly full for a change, he squatted on the shore with his hands folded contentedly over his sagging paunch and stared at us like some wise old basilisk. I had seen endocranial casts of his kind, though, and knew that his bliss was one of ignorance, not the wisdom of the ages.

We left him there later in the morning, squatting in the sand with his lake full of fearful hadrosaurs. His larder would be stocked for years to come.

We radioed Jack and continued north, toward Canada. There had been a sizeable dinosaurian population there. James wanted to know why. Also, he was now convinced that we had arrived in the Late, or Upper Cretaceous. All that remained was to clarify his identification of certain sedimentary units. We might be in the Campanian or Maestrichtian. Of the two, the Maestrichtian was the latest. At its close the dinosaurs had faded out rather abruptly and the diversification of the mammals had begun. To have arrived at this period in time would have been an almost outlandish stroke of luck.

The pressure began to get to James. He fidgeted endlessly, now.

As we flew north the palms dropped out of the forest complement. Conifers and oaks predominated. The cycads held on stubbornly. But they looked stunted.

Jack called us around noon. He had brought down a sauropod with his tranq gun. Most of the giants were extinct in this late age. Apparently someone had neglected to inform this particular individual. It wasn't one of the really big sauropods, anyway.

Jack identified his prize as being a Tenontosaur. A surprising holdover from the Lower Cretaceous. Herbivorous, partially bipedal with a large head, this one was no more than twenty-five feet long. And blind stupid, Jack reported. He had nearly been trampled underfoot as the big beast had blundered away to freedom after receiving the antidote.

James congratulated his partner excitedly. But the conversation was a brief one as we sighted our first horned dinosaurs.

These ceratopsians were formed up in a large herd, proving that social behavior is not solely dependent on brain size. Once it had been said that the triceratops, and others of his kind, had been too stupid to herd. Now we knew better.

They were on a hillside cropping bushes, small trees, and anything else that got in their way. They were huge, surprisingly nimble eating machines that made goats look picky.

They also had a couple of attendant carnosaurs.

James decided that they were gorgosaurs. I didn't argue. I've never been able to see that much difference between old Gorgo and the Tyrant Lizard. Both of them had obscenely big mouths, and enough teeth to make a dentist beam with joy.

The ceratopsians, as dumb as they were, hadn't missed that point.

These were some of the largest of that breed: Pachyrhinosaurs. They didn't have horns. They weren't impalers. They butted with a gaint, ram-like boss which sprouted from the top of the skull like a granite boulder. The neck frill which protected the spine from being bitten through was short and capped by two short spines. Hooking with these could still lay open an incautious predator's belly.

These were formidable beasts. And that was undoubtedly why the carnosaurs were keeping their distance.

But not all of the herd was made up of full-grown adults. There were youngsters in the center. I couldn't decide if this was instinct, or just dumb luck. They appeared soft and helpless. The ram was just a bump on their forehead.

The herd and the carnosaurs were both ignoring the helicopter. I asked Rogers to keep his distance anyway, and started filming. Nothing very interesting happened for quite some time. We followed the herd in its long, rambling march.

Then one of the youngsters decided that it was thirsty. It broke ranks to scramble toward a small stream that cut through the plain. The adults didn't make any move to stop it, either. I'm not even sure they noticed.

The carnosaurs did. The largest made a quick, waddling dash and broke the youngling's back with a snap of his great jaws. It wasn't much of a contest.

The herd ignored the killing. Apparently the adults only got riled by a direct confrontation. A little bit of natural selection was only part of the game.

Rogers circled while the carnosaur ate his fill. After he wandered off, Number Two waded in and polished off what remained. All he left was a bit of bony skull; causing James to speculate that this might be why so few juvenile fossils are discovered. Apparently carnosaurs made efficient garbagemen.

We followed the herd for most of an afternoon, getting to know the reactions of the animals. I guess they reminded me of rhinos in their manner of moving and feeding. They were certainly short-tempered enough to double as rhinos.

Later, we turned west to examine a range of hills that seemed to reach out toward the distant coast. Rogers felt it might be a landbridge to the Cordilleran. The fossil record suggested the existence of such a bridge.

Finally, just before dark, we landed in a lush valley

nestled in among these same hills. We spent the next two days in exploration. James and Rogers were impressed. So much so that they ordered Jack, over my objections, to fly the shuttle north to join us.

A permanent camp was formed. The copter and shuttle were parked atop a ridge of sandstone that obtruded from the talus-strewn slope of a large mesa. The big dinosaurs couldn't reach us here, and the little ones wouldn't want to. Everyone was happy.

The team split up, with everyone concentrating on his own particular field of endeavor. Jack and James seemed to vanish, but I did see Rogers in the morning over breakfast. He was mapping strata that wouldn't exist in our time. And I was playing ethologist in the daytime, and astronomer by night.

Also, I had found myself a pack of dromaeosaurs.

Pack was the correct term. They were more properly a pack than the ceratopsians were a herd. They were active hunters, extremely efficient and bloodthirsty. They were smart, too. Their brains were highly developed, probably to the avian level of the emu, or other large ground birds.

Slightly smaller than a man, they were bipedal runners who preyed on the young hadrosaurs that populated the valley. Sometimes they hunted in concert and dragged down the adults.

Their favorite method of attack was to run some poor beast into a thicket, corner it, and make the kill with fangs and claws. They were well equipped for this. Each of the killers had an enlarged talon on the second toe of the foot. They used it like a large knife, and it was an effective instrument for disembowelment.

I filmed several hunts, though they weren't anything for

the Sunday animal lover's entertainment feature. Apart from loud and excited hissing, each kill was carried to its conclusion in grim silence. My civilized nature was both repelled and fascinated by the stark bloodiness of it all.

Perhaps that was what made me concentrate my studies on them.

One day, while I was hoping to record some mating duels, I came across a solitary spoor crossing one of the main runs that led down to a stream in the lowest part of the valley. There was a dense stand of cycads on each side of the trail at this point. I had thought them to be impassable. Apparently they weren't. The prints in the recently disturbed dust said that much.

The dry trunks were thick with the remnants of old, withered fronds. A large, fat-bodied spider moved sluggishly out of my way as I rustled about in the litter. The opening proved to be a narrow gap between two dead stumps. Drooping fronds from the other plants had concealed it from my casual view.

I squeezed through. Before me was a cleft with low walls of sandstone. The red of the rock contrasted sharply with the dark green of the grape vines that grew so thickly everywhere. They were tangled on the rock floor, and streamers crisscrossed the cut. But something passed through here regularly. The trail was dim, but it was there.

The slope of the cleft was upwards, toward the back of the mesa. Eventually, it opened out onto a broad shelf that was part of an eroded buttress. The grape vanished and was replaced by rank, sun-hardy plants. The buttress had a low cave at its base. A stream ran out of it and spread across the shelf in a shallow pool before spilling off the shelf and down a cliff toward the valley floor. Prints were everywhere. The pale mud was thick with them, and a good many led into the cave.

I had left my tranq gun behind to be able to carry another camera. There were no large carnosaurs in the valley, and the dromaeosaurs had gotten used to my presence. It seemed a needless encumbrance. Now, I wished that I had brought it along as I found myself facing the unknown unarmed.

The prints told me that I was larger and heavier than their owner. So, with nothing else at hand, I picked up a dead and seasoned branch that seemed as though it would prove useful as a club and pushed on into the gloomy recess of the cave.

I had no light, so I stepped to one side just within the entrance to let my vision adjust to the darkness.

It was a large cave. The stream flowed through limestone, and it had eaten out quite a grotto. There were grotesque formations dangling from the low ceiling, and spikes growing out of the puddled floor. The stream gurgled out of the black depths of the cave. But it wasn't the stream that interested me. Almost at once I became aware that I was being watched. Gradually, my eyes picked a dim shape out of the shadows of the opposite side of the cave.

It was a slim and graceful dinosaur squatting on a sand-covered ledge. By her very attitude I assumed that she was a brooding female, though I couldn't see any eggs, nor even a nest.

But there was a nest. A small one formed out of the gravel at her feet.

She was frightened of me, but she didn't leave her eggs. That impressed me.

Since we had arrived we had been treating the life forms we had encountered as resurrected museum exhibits, not really as living beings even though it was ourselves who were the aliens to this time. Now, abruptly, I realized that here was a being who, like myself, knew and enjoyed life. It takes brains to be frightened for something other than one's self.

Dinosaurs didn't really have much to be frightened with. Even the dromaeosaurs, as bright as they were, could not surpass an ostrich, or emu in genius. And birds were only instinctual machines.

And yet she was frightened for her eggs.

I stepped back to reassure her, and after a moment she did seem more calm. But she kept a wary eye on me.

The interior of the cave was too dark to allow filming. All I could do was pick out details of her anatomy so as to preserve them in my memory.

At first glance she was just another dromaeosaur. Then you noticed that the back of the skull was round, and the eyes faced forward. The jaws, though large, were more reduced than in other theropods. Perhaps the jaws were used less as an offensive weapon, and more as a mastication device. The hands, already extremely dexterous in the dromaeosaurs, had developed an opposing digit in the enlarged little finger. The claws were reduced in size. I had to fight down the impression that I was looking at the dinosaurian equivalent of Australopithecines. No dinosaur was that intelligent.

But even so, this was a find. James would be beside himself when I showed him this new genus.

I began backing out of the cave very slowly.

Then something hit me from the rear like a bolt of hissing lightning. I felt my jacket being slashed open and spun before the flashing foot that I knew had to be there could tear into something vital. I fell, and my attacker was forced to come round in front of me. I struck out . . . felt my fist smash into something warm, hard, and scaled, and all at once I was free.

Hastily I struggled to my feet. Before me on the floor of the cave was the mate of my dinosaur. Between us, staining the stream red with its blood, was the headless carcass of a young hadrosaur. Well, I thought, birds bring prey to their nesting females. Why couldn't some dinosaurs do the same?

It's easy to give an animal credit for more intelligence than it really has.

The creature was only stunned. It lurched back to its feet before I could turn and make my escape. And it destroyed all my preconceptions about dinosaurs with one simple action. It picked up the club I had dropped and swung it at my head.

I retreated precipitously from the cave into the sunlight.

The dinosaur followed me, but he stopped in the mouth of the cave.

"I have no intention of harming you, or your mate." My words were soft and intended to calm the creature.

He replied with a loud hiss to show that he was still angry. His was a basic kind of logic: You mess with my mate, I break your head. There's no arguing with that kind of reasoning. My only option was to retreat. If he would let me.

My luck held. He did.

All the way back to the camp I was lost in thought, and it almost got me run over by a thirsty ankylosaur built like an antique Volkswagen with spines.

I knew I couldn't tell James. He'd never believe me. Jack wouldn't either. Both men were steeped in the accepted dogma of paleontology. Dogma changes, but not swiftly, and not by the quantum leap that this required. Getting either one of them to accept the idea of an intelligent dinosaur would be almost as easy as convincing the Pope that God was dead. Rogers wouldn't be easy, either. But I had to share the secret with someone, and Rogers, being a geologist, might have a more open mind about life.

The following morning, on the pretense of examining a curious outcropping of stone, I brought Rogers along as I returned to the cleft. We fought our way through the grape-vine jungle and up onto the shelf.

I stopped him well away from the cave. I didn't want us attacked.

"Where's this outcropping?" Rogers inquired doubtfully, gazing at the cliff before us.

I didn't answer. I was shining a flashlight beam around the interior of the cave. It was empty. The shelf was bare. No eggs, no club, no bones. They had moved out during the night.

Wisely, I told Rogers nothing. Instead, I showed him a rather ordinary limestone lens embedded in the cliff that reared over our heads.

He was not impressed. He left muttering unkind things about the judgment of laymen.

A week passed. We were all busy, and my sighting of the intelligent dromaeosaur began to take on the aspect of a dream. I was no longer sure I had really seen it.

I went back to my studies on the taloned killers.

One day, while I was filming a hunt, however, something happened that restored my convictions.

One of the runners had split from the main pack, which raced off in pursuit of an aging hadrosaur. Apparently it had detected another spoor. As it paced along a narrow trail through the dark and gloomy forest, I followed.

A hadrosaur was down in a tiny clearing dappled with shafts of sunlight. It was a large one. Another dinosaur was in the process of dismembering the body. It was the male. I knew it at once, even before seeing the crude stone knife it held in one hand.

The "wild" dromaeosaur attacked at once, leaping over the carcass toward the other with a hiss like an open valve on a steam engine.

The knife wielder jumped to one side and stabbed. The stone tool had a point that was too blunt to do much more than damage the skin. But the impact knocked the attacker down. He stayed down, because I used my gun to tranquilize it.

I stayed out of sight behind a tree while the other finished his job of butchering the hadrosaur. Then he started on the dromaeosaur. Between the two carcasses there was more meat than he or his mate could use in a week. As he staggered off with his gory burden, the scavengers began arriving in twos and threes.

Again I followed, using binoculars to keep him in sight without being seen myself.

The new nest site was in a cave a mile down the valley, where the cliffs were taller. I hung around making observations until just before nightfall. Then I returned to camp. No one was around. I ate and went to bed. Didn't sleep much, though. I was too excited for that.

The next morning I returned to the vicinity of the cave to continue my study.

Fascination has many meanings. James would not have characterized these dinosaurs as having very many human virtues. The male, and probably the female when she was off the nest, killed whatever they needed without the slightest remorse. And they were efficient killers. But they weren't human beings, and they lived in a world much different than ours. I didn't judge them, I only watched.

Being unable to work directly with them, I was unable to make an estimate of the male's intelligence. I didn't doubt that, with the exception of us, his kind were the smartest beasts on the planet. But they were rare. A careful search showed that they were alone in the valley, and as much of the surrounding area that I was able to search.

As times passed, I began to feel a certain custodial inclination toward these runners.

By now we knew what time we were in.

That afternoon, James and Jack held a brief meeting. The close of the Maestrichtian is arbitrary because the boundary is not a change in sedimentation, but rather a sudden absence of dinosaur bones. By chance, our journey had brought us to this period. An age was drawing to an end. We accepted this, but it brought about a change in our attitudes. We began to view things with nostalgic eyes. Much speculation was put to discovering the cause of the coming extinction.

Jack and James were convinced that it had already been in effect for some time. There were seasons in the

Mesozoic year. But they were mild. Even the winters were balmy. But now winter meant a time of growing cold.

The mid-continental sea was shrinking steadily as the Laramide Uplift continued, forced by the slow compression of Cordilleran America into the west coast of Cratonic America, impelled by the subducting Pacific plate. As the land rose, the climate and environment were being changed. Warm-blooded though they were, the large dinosaurs were without insulation. They were too big to den, could not hibernate during periods of cold, and so some of them had taken to migrating. We had already seen vast herds moving south along the river margins.

Gradually, our group drew together almost as though we had begun to need each other's company. In the evenings we sat around a fire listening to the hootings of feeding hadrosaurs while we discussed their demise.

Rogers enjoyed putting himself in the role of devil's advocate. He doubted that the dinosaurs would become extinct merely because of climatic changes. No matter how cold it got, the tropics would remain a suitable domain. There was no reason why the dinosaurs already living there would not survive even an ice age. And why couldn't they produce insulation? The deterioration of the climate would take millions of years, time enough to adapt. Hair was merely a modification of reptilian scales. If this had happened once, it could again. Had not the mastodons and mammoths grown dense mats of hair during the ice ages and lost it once the weather had moderated?

Jack jumped on that. Elephants had rudimentary hair

even in our time. And though we ourselves appear naked, we possess the same number of hair follicles as any other primate. The difference lies in the density of the individual hair strand. It had been an easy task for the naked mastodon to sprout a rug. The dinosaur would need much more time. They had not found it.

"Perhaps they should have invented clothes," Rogers joked lightly.

"That wouldn't have helped either," I told them flatly.

I had been in a black mood all day. The others hadn't missed it. James glanced at me uncertainly as I tossed a stellar radiation chart across the dinner table. The normal pattern of traces was overwhelmed in one corner by a swollen, cancerous blotch of white.

"That's GO538," I told them. "You couldn't see anything wrong with the naked eye, but it's gone supernova."

My companions stared upward as one into the shining, star-flecked blackness of the night sky.

"We're safe for some time," I chided them. "The radiation storm won't get here for at least a year."

"How far away?" James wanted to know.

"I'm not sure. Maybe a couple of light-years. There's nothing left of it in our time, only a black dwarf whose hard radiations were discovered by accident during a solar study. The radiation shell of the explosion vanished into deep space millions of years ago."

Rogers was the first to catch on.

"The radiation will play hell with the upper atmosphere. I wonder what it will do to the animal life."

"Only the smallest forms will survive," I guessed. "Turtles, snakes, lizards, crepuscular mammals, fish.

Creatures that tend to hide in the ground by day, or night, or are shielded by water. Anything larger than a dog that stays continually out in the open will find itself fighting cold and radiation sickness."

"Lord," Jack breathed aloud. "Just like wiping a slate. It's going to be a whole new ball game."

James, possibly because he was the practical one among us, had thought of another aspect.

"We can't hang around until the front hits. The radiation shielding in the shuttle wasn't designed to block off that kind of energy. And the radiation belts around Jupiter are going to flare up like neon tubes when the storm starts sweeping past. We're going to have to close this trip out early. When can you be finished with your study, Bill?"

"About a week. Most of the star charts have been made. The computer can correlate them in space just as well as here."

"Okay. We'll use you as the deadline. The rest of us will wrap things up and get ready to leave."

I've never known a week to go by more swiftly.

The mood was grim, like waiting around for an execution. It was impossible to avoid the idea that somehow an entire class of life had been weighed and found wanting. Perhaps that was merely mammalian chauvinism, but as Jack had said, the slate was about to be wiped.

We were far too busy to worry, though.

I only had time for one more visit to the cave before we took the shuttle up and began refueling from the barge. I can't say my runners were glad to see me. I was forced to knock them both out before I could get free.

But there was something I knew I had to do. I'm not sentimental in the least, so I don't know what drove me to do it. But there seemed to be a need. Certainly it was against regulations.

Our last few hours in the Mesozoic were spent staring at the cloud-bloated eye of Jupiter as we spiraled in for the jump home. There's no doubt in my mind why it's called the King of the Planets. Jack went so far as to call it a god, but he's impressionable.

No god would be so puny as to lock himself within a mere planet.

Rogers says that, and I agree.

Nor would a god deny himself the right to change his mind.

I no longer feel our arrival was due to chance.

We made it back all in one piece. The return brought mixed reactions. But the eggs should hatch in a day or so. There are five of them. I'm hoping that there's a good proportion between males and females. Our runners need a chance.

James and Jack have already declared themselves uncles.

# During the Jurassic

## by John Updike

Waiting for the first guests, the iguanodon gazed along the path and beyond, toward the monotonous cycad forests and the low volcanic hills. The landscape was everywhere interpenetrated by the sea, a kind of metallic blue rottenness that daily breathed in and out. Behind him, his wife was assembling the hors d'oeuvres. As he watched her, something unintended, something grossly solemn, in his expression made her laugh, displaying the leaf-shaped teeth lining her cheeks. Like him, she was an ornithischian, but much smaller—a compsognathus. He wondered, watching her race bipedally back and forth among the scraps of food (dragonflies wrapped in ferns, cephalopods on toast), how he had ever found her beautiful. His eyes hungered for size: he experienced a rage for sheer blind size.

The stegosauri, of course, were the first to appear. Among their many stupid friends these were the most stupid, and the most punctual. Their front legs bent outward and their filmy-eyed faces almost grazed the ground: the upward sweep of their backs was gigantic, and the double rows of giant bone plates along the spine clicked together in the sway of their cumbersome gait. With hardly a greeting, they dragged their tails, quadruply spiked, across the threshold and maneuvered themselves toward the bar, which was tended by a minute and shapeless mammal hired for the evening.

Next came the allosaurus, a carnivorous bachelor whose dangerous aura and needled grin excited the female herbivores: then Rhamphorhynchus, a pterosaur whose much admired "flight" was in reality a clumsy brittle glide ending in an embarrassed bump and trot. The iguanodon despised these pterosaurs' pretensions, thought grotesque the precarious elongation of the single finger from which their levitating membranes were stretched, and privately believed that the eccentric archaeopteryx, though sneered at as unstable, had more of a future. The hypsilophodon, with her graceful hands and branch-gripping feet, arrived with the timeless crocodile—an incongruous pair, but both were recently divorced. Still the iguanodon gazed down the path.

Behind him, the conversation gnashed on a thousand things—houses, mortgages, lawns, fertilizers, erosion, boats, winds, annuities, capital gains, recipes, education, the day's tennis, last night's party. Each party was consumed by discussion of the previous one. Their lives were subject to constant cross-check. When did you leave? When did *you* leave? We've been out every night this week. We had an amphibious baby sitter who had to be back in the water by one. Gregor had to meet a client in town, and now they've reduced the Saturday schedule; it means the 7:43 or nothing. Trains? I thought they were totally extinct. Not at all. They're coming back, it's just a matter of time until the government . . . In the long range of evolution, they are still the most efficient . . . Taking into account the heat-loss/weight ratio and assuming there's no more glaciation . . . Did you know—I think this is fascinating—did you know that in the financing of those great ornate stations of the eighties and nineties, those real monsters, there was no provision for amortization? They weren't amortized at all, they were financed on the basis of eternity! The railroad was conceived of as the end of Progress! *I* think—though not an expert—that the pivot word in this over-all industrio-socio-what-have-you-oh nexus or syndrome or whatever is *overextended.* Any competitorless object *bloats.* Personally, I miss the trolley cars. Now don't tell me I'm the only creature in the room old enough to remember the trolley cars!

The iguanodon's high pulpy heart jerked and seemed to split: the brontosaurus was coming up the path.

Her husband, the diplodocus, was with her. They moved together, rhythmic twins, buoyed by the hollow assurance of the huge. She paused to tear with her lips a clump of leaf from an overhanging paleocycas. From her deliberate grace the iguanodon received the impression that she knew he was watching her. Indeed, she had long guessed his love, as had her husband. The two saurischians entered his party with the languid confidence of the specially cherished. In the teeth of the iguanodon's ironic stance, her bulk, her gorgeous size enraptured him, swelled to fill the massive ache he carried when she was not there. She rolled outward across his senses—the dawn-pale underparts, the reticulate skin, the vast bluish muscles whose management required a second brain at the base of her spine.

Her husband, though even longer, was more slenderly built, and perhaps weighed less than twenty-five tons. His very manner was attenuated and tabescent. He had recently abandoned an orthodox business career to enter the Episcopalian seminary. This regression—as the iguanodon felt it—seemed to make his wife more prominent, less supported, more accessible.

How splendid she was! For all the lavish solidity of her hips and legs, the modelling of her little flat diapsid skull was delicate. Her facial essence seemed to narrow, along the diagrammatic points of her auricles and eyes and nostrils, toward a single point, located in the air, of impermutable refinement and calm. This irreducible point was, he realized, in some sense her mind: the focus of the minimal interest she brought to play upon the inchoate and edible green world flowing all about her, buoying her, bathing her. The iguanodon felt himself as an upright speckled stain in this world. He felt himself, under her distant dim smile, impossibly ugly: his mouth a sardonic chasm, his throat a pulsing curtain of scaly folds, his body a blotched bulb. His feet were heavy and horny and three-toed and his thumbs—strange adaptation!—were erect rigidities of pointed bone. Wounded by her presence, he savagely turned on her husband.

*"Comment va le bon Dieu?"*

"Ah?" The diplodocus was maddeningly good-humored. Minutes elapsed as stimuli and reactions travelled back and forth across his length.

The iguanodon insisted. "How are things in the supernatural?"

"The supernatural? I don't think that category exists in the new theology."

*"N'est-ce pas?* What *does* exist in the new theology?"

"Love. Immanence as opposed to transcendence. Work as opposed to faith."

"Work? I had thought you had quit work."

"That's an unkind way of putting it. I prefer to think that I've changed employers."

The iguanodon felt in the other's politeness a detestable aristocracy, the unappealable oppression of superior size. He said, gnashing, "The Void pays wages?"

"Ah?"

"You mean there's a living in nonsense? I said nonsense. Dead, fetid nonsense."

"Call it that if it makes it easier for you. Myself, I'm not a fast learner. Intellectual humility came rather natural to me. In the seminary, for the first time in my life, I feel on the verge of finding myself."

"Yourself? That little thing? *Cette petite chose?* That's all you're looking for? Have you tried pain? Myself, I have found pain to be a great illuminator. *Permettez-moi.*" The iguanodon essayed to bite the veined base of the serpentine throat lazily upheld before him; but his teeth were too specialized and could not tear flesh. He abraded his lips and tasted his own salt blood. Disoriented, crazed, he thrust one thumb deep into a yielding gray flank that hove through the smoke and chatter of the party like a dull wave. But the nerves of his victim lagged in reporting the pain, and by the time the distant head of the diplodocus was notified, the wound would have healed.

The drinks were flowing freely. The mammal crept up to him and murmured that the dry vermouth was running out. The iguanodon told him to use the sweet. Behind the sofa the stegosauri were Indian-wrestling; each time one went over, his spinal plates raked the recently papered wall. The hypsilophoden, tipsy, perched on a bannister: the allosaurus darted forward suddenly and ceremoniously nibbled her tail. On the far side of the room, by the great slack-stringed harp, the compsognathus and the brontosaurus were talking. He was drawn to them: amazed that his wife would presume to delay the much larger creature; to insert herself, with her scrabbling nervous motions and chattering leaf-shaped teeth, into the crevices of that queenly presence. As he drew closer to them, music began. His wife said to him, "The salad is running out." He murmured to the brontosaurus, "*Chère madame, voulez-vous danser avec moi?*"

Her dancing was awkward, but even in this awkwardness, this ponderous stiffness, he felt the charm of her abundance. "I've been talking to your husband about religion," he told her, as they settled into the steps they could do.

"I've given up," she said. "It's such a deprivation for me and the children."

"He says he's looking for himself."

"It's so selfish," she said. "The children are teased at school."

"Come live with me?"

"Can you support me?"

"No, but I would gladly sink under you."

"You're sweet."

"*Je t'aime.*"

"Don't. Not here."

"Somewhere, then?"

"No. Nowhere. Never." With what delightful precision did her miniature mouth encompass these infinitesimal concepts!

"But I," he said, "but I lo—"

"Stop it. You embarrass me. Deliberately."

"You know what I wish? I wish all these beasts would disappear. What do we see in each other? Why do we keep getting together?"

She shrugged. "If they disappear, we will too."

"I'm not so sure. There's something about us that would survive. It's not in you and not in me but between us where we almost meet. Some vibration, some enduring cosmic factor. Don't you feel it?"

"Let's stop. It's too painful."

"Stop dancing?"

"Stop being."

"That's a beautiful idea. *Une belle idée.* I will if you will."

"In time," she said, and her fine little face precisely fitted this laconic promise; and as the summer night yielded warmth to the multiplying stars, he felt his blood sympathetically cool, and grow thunderously, fruitfully slow.